D1435343

GUN BULLDOGGER

In Pony Kirk's native Texas, when a man wanted something—a steer or a pretty girl or a scalp—he took it.

The rustlers of One End Creek wanted beef on the hoof. Floyd Milton wanted Connie Hall. Bully Witt wanted Pony Kirk's scalp.

All Pony wanted was to keep what was his. That meant he had to fight. And Pony knew how to fight. They called him the Gun Bulldogger.

Eugene Cunningham grew up a Texan in Dallas and Fort Worth. He enlisted in the U.S. Navy in 1914 serving in the Mexican campaign and then the Great War until his discharge in 1919. He found work as a newspaper and magazine correspondent and toured Central America. He married Mary Emilstein in 1921 and they had two daughters, Mary Carolyn and Jean, and a son, Cleve. Although Cunningham's early fiction was preoccupied with the U.S. Navy and Central America, by the mid 1920s he came to be widely loved and recognized for his authentic Western stories which were showcased in *The Frontier* and *Lariat Story Magazine*. In fact, many of the serials he wrote for *Lariat* were later expanded to book-lengths when he joined the Houghton Mifflin stable of Western writers which included such luminaries as William MacLeod Raine and Eugene Manlove Rhodes. His history of gunfighters—which he titled *Triggernometry*—has never been out of print and remains a staple book on the subject. Often his novels involve Texas Rangers as protagonists and among his most successful series of fictional adventures, yet to be collected into book form, are his tales of Ware's Kid and Bar-Nuthin' Red Ames, and ex-Ranger Shoutin' Shelley Raines. Among his most notable books are *Diamond River Man*, a retelling of Billy the Kid's part in the Lincoln County War, *Red Range* (which in its Pocket Books edition sold over a million copies), and his final novel, *Riding Gun*. Western historian W.H. Hutchinson once described Cunningham as "as fine a lapidary as ever polished an action Western for the market place." At his best he wrote of a terrain in which he had grown up and in which he had lived much of his life, and it provides his fiction with a vital center that has often proven elusive to authors who tried to write Western fiction without that life experience behind them. Yet, as Joseph Henry Jackson wrote of him, "everywhere he went, he looked at life in terms of action, drama, romance, and danger. When you get a man who knows what men are like, what makes a story and how to write it, then you have the ideal writer in the Western field. Cunningham is precisely that."

GUN BULLDOGGER

Eugene Cunningham

GUNSMOKE

First published by Collins

This hardback edition 2001
by Chivers Press
by arrangement with
Golden West Literary Agency

ISBN 0 7540 8151 6

British Library Cataloguing in Publication Data available

Printed and bound in Great Britain by
BOOKCRAFT, Midsomer Norton, Somerset

CHAPTER I

"Ojo means eyes—"

PONY KIRK SAT COMFORTABLY on the pine needles. His legginged legs were wide apart. His bare yellow head he held on one side. He was scraping at a thin piece of hard, white bone. Pat Curran sprawled as comfortably, watching, yawning frequently.

"Me for Ojo, the night," he said at last. "Oh, it's a fi-ine, handsome young man you are, Pony. And that's as blue a sky over the mountains as ever blue could be. And we've got bacon and beans and coffee and venison and even whisky in camp. And there's never the sign of a Bully Witt or a Curly Horton or anything else crooked wearing a sheriff's or a deputy's star, on our trail. But— still—with it all—"

Pony fitted the bone to his pistol frame, then took it away again. He polished it on his leggings and lifted steel-gray eyes to the lanky redhead.

"I was the one that picked this camp," he reminded Pat. "You can bet it wasn't picked to be handy for Sheriff Bully Witt and that bushwhacking gang he's put officer stars on."

"Yeh. Well, like I was saying, everything's fine. But—"

"But Berta Schwartz ain't here," Pony drawled. "And, being the wild-eyed Irisher you are, if you don't see your beauty once a week anyway, you ain't fit to live with."

He bored a hole with the point of his sheath knife in

the bone, picked up the mate to it and put both on Colt frame.

"There! As nice a pair of bone handles as I could buy for twenty dollars, anywhere in this Territory. So—you've got to hit Ojo—a town just swarming with stars—stars on the ground, not in the sky. Pat! Pat! Sometimes I think you're a plumb nitwit, but mostly I know you're that same!"

"She's the prettiest thing I was ever setting sinful eyes on. Why don't you like Berta, Pony? Why?"

"Don't like any woman, for steady diet. Berta's pretty—more like her Mexican mother than like that ugly Dutchman, her father, I'll bet. But we've been on the dodge a year and—"

"Yeh. Yeh, I'm remembering. I'm remembering! *We* would try to be cowmen, we would. Without the say-so of Bully Witt. So he dealt us misery. Then we had our gunplay with Witt's sidekick, Johnson of the Cross J. You killed Johnson fair enough, but 'twas all Bully Witt was asking. A chance at us—at you!"

Pony tightened the handle screw and spun his Colt by the trigger guard. He looked blindly across this mountain camp as if he could see Ojo, the drowsing county seat, twenty miles below on the winding Rio Ojo.

"And that scoundrelly Felix Avila lied about the killing! He cleaned Johnson's gun and reloaded it and swore I shot his boss in the back, that Johnson didn't fire a shot. And that you helped me bushwhack Johnson. So—we're charged with murder and if we're caught we hang. And *so* my nitwit *compañero* wants to walk right into the jail at Ojo—to see a girl!"

He got up and replaced the Colt in its low-swung holster, put the long knife back in its sheath under his shirt, between his shoulder blades. He crossed to the coffeepot set upon the stones of their fireplace and poured a cup of warm coffee.

"You ever stop to think what *ojo* means?" he asked Pat, without turning. "It means *eye*. Only, this Ojo down the hill means *eyes*. Lots and lots of eyes. Bully Witt's—and his deputies'—and twenty men Anglo and Mexican who either don't like us or want Witt's favor. Even Schwartz ain't fond of you. Berta—well—"

"Don't you be saying it, Pony!" Pat interrupted him. There was an edge to his voice. "We're partners; we're friends; we're *very* like to pass in our checks together, one day. But not from you, more than any other, will I hear anything said about Berta. She's maybe *not* all a mother'd be picking for her son to marry. But straight she is! I'd put my life in her hand—"

"You mean, you *will* put your life in her hand, tonight. But I'm done talking. If you will play the *tonto*, you will! I'll ride part way with you. As far as Mig Chacon's."

He looked up at the sun, just tipping Crow Peak in the west. It would be sundown in two hours.

"Big Mig and Little Mig ought to have something to say, by now, about Flying W steers. That's one debt I'm going to collect before we build our cloud of dust, leaving the Territory! Bully Witt got more than three hundred of ours when we had to run. And we've got two hundred of his, so far—"

"Two hundred and twenty-three, the tally stands," Pat said, grinning. "But, of course, *he* could sell ours at market prices and on his we're having to take the offer for *rustled* stock. How many'll we be needing, to make out the debt?"

"About a hundred—of his biggest and best," Pony estimated. He grinned, also, if unpleasantly. "And then—we'll dig up the money over in Dog Canyon, add it to what we get this time, and split the breeze for Old Mexico. And if you want to take Berta Schwartz along, *bueno!*

I won't mind her, when the Bravo's between us and Bully Witt."

They cooked supper, fried venison and bacon and beans. There was no bread, but neither of these human wolves felt the lack of it. In a year of outlawry they had not slept six times beneath a roof. Often, a half-dozen meals had done them for a week. They had ranged the Territory's length and breadth, accepting favors from their few friends, snatching what they could from their many enemies.

Pony's tall black horse and Pat's buckskin were grazing on a tiny flat beyond the camp. Pat got them when they were done their meal. They saddled, looked carefully at the Winchesters, and rammed them into the scabbards. Pat grinned and set his shapeless old hat carefully over one gay, green eye. Then he swung into the silver-trimmed saddle to which he had clung through many a tight scrape and long chase. They rode downhill.

It was not yet dark. Tawny rock squirrels and tiny chipmunks ran across the almost invisible trail they followed. Flickers and woodpeckers hammered the trees and one particularly curious bluejay swooped back and forth almost at the horses' noses. A pair of does made crashing noise in the underbrush of an arroyo and raced off toward the safe heights. It was like a land that men had never crossed.

Miguel Chacon's little ranch lay a mile off the Jupiter-Ojo road into which Pony and Pat came from their mountain trail. At the side road to Chacon's the two drew in. The September moon now was bright; Pony looked at Pat and shook his head.

"Go on!" he said resignedly. "Nothing else'll do you, so fog it. But—"

"Yeh! Yeh! I'll be careful," Pat promised, laughing. "I know all the story you want to unwind."

He jerked up a hand by way of farewell and rammed the hooks to his buckskin with a cowboy yell.

"*Yaaaiiiaaah!* Cowboy! Going to town!"

Old Miguel came down to the log corral behind his 'dobe house at Pony's whistle. He was a short, immensely wide man, grizzled, seamed of face. His father had been a Mexican, his mother a woman of the Apaches, and in him—as in his bright fifteen-year-old son, Little Miguel—the best qualities of both races showed.

"All is good," he told Pony. "None but my family is in the house tonight. Little Miguel is in Ojo looking for a son of my cousin. When he comes with Miguelito, this José, we will be enough to drive those steers of the Flying W. Witt's vaqueros have gathered two hundred and more of his biggest and heaviest, in the low pasture of the Flying W. They expect no danger, I think; the steers range and graze slowly; the men—there are only three in the pasture now—sleep in that little house by the spring. We know that little house, *amigo*—"

Pony got a quart of whisky from an *alforja* behind his saddle and uncorked it. Mig Chacon took it, drank, handed it back. Pony drank in his turn and they walked twenty yards to where they could sit comfortably upon a cottonwood log and have a low bluff at their backs, while their position commanded a view of the land beyond the house.

They drank and smoked. Occasionally the rancher spoke of his spying upon the sheriff's ranch, and upon the Cross J which had been the property of Sheriff Witt's friend—some said his partner in crime—Johnson. Pony asked in a flat voice about Felix Avila, the foreman who had lied about the killing of Johnson.

"He is there—and elsewhere. The Cross J is managed by the bank. That rascal, Avila, is the foreman."

"The bank. Which is the same as saying Bully Witt

and the storekeepers Shea and Rosen. The three of them own the bank. But, about Avila— It would be good to ride over to the Cross J and kill him. A liar who will swear away a man's life is good only for killing. I would have done this long ago, if only I could have found Avila."

"It will be hard," Mig Chacon said slowly. "Always he has two or three men with him. He stays in the open, out of shot from rock or bush. I have watched him by the hour. For it was also my thought to kill him. When he rides away from the ranch on business, one might find the chance. But how to know when he goes; where he goes—"

He shrugged and drank. Pony nodded dourly. He was not happy tonight. Even in his year of outlawry he had managed to keep some of the cowboy cheerfulness which had marked him from Texas to Milk River, before ever he came to the Territory as a stock detective and, under the name of Chance Fielder, bought a little ranch. But now even the prospect of getting some of his own back from Bully Witt could not lift his spirits. The whisky did not help.

As Chance Fielder he had used the ranch for cover and from it he had finished his work of breaking up Alec Sells's gang of thieves. But he had not sold the ranch, afterward, as he had intended in the beginning. Keeping the name by which the Territory knew him, he had taken Pat Curran for partner. Bully Witt, he thought, had always suspected him of bringing about Alec Sells's death and the scattering of the gang—and it was open rumor that Witt had regularly bought stolen stock from Sells.

And he told me in Shea and Rosen's store he'd break me, Pony thought, as he stared across the moonlit yard. *And he was just about calling the turn. He's beat me. Even if only one man in the Territory knows that*

"Chance Fielder's" real name is John "Pony" Kirk of Texas, a warrant might pop up just anywhere I'd go. The truth about my name would leak out.

"Don Pat?" Mig Chacon said inquiringly, breaking in on the gloomy train of thought. "He—is in Ojo tonight?"

"In Ojo. With Berta Schwartz."

"A man's womaning is his own affair," Mig Chacon said wearily. "But I do not like this. It has been said— but you know that Berta and Johnson were *very* good friends. I think that Witt knows of Don Pat's feeling for the girl. Knowing it, he will talk to her. And he will have her father talk to her. It is not good. It is, in fact, very bad!"

"Pat met her at the *baile* of the Carrascos six months ago," Pony answered moodily. "We went—perhaps because we had drunk enough to make fools of us. We would show Bully Witt and all his killers that we were not to be kept always in the mesquite like hunted wolves. Pat saw Berta and she rolled those great eyes at him and held him very close in the dancing and— Since then she has been his *querida*. He would quarrel with me if I said to him he must not go into Ojo to her arms. But he has what we Anglos call 'the luck of the Irish,' *amigo*. He puts his head into the jaws of *El Tigre* and, where you or I would die, he goes away laughing—and perhaps with a whisker or two jerked from that tiger's muzzle. He will come at dawn."

"*Sí! Sí!* He will come here at dawn," Mig Chacon echoed quickly. "He will come singing that song of the queer creature he calls a 'mavourneen' and he will laugh at us for that we had fear. About these steers— I will send Little Miguel to you at your camp within two, it may be three or even four, days. With you and Don Pat and the three of us from this house, we will catch and bind those vaqueros in the little house by the spring. Then we will drive the steers over the *malpais* to Lost Valley and there our buyer will come."

"*Bueno!* Now, I will put my horse into the piñon thicket and we will sleep. I know that your house is my house, *amigo,* but I cannot be easy when walls are about me. The wolf that has once been caught, but escaped, you know, he will not lie in a cave. Let us finish the whisky. It has no bite, tonight!"

They emptied the bottle, standing at the corral. Then Pony swung into the saddle and rode back, up and over the little bluff, until he found a comfortable place to sprawl. Dan, the big black gelding, nibbled at such browse as he could find at the end of the lariat with which Pony staked him.

Pony was long getting to sleep, but when he dozed it seemed to him only a moment before running feet pounded below him and his name was called in a tone to jerk him wide awake.

CHAPTER II

"I am a lone wolf—"

IT WAS YOUNG MIG CHACON, with his father only a few feet behind him. Pony did not wait for them to climb the bluff, but slid over it. The boy was panting.

"Don Pat!" he gasped. "In Ojo—I was there—Curly Horton—Berta Schwartz sent word—Horton killed him!"

Pony shook his head as if he could clear it by the physical jerk. It seemed unreal. In spite of his fears, his forebodings, he could not believe that gay Pat Curran had pushed his head once too often into the tiger's mouth.

"You said—Berta sent word," he mumbled. "You mean

she—she sent word to Curly Horton that Pat was with her?"

"I was in the back of the Open Eye, watching the game of faro and listening for anything I might hear. Horton was at my very side. Pico, the boy who works for Berta's father about the house, he came in and whispered to Horton. I could hear only a few words. But Pico was saying that Berta wished him to know that Don Pat had come once more to her house; that he was there at that moment. So much I must put together from the words I heard. Horton went quickly out by the back door. I went out, too, but he was at the Schwartz house before me. And as I reached the house I heard shots at the back. Don Pat was killed within the house. I think he did not have pistol in hand at the time. Horton, of course, said that Don Pat would not surrender; that he fired the first shot."

He waited, but Pony only stood staring straight ahead. It still was incredible that Pat Curran lay dead in Ojo. He shook his head at last.

I am *a lone wolf, now!* he thought. *What to do? Witt will probably think that I'm near town; that where Pat was, I would be. He knows me well enough to believe that I'll do something about this. So, tonight, they'll be forted and waiting for me.* Bueno! *I'll give Bully Witt a surprise. I'll kill Curly Horton for that murder, but I'll kill him when I'm ready—kill him and Felix Avila both, when I'm ready. First—*

"It was hardly more than two hours past," young Mig was saying. "I talked to that Pico for a little while and so I came to believe that Horton slipped through the open back door into the house and killed Don Pat without warning. And I saw them carry Don Pat to the store of Shea and Rosen and put him upon the counter for the town to see. Then my cousin José and I rode fast back here. What do we do, *amo?*"

"We ride for the Flying W," Pony told them both in a slow and deadly drawl. "With José, we ride for the little house by the spring. Tomorrow night—tonight, I mean, for it is two o'clock, now—we will take those steers to Lost Valley and get from Jink Lowrey the price. Then—"

The Chacons, father and son, grunted agreement. Pony sent young Mig for Dan. At the house he looked at José, a tall, slender, daredevil sort of youngster. José in his turn fairly gaped at this most famous of Territorial outlaws. They got cooked food from the Chacon kitchen and young Mig and José roped fresh horses and shifted saddles. Then the four of them rode off westward—toward the Flying W, thirty miles away.

With dawn they were in the hills. They had not ridden fast, for there was time to spare and there would be need of the horses' strength after the steers were dined out toward the *malpais*. So in late afternoon they sat comfortably in an arroyo five or six miles from the spring where the Flying W kept a line camp in a tiny 'dobe house.

Young Mig and José talked, but Pony sat grimly quiet and old Mig watched silently. They ate beef and brown beans and *tortillas* and smoked. Dusk came, as if all the flat golden canopy of the western sky were curtained instantly, magically, by a violet sheet. Every canyon and arroyo of the mountains became for an instant a stripe of black velvet upon the lavender slope. Then light faded and all the land was gray, and the sky above it.

"Let's go!" Pony grunted. "It will be very dark, out of the moonlight, within an hour. But, first—"

He got his last quart of whisky from the *alforja* and they had a drink around, then mounted. Old Mig Chacon had spied upon this range until he knew it as he knew his own little holding. He led the way easily and certainly. Two hours later they sat the horses in a motte of cottonwoods on the tiny stream that ran from the spring by the 'dobe house. The moonlight made the hundred yards of flat between trees and house almost as plain as in the day. But the 'dobe had been built for shelter, not ventilation. They faced an end and side that were windowless.

Pony swung down and took off his leggings. He left the Winchester on his saddle and the others followed his example. Then they moved slowly out of the trees, afoot. No sound came from the house, and when he had listened at the corner for two or three minutes, Pony tiptoed around to the door. Now he could hear snoring. Old Mig was at his elbow. He nodded.

Pony stepped inside the single small room and old Mig and the boys slid after him. A man sprawled at Pony's feet. He bent.

"*Bueno!*" he called. "Take them!"

There were startled grunts from the wakened riders; savage snarls—none so savage as young Mig's—from the Chacons. Then old Mig said calmly that he had *his* man.

"Into the light with them," Pony ordered. "We will tie them where we can see to make good knots."

When each man had been bound with hands behind him, they were marched up to the trees and their ankles lashed with the rawhide strings brought from Chacon's. Then they were tied to the trees and Pony led his band away.

It was not difficult to start the scattered steers moving. Pony made no effort to clean the pasture. He estimated that they had a hundred and fifty head in the bunch which began to move toward the *malpais* five miles away.

They'll do, he told himself without interest. *If I wasn't set on evening the score with Bully Witt, I wouldn't bother with his stuff, now. But Jink Lowrey will hand over a thousand or fifteen hundred for 'em and I'll pay off Mig and the boys, dig up the other money and—*

One corner of his hard mouth climbed. Witt and Horton had expected him to show in Ojo. He was certain of that. But since he had not rushed in as soon as Pat Curran was murdered, they would wonder. In a few days they might think that he was scared out of the country.

And then I'll rouse Curly out of that notion! he promised himself grimly. *And that'll be Curly's last rouse.*

The steers went on through the day. The rugged hills into which they were pushed rarely saw riders. But in turn young Mig and José rode off to the side and studied the country from high lines. That night the bunch was held in a box canyon. The second day went as quietly as if the raiders were no more than ordinary riders driving cattle for honest wages. Old Mig said as much and Pony nodded.

"That in truth is just what we are. To take back from a thief what he has stolen from you is not stealing. I hope that Lowrey is waiting for us. He said last week that he would be at the cabin within six days."

Coming into Lost Valley very cautiously, Pony and old Mig rode well ahead. The steers slouched forward as if they smelled the water of the little spring. This was part of Jink Lowrey's holdings. The buyer used the canyon, and the valley into which the canyon widened, for stock not ready to be inspected. Only two or three riders, well paid and tight-mouthed, ever rode this way.

"There he is," Pony said when they could see the cabin beyond the spring. "Couple of his hardcases with him. Trust Jink never to trust himself alone with the men who sell him cattle! He would shoot us in the back, so he believes that we would shoot him in the back."

The buyer lifted a long, thin arm in greeting. He was a storklike man except in face—which Pony thought resembled a buzzard's head. He shambled out from the cabin door, leaving behind him two cowboys whose eyes differed in color, but owned the same fixed watchfulness of stare.

"Hi!" Lowrey called. "Got 'em, huh? Y'ain't disappointed me yet. Wisht y'd made it a week quicker, though. Had a dicker on, then. But it blowed up. Too bad! Could've give y' more'n I can afford to offer today."

He had a high, rasping voice and a way of giggling that irritated Pony.

"You'll still be able to pay my price," Pony drawled. "I heard you got a bigger beef contract over at Fort Lowe. These big—Barred Double Diamond steers—they *will* be Barred Diamonds when they come out of here, I take it?—ought to fill in fine on that contract, and even help on the tally at the Agency. Except, of course, that they're too good for the feather dusters. Too heavy. It has been said, Jink, that you and the agent are hell on scales; got one up there that tips eight hundred pounds when a dog trots across it."

Lowrey giggled again, but turned to his men and nodded.

"Give these fellas a hand to line 'em out for a tally and a look. Push 'em by me and on into the Hollow."

He stood with Pony while the steers went past, his shrewd little eyes bright. When the last of Witt's Flying Ws had gone into the upper canyon he looked at Pony, started to say something, then stopped with sight of Pony's thin smile.

"Two thousand," Pony said evenly.

Lowrey broke into a storm of protest. Pony shrugged. The men came up, the Chacons and José, the two silent cowboys. The argument went on bitterly. At last Pony nodded.

"Fifteen hundred, then. I'll take it because I've got to head north. I want to see the east bank of the Rowdy lying 'way west of me. You know about Pat Curran?"

He was very conscious of those sharp little eyes and he kept his face blank while he made a cigarette. If Jink Lowrey followed his usual habit, it would not be long before Bully Witt in Ojo would hear that "Chance Fielder" was heading for the Rowdy River country, leaving the Territory.

"Uh—yeh, heard about him," Lowrey admitted. "But I didn't want to mention it. Well, reckon y' right about hitting for the Rowdy. Y' raised more hell than anybody ever done in the Territory. But ary man's string of luck's bound to run out somewheres. Stick here and y'll go like Pat. Uh—where'll we meet for me to pay y' the money? How about my place in Jupiter? Y' could slide up—it's on the edge of town—say, one night a week from now and—"

"Oh, I couldn't do a thing like that!" Pony said gravely. "You just don't know what a scary man I am, Jink. I'd likely keel over dead a dozen times before I ever got to your door. I—would lots rather have the money right here, right now."

One of the cowboys, smallish, dark, made the slightest move of right hand. Pony stared at the hand, then at the thin face. The cowboy lifted the hand to rub his cheek.

"But—" Lowrey began.

"But you've got it here and you'll pay it here," Pony checked him. "You knew well enough I'd want it on the barrel. Fifteen hundred, Jink. Tonight."

He watched the three of them. He knew that old Mig had English enough to follow the talk and that young Mig had even more understanding. He watched Lowrey and the two cowboys and trusted the Chacons to do the same. There were small scuffing sounds behind him to indicate movement. The pair moved carelessly to left and right, to stop on right and left of Pony. Lowrey looked uneasily at them, then shrugged and giggled.

"A' right! I was just going to say it'd be handier the other way. But if y' got to have it right now, y' can have it."

"We'll take it and hightail. It's got too hot for me."

CHAPTER III

"This is the Law"

PONY LEFT THE CHACONS and José at the ranch of a distant cousin of old Mig's. They nodded and he lifted a hand in return. There was no more formality about the leave-taking than that. The gold had been divided. Pony intended to get the other hoard from Dog Canyon before looking for Curly Horton.

"We will go with you," Mig told him. "You need only say that it will be of help—"

"No, one man riding fast is better than more men, in the mountains. There will be no fighting. You will be better in your own house. Bully Witt may come asking if you have ridden with me—toward the Flying W."

"If he comes," Mig said with a slow-grin, "I hope that he is satisfied with what he hears."

"If you go to Ojo," young Mig put in suddenly, "watch for a new deputy. I heard when I was there that one came from Faith and was made deputy by Bully Witt. I did not see him nor do I remember his name. But he told Witt, I heard, that you and others would now find warrants served, if out of the muzzles of a shotgun."

"I'll watch," Pony grunted without interest. "Now, I go to Dog Canyon. I will see you all or—I will not see you all. *Hasta luego!*"

He slept one night in the camp he and Pat Curran had made. But it was not pleasant to sit there, or lie there, remembering how Pat had set his hat rakishly over an eye and gone singing down to the treacherous arms of Berta Schwartz. He took such food as he needed, cached everything else, and rode over dim trails to the ancient outlaw hangout in Dog Canyon.

There was a boulder-studded flat with only one road up to it. The ruined rock house had harbored many a wanted man over forty years. Pony knew it well. He and Pat had used it a dozen times within the year. And among boulders behind the old house they had buried some twelve hundred dollars in gold pieces.

He did not intend to stay overnight there, when near noon he sent Dan easily up the steep and narrow trail to the flat. He swung down at the house and looked in. Only his footprints and Pat's showed in the dust of the roofless shell. He went around to the boulders. The two of them had levered up a big one, using a thick pine branch to manage the weight. He wondered if he could shift the boulder alone.

He worked at it for a while, then began to dig at the side of the great rock. Two hours passed before he had the leather bag in his hand, moodily jingling the coins.

Pat always said he didn't have a soul in the world, he thought. *Nobody to take his half of it. If I could just put it all into shells and man-hire, I'd like to come in here with a good half dozen and wipe Bully Witt and his killers off the map. But he and Shea and Rosen and their bunch have got the straight line to the governor's ear, up at Faith. He'd have the soldiers and U.S. marshals swarming around us—*

He leaned tensely forward. Faint, bell-mellow, somewhere below the level of this little mesa, there was the clink of an iron shoe on rock.

Pony went at the run around the house, tossed the gold down beside black Dan and continued to where he could look down the trail from between two pillars of rough stone. He could see nothing, at first, but there was more sound of horseshoes on rocks. He thought of Bully Witt and the Flying W cowboys. It was barely possible that, having missed the steers from the lower pasture, Witt had thought of Dog Canyon and led his warriors that way.

He went back to the house and got his carbine and the box of shells from his saddle. He was frowning when he returned to the watching-place. If that should be Witt, this was the tightest place Pony Kirk had ever known. He could hold the mesa singlehanded, almost indefinitely, but he could not leave the mesa. Attackers had only to bottle up the steep trail and let him shoot away his ammunition, eat his food. And he had no water. That was below, at the foot of the trail.

He opened the shells and pushed the Winchester between the boulders. Now he could see underbrush waving, near the bottom of the slope.

"Plenty of 'em!" he muttered. "And they've probably cut my trail— Moving each way; getting behind the rocks—"

"Oh-h, Fielder!" a strong voice called from the masking brush below. "I know you're up there. This is the Law. Better come on down."

Pony said nothing, but studied the rocks and brush. He was in no immediate danger. Anyone charging up that trail would be facing certain death, while he behind his pillars was safe from their lead.

"This is Merl Couch, deputy from Ojo," the voice called calmly. "Better come down. I'll see that you get safe to the jail. This is wind-up for your twine. Might's well believe it."

"Oh, I couldn't do that," Pony answered, with equal calm. "I don't like jails, even good jails. And one with Bully Witt and Curly Horton around it— Why, it'd smell like a skunk den, and I'm a clean, moral man. Uh-uh! Is Curly down there? I want to name a slug for him."

"No. Curly's in town. I'm rodding this spread. Got a dozen men in my posse. You haven't got a Chinaman's chance, cowboy. I don't want to kill you, but I promised to loop you. And that's what I'm going to do."

"A posse—" Pony said. "Sure that's what it is? If it's a bunch of those barroom warriors and saloon bums from Ojo, better hobble 'em. They'll break down the timber when the first shot's fired. Not one of 'em ever busted a cap unless he could see the broad of the other man's back. They—"

There was a chorus of snarling and out of the brush a volley roared. Lead sang and buzzed and whined on rocks up the slope and over Pony's head. He grinned wolfishly and looked from right to left. When a patch of red showed briefly to the side of a boulder he squeezed the trigger. A man yelled; the red patch jerked farther into sight, then back again. But a slug rang on the rock a yard from Pony. A second shot and a third were as accurately fired.

Pony withdrew and listened to the ragged bellow of the posse's shooting. When it died away he crawled a yard forward and bounced a half-dozen slugs off rocks without troubling to hunt targets. Waving of the brush showed that the posse was at least worried by the ricocheting lead. Couch called to him again.

"Not a bit of good! We can starve you out. Show some sense, cowboy! Have to give up in the long run. You don't want to be wasting my time like this."

"Bully Witt's getting a sight better deputies than usual," Pony muttered. "That's a cheerful hairpin, that Couch. Let's see what I can do."

He shifted aim after studying the place from which the new deputy's voice came. Three fast shots produced violent movement in the brush. From a new place Couch yelled, "Not bad! But you'll have to do lots better. Come on, Fielder! Nobody will bust a cap while you're coming down."

"Can't be done," Pony told him in kind. "Why don't you come up? Bring your war and put her in the pot. I'll put the big skillet in the little skillet and fry the dishrag for you. How's that bunch of bushwhackers doing? Learned how to shoot at a man's *face*, yet?"

As the afternoon wore on toward dusk, Pony went to Dan and got food. He ate and smoked and kept his watch. Occasionally, he thought of a new insult to hurl downslope at the men of Ojo, and usually his yell roused a burst of harmless firing. He shot only when he thought he saw a target among those moving incautiously from rock to rock. For he had less than thirty shells, now. From time to time Merl Couch renewed his promise of protection to Ojo.

Beginning to feel like old compadres *with him,* Pony thought, near dark. *But that won't keep him from dusting me when he sees a chance. And—come dark, just anything might happen.*

He considered mounting Dan and making a headlong run of it. But the slope was both steep and rocky. At the bottom the big horse would plunge into the brush among those boulders. It would be little less than a miracle if he kept his footing.

"How things go, I reckon," Pony told himself, looking over the rim of the little mesa, off to where a misty haze of mountains showed, twenty and more miles away across the greasewood flat to southwest. "If I had come straight here after leaving Mig I'd have had the money and been halfway to Ojo by now. Couch and his coyotes would've found nothing but our tracks. But I didn't do that and so—"

He shrugged. It seemed quite possible that here "Chance Fielder" would join Pat Curran. But he was not a man to be unnerved by the prospect. Some of those hired killers of Bully Witt, down there, would side him on the road.

He caught a glimpse of movement and drove two careful shots into the brush and waked a volley in reply. Only the lead which he had come to identify as Merl Couch's came close to him and he was certain that one overbold posseman had been hit in the arm.

The sun clung to a western peak, then slid behind it like a great gold piece. Pony tensed a little. Not long, now, to wait, if Couch could rouse his men for a charge in the dark. Or—Pony thought, putting himself in the deputy's place—he might try a quiet climb up in a single-handed attack.

When dark had come he could see the reflected light of the posse's supper fire. The moon would not light the trail for more than an hour. Now was Couch's time, if he had made a plan. He leaned against his pillars of rock and watched.

Over at the stone house Dan moved suddenly, and mechanically Pony turned. He stiffened incredulously, shrinking back into the deeper shadow, lifting the carbine. A small, quick figure showed by the black horse.

"What the devil?" he breathed. "Nobody has sneaked up the trail—and that's the only way up—"

From Castle Rock to the Hole-in-the-Wall, the high-line riders knew Dog Canyon. And always it was said flatly, in discussing hide-outs, that only by the northern side, by that winding trail, could the tiny mesa be gained.

The man disappeared, then came past Dan. He was stooping, coming almost at the run toward Pony. But his feet were silent on the rocky ground. Pony lifted the Winchester a little more, then suddenly let it sag.

"Mig!" he whispered. "Why—Mig, how did you sneak up here?"

Young Mig laughed softly and moved over to peer down the slope through the darkness.

"I came to bring you a letter. But I heard the firing and so I looked to see who fired at you. When it seemed that you were held up here, I rode far around and climbed by a path that my father once showed me. And by that same trail, *amo*, you—and your horse—may leave the mesa."

"But—" Pony began. Then he laughed. *"Muy bien!* Why should I waste our time? You have proved that I do not know all that may be known of Dog Canyon. First, I will stir up the coyotes."

He rained lead down in the general direction of the posse and when they returned the fire savagely, harmlessly, he and Mig trotted across to Dan. Pony recovered his sack of gold and stowed it to balance the other money in an *alforja*.

"Let me take the bridle, *amo!*" Mig suggested. "This trail can be seen neither from above nor below, unless you know where to look. I will go first, with Dan—"

There was a clump of wind-gnarled junipers on the rim of the mesa, surrounded by a jumble of red boulders. Mig led Dan confidently through the great rocks and past the stunted trees. Still, Pony could see no way ahead of him to descend the hundred-odd feet of cliff that had always looked so sheer. But there *was* a narrow path—it clung to the cliff and, halfway down, began almost an easy incline.

"Now!" Mig whispered at last. "We are down. I had not thought that you knew nothing of this back door. My father would have told you, or I would have shown it. But, *no es importe*, now. My horse is yonder. Hear them shoot! I think that they will be much surprised when at last they come up to the mesa top and find you gone."

"That new deputy is a good man, I think. It may not be beyond him to find Dan's trail. But—no matter. What is this of a letter? Where had you it?"

"A man brought it from Jupiter to my father. He said, this cowboy, that it had been given him by one in Jupiter to deliver to Miguel Chacon. He rode away, then. None of us can read, so my father called upon Segundo, who is my cousin who went for a time to school in Faith. Segundo said that it was for my father. But within that cover was another letter, addressed to Don Chance Fielder. So—"

Pony held the soiled envelope up where the moonlight showed the writing. And with sight of Terry Verner's name he understood. Except for Pat Curran, Verner had been the only man in all the Territory to know that Chance Fielder was really Pony Kirk. He slipped the envelope into a pocket and mounted. Mig got his horse, and as they wound in and out through boulders and brush, he looked often and curiously at the silent Pony, who rode sometimes before him, sometimes well ahead. At last, it seemed that he could hold in his questions no longer.

"What, now?" he asked. "You have in your hand the money from the steers and, if it is not so much as Bully Witt stole from you, if there is no payment for the ranch you cannot work, it is yet a great deal. Or so it seems to us, my father and me. There is no need, now, for you to stay here in the Territory, where behind every rock and mesquite may be the Winchester of an enemy. You will go, amo?"

"We will see. Now, we ride to lose our trail."

They rode on for a time and when Pony spoke again, it was in English, more to himself than to the boy.

"Yeh, we had best tangle our trail. I mistrust that happy young Deputy Couch. He's done more in a week than Witt and Horton managed in a year. And he shoots damn straight! I've got a call to pay, now, down at Ojo. I want to wander down that way for a wawa with Curly Horton. After that—I'll see. If I can see anything, then, but the Pearly Gates—"

"Your talk, then, to Jink Lowrey at Lost Valley?" Mig said, but nodding wisely. "It was nothing but dust in the face of Bully Witt? You had no thought of going to the Rowdy?"

"It was only dust in Jink Lowrey's face and, so, in the face of Bully Witt. Tomorrow night, if you will help, I stop on the edge of Ojo and wait for you to find Curly Horton. Then you will come out to me and—whatever can be done, I will do!"

"You have only to say what I am to do and, if I can do it, the thing is done!" Mig promised earnestly, leaning and nodding. "My father says the same, for himself. Tomorrow night I will scout Ojo for Curly Horton; I will tell you where he is to be found. Then—you will kill him!"

CHAPTER IV

"These are snakes"

OJO LAY LIKE A DAPPLED YELLOW SNAKE in the pale moonlight when Pony and Mig stopped their horses in a motte of cottonwoods and looked down the valley of the Ojo River. Pony thought that their trail from the hills was sufficiently tangled to puzzle even the efficient Merl Couch. Nor had they turned, this time, toward the

Chacon house.

"Bully Witt's liable to remember that Big Mig was always a friend of mine; liable to comb the place any time," Pony told himself. "And if he should happen to ride up with that bunch of killers he always has got behind him, and they found even a hint of my using around Mig's, I wouldn't put it past Witt to do a murder right there."

Young Mig was like an eager hound puppy, now. He leaned forward against the big horn of his Mexican saddle and stared at the sprawling town along the Ojo.

"You will wait here, *amo?*" he asked. "Then I will go into town; none will guess what I come for. I will hunt out this killer of our friend and come back."

"Bueno!" Pony grunted. "Then—depending on where you find him—I will make my plan. Go, now. Be careful, *muchacho;* these are snakes we walk among."

After the boy was gone downslope to the trail, he sat quietly, shielding the coal of his cigarette within cupped hand, watching that section of the Jupiter-Ojo road a hundred yards away. In an hour he saw several riders, going or coming. But none showed interest in the cottonwoods, so he was free to think, casting backward and forward over his life as he had lived it and as he planned it, now.

"Mexico's my best bet, I reckon," he told himself. "I could head for the northern ranges again; cross into Alberta. But Mexico's closer. Terry Verner can keep me posted about affairs on this side—"

Thought of his only close friend remaining in the Territory reminded him naturally of that letter from Verner, the letter Mig had brought and which he had pushed into a pocket for reading in a more leisurely moment. He moved farther back, until the cottonwoods were between him and the road. In a shallow arroyo, hardly

more than a ditch, he made a tiny fire of very dry twigs
and opened the envelope.

There was still another within this cover—an envelope
postmarked *Vasko, Texas,* and addressed to him under
his real name. It had gone, more than five months past, to
the 8 Lazy 8 at Landusky. There were four steps in its return southward, the last from Sam Myres's saddle shop
at Sweetwater, to Terry Verner's freight corral in Jupiter.

"Vasko," Pony grunted. "That's old Cousin 'Roaring
Red Roy' Kirk's post office! His horse outfit's out from
there. Now, what is it he brands? Two Bench! That's it.
And what would he be writing to me about?"

He leaned closer to the little blaze. In the same copperplate handwriting of the address on the envelope were
two neat paragraphs.

Dear Cousin John:

*Of the direct line of that John Kirk who is founder of
our family in America, my investigation shows only four
survivors. Of these, you and I are the closest in relation,
since your father was my first cousin. The others are
Floyd Milton, a distant cousin, and Constance Hall (who
writes this letter for me), a cousin even more distant.
Only four of our line. Only you and I bearing the Kirk
name.*

*After my wife's death, last year, I thought much about
this. You three, Floyd and Constance and yourself, are
my only kin. You are the only Texas representative. I
decided to invite all of you to make lengthy visits to me.
Floyd and Constance are already here on the 2 Bench.
I have just discovered your whereabouts and am writing
now to ask you, also, to come to Vasko and the ranch. I
am getting old and it seems that an old man turns naturally to his kin. Will you come and visit me?*

"Old Roaring Red Roy!".Pony said absently. "Dad used to tell about his hell-raising. And now he's got close to the end of his twine and begins to hunt around and chouse out his blood-kin. Floyd Milton— Must be one of the outfit in Cleveland. Constance Hall, I never heard Dad speak about. And *she* wrote the letter—never was a Kirk could herd the language and shape it up like this. And you can tell Red Roy didn't do a thing but sign his name. Looks like there's maybe a kick in the old boy, yet—you could believe he *shot* that 'Roy Kirk' onto the paper, or banged it on with a club."

He lifted his eyes and, with sight of the cottonwoods and big black Dan grazing in the moonlight, he laughed harshly and crumpled the page of copperplate script.

"Pay 'em a visit!" he snarled. "Old Roaring Red Roy *don't* know a lot about his relations, and that's gospel. The visit *I* have got on my mind certainly won't take me to Vasko, no matter where else I land! And it's not kinfolks I'm going to see, on the Two Bench or anywhere else—"

He heard a horse coming fast and tossed the paper into the dying fire. It was Mig riding toward the cottonwoods —Mig or someone else very bent on making this particular spot. Pony trotted to where he could see, carbine across his arm. Mig was within thirty yards, excitement plain in the way he carried himself in the saddle, ancient single-shot rifle importantly across his arm.

"*Amo!*" he gasped, sliding the horse to a stop. "He is in the store of Shea and Rosen. Bully Witt is not in Ojo tonight. Curly Horton is alone with the *tienderos*. They talked of some business he was to do for them. They had out a jug of whisky. I think that he will not leave before you can reach the store."

"*Bueno!*" Pony grunted, frowning. "If it is not the exact place I would have chosen for facing him, it will do. Were there many in the store?"

He was scooping up his reins as he talked, passing them over Dan's thick neck, hunting the stirrup.

"Not many, and they in the front of the place," Mig said as Pony settled himself and shoved carbine into scabbard. "I looked there, through the front door, as I left. Shea and Rosen and Horton are in the back, in that little place among the shelves and boxes which is the office of the store."

Pony considered the town as they rode toward the distant lights. It was many months since he had shown his face in Ojo. Not many men there had seen him recently; not many men could be there who had faced him for those months spent on the dodge. No need to be too cautious about riding in.

So he turned into the road and spurred boldly up it like any thirsty cowboy impatient to charge the first saloon. But on the edge of town, almost in front of the Flag Saloon, he drew Dan down to a walk and grunted at Mig. Obediently, the boy whirled his horse and trotted off to the right, toward the Mexican quarter of Ojo. Pony continued along the street—that part of the road which ran between Ojo's forty-odd business buildings or important residences. He rode hunched as Dan foxtrotted, the very statue of a rider weary from miles in the saddle. He saw men here and there in the light from windows and open doors. But none gave him more than a passing glance and he rode past Shea and Rosen's big 'dobe with quick glance at the scattering of buyers, then jogged on out of Ojo.

Once away from the town he turned left and back, to come up behind the store. The September night was warm and the back door was open. He left Dan with reins fastened in a slipknot, behind a store shed of the partners. Then quickly, walking like a wolf to a seen kill, he crossed to the store and listened. There was no sound inside that did not come from the clerks and customers. He looked into the dusky rear of the great room, where bales and boxes were piled almost to the ceiling, only a wide passage being open between the merchandise heaped everywhere. He slid noiselessly inside.

From frequent visits to the store, he knew the partners' "office," no more than an alcove, an open space left between stacked boxes, holding safe and table and chairs. He watched a Mexican clerk and two cowboys at the counter under a hanging light far front, seen as through a telescope down the passage he followed. The three were intent upon a Winchester, passing it from hand to hand, working the lever, sighting it.

But from the alcove, thirty feet or so ahead of him, carried the murmur of voices. He went slowly that way, listening to Shea's oily brogue, catching the phrases "fat steers" and "over on the Tecolote," then Rosen's harsh, accented voice, agreeing with "*ja ja!*" and something about Tecolote steers always being fat. He stopped, listening strainedly.

"Yeh!" a third voice drawled. "But me, I never did like that 'Owl' country. Folks over there got too much *tecolote* in 'em; see too damn good at night, over a front sight. Damn owls!"

Pony went quietly on, touching his six-shooter to see that the hang was right. He stepped into the ten-foot-wide opening to face the three men. But he had lost, this time. Not Curly Horton, but a hard-faced little cowboy, was third man here. He squatted, smoking, on the floor. The partners sat at their kitchen table desk, between it and the side wall.

"*Gott in himmel!*" Rosen breathed, china-blue eyes widening as he gaped at Pony. "Der man—himsellufs!"

Shea was of another caliber, a lanky, lantern-jawed

"black Irishman" who had been soldier and miner and teamster before settling in Ojo. His narrow dark eyes were steady on Pony's face, the only sign of emotion about him being the tightening of thin mouth. His long, hairy hands were on the table before him. They did not move. The cowboy only frowned slightly, then looked at Rosen and Shea in turn.

"Well!" Shea said evenly. "And this would be what ye might call a surprise!"

"Expected me before, I reckon," Pony drawled. "Expected me to hear about Pat Curran and come running—right into a nice, Ojo-style bushwhacking. I wasn't having any!"

"Undt—whats iss it you want, Fielder?" Rosen stammered. "*We* dond'ts do noddings to you! We—"

"Who bought the stock off our place—mine and Curran's—when Bully Witt cleaned the range? Don't bother about lying, either; I know you two thieves got everything, then handed Bully his share. It was a put-up job and I damn well know it!"

"Ye never heard of sich a thing as a writ, maybe?" Shea thrust in calmly. "Or maybe a coort order, huh? Witt had 'em all. We was asked to bid on the stuff he'd saized. We bid and the bid was took. And, so—"

Pony had his back to the boxes, where he could watch the passage toward the front, yet face the three. Contemptuously, he looked from partner to partner, thumb hooked in slanting shell belt. The cowboy was motionless, hand at his mouth, pinching a cigarette. He drew in smoke; released it. He was like a man sitting in a theater, intent upon a play.

"Suppose I tell you I don't give a hoot about all the writs and orders and warrants Bully Witt can pack?" Pony demanded between his teeth. "With the kind of justice the three of you whittle out of clothespins, around

Ojo, he could get a warrant for the governor by just asking. Suppose I tell you I drifted in, tonight, to collect three thousand dollars from you, Shea, and you, Rosen, and from Witt?"

"Tell us!" Shea invited him, almost indifferently. "It won't be making the bitsiest bit of difference, Fielder. Ye couldn't collect it because it's not here, nor even the little part of it. Ye'd find eighty or maybe a hundred dollars in the store. And if ye *kill* us, ye'll find no more."

"Where's Witt?" Pony grunted, scowling.

"Bear Paw, it might be. Or maybe he wint on to Jupiter."

"And where's Curly Horton?"

"And how would I be knowing? Sure, he walked out no more than twinty minutes back, like a man with something big on the mind of him. He—"

It was Rosen's face, not Shea's iron mask, that warned Pony. Into the pale eyes a light seemed to flicker—a triumphant glitter. And Rosen was looking past him, Pony observed, looking toward the dark rear of the store. He slid to the left and whipped out his Colt and struck with the barrel as the wind from a descending knife and hand touched his face. Squat, one-eyed Ygnacio Lopez, handy man of the store, reputed to be Shea and Rosen's killer, drove his knife in a short arc through that space where Pony had been, and deep into a box, with muffled grunt.

Pony's pistol barrel licked across his cheek, was jerked back and crashed full upon his skull. He dropped soundlessly at Pony's feet.

Sure of his harmlessness, Pony turned the Colt to the left. Rosen had not moved—except to shiver. Shea had a long hand out of sight beneath the table. The cowboy was on his feet, hand at the front of his shirt. But Pony's Colt froze them where they were. Then Shea lifted his hand to the table; the cowboy's hand fell away from the gap in his shirt.

"You don't seem to be hiring the right kind of hands," Pony told the partners meditatively. "I reckon the trouble with you all is, you think, because a man's a scoundrel no decent polecat'd walk with, he can do your jobs. You think, because a man's willing to cut a throat for hire, he's *able* to cut a throat."

He shook his head. Rosen was looking hopelessly at the sprawling Lopez. Shea faced Pony with bushy brows drawn down. The cowboy pressed back against the boxes and kept his hands rigidly against his thighs.

"I'll pay you a compliment, Shea," Pony went on evenly. "You're a filthy son of a dog who'd double-cross his own mother—the same as Rosen. The smell of you turns my stomach. But you're the best man of *The Three Thieves of Ojo!* You ought to do more of your own dirty work. It'd be better done. Rosen's got the backbone of a white slug. Witt's got no brains. You will have to do some of your murders with your own hand, or Rosen and Witt'll hang you!"

From the passage, where Lopez had been, carried the tiniest scuffing sound. Pony moved as if hurled by a spring. He could do only one thing—jump and spin about, back open to attack from the front of the store, but facing that sound and, too, keeping the trio in the alcove on his right and in view.

Curly Horton had come back, through the rear door. He was jumping for the open side of the alcove when Pony crossed it, and his Colt was out. They fired almost together, but Pony dropped the hammer on a second shell, and Curly Horton staggered and dropped his pistol after the one shot. He jerked with impact of that second slug, half fell, half ran, into the office, to cannon into the cowboy, now jerking a gun.

Pony squatted flashingly, for out of the blur of movement on his right, he had seen Shea lifting a pistol. The roar of it drowned the whine of that slug going over him. He snapped a bullet at the oil lamp beyond Shea in a wall bracket. The lamp exploded and flaming kerosene rolled in a sheet down the wall and across the table. Instantly, someone yelled in pain. He twisted, then, to fire up the passage at the big hanging lamp in the store. Clerk and customers had vanished from the counter. The lamp went out and he ran down the passage, to jump through the back door. Mig's voice lifted shrilly from behind the shed.

"I have Dan, *amo!* Loose! Quick, for the town comes!"

CHAPTER V

"You cannot kill twice"

IN THE THICK PINON GROWTH of Table Mountain, Pony and Mig tangled the plain trail left from the county seat and pointing east toward Jupiter. Then Pony turned north across trailless range and with dawn the two made camp, high in the hills.

Pony had hardly spoken since swinging up on Dan for the run out of Ojo. Mig had asked one question and he had answered curtly that Horton was dead.

Now, the boy took Pony's carbine with inquiring lift of dark brows. He slipped into the trees and presently shots sounded. Pony hardly listened. Curly Horton was dead. One thing, at least, the Territory would know—that not always could a murderer of the Horton stripe swagger it after his cowardly kill, untouched by punishment!

But there was still the lying Felix Avila, Bully Witt's willing tool. Avila was responsible with Witt for loss of

the ranch, for Pat Curran's death, for Pony Kirk's outlawry. Pony found himself now brooding upon Avila.
The Mexican had been sole witness, that day on Cross J
range when he and Pat Curran had met Johnson, and the
Cross J owner, slow on the draw for once in his life, had
died under Pony Kirk's slug.

"I can't even say that Bully Witt talked Avila into
lying about the shooting," Pony reminded himself, as he
had done many times in the past year. "Avila cleaned
Johnson's gun and swore that I shot Johnson in the back
and Pat shot at him. If Witt had told Avila to do all that,
I would've killed a sheriff long ago. But—I can't say that
he did."

A half-dozen times he had shifted aim to avoid killing
Witt. He might shoot a posseman and somehow, sometime, come clear of the charge. But the death of an officer at his hand, while he resisted arrest, would mean
outlawry forever. So, since he had never been sure that
Witt had done more than take advantage of Avila's lies,
he had held his fire even when hard pressed. Only Alec
Sells and Johnson and, now, Curly Horton, could be
charged to his account. Given altered conditions in the
Territory, a fair trial, he thought that he could be ac-
quitted of any charge against him. But—

"I can't do it!" he said at last, between his teeth. "I
can't leave without settling Felix Avila, even if it means
staying on the dodge the rest of my life. He had as much
to do with killing Pat Curran as Curly Horton did."

Mig came back, carrying squirrels. They broiled them
and ate and wiped their hands on the grass.

"You did not hurt Shea and Rosen?" Mig asked at last.

"No," Pony said wearily. "Except, perhaps, by making
the lamp explode and causing Shea to be burned by the
oil. They deserve to be killed, like Witt, but I cannot
shoot at men who do not come at me with pistols drawn.

I would make a very poor officer, in Ojo! There was a cowboy there, a man I do not know. I think he shot at me, that Shea also shot at me. But I fired only at Horton and he came to kill me. We shot almost together, but— he missed."

"It was Don Pat," Mig said with a grave nod. "He stood beside Horton and jogged his Colt. Those things happen, *amo*. But, now? We will go to my father's house?"

"Only for food. Then I ride to kill Felix Avila."

"Avila! But—but, *amo!* He is on the Cross J, with many men always about him. You could not come to face him without being shot by many guns."

"There is a way," Pony told him calmly. "There is always a way. I will not leave the Territory until I have killed Avila—or failed so that I cannot kill him, or leave."

They were above Miguel Chacon's house in midafternoon. Pony scowled down the slope, then turned to Mig.

"It seems quiet. I think none but your people are there. But I will stay here, Miguelito. No trail of mine will go to the house. So, if Bully Witt comes, there will be nothing for him to find. Ride down and bring back something to eat. And tobacco, if any is in the place."

Mig stared curiously at him, seemed about to speak, then nodded and rode his sorrel down through the brush and stunted piñon trees. Pony sat, making a cigarette of his last tobacco, smoking moodily. By tomorrow he would be hidden on the Cross J. No matter how long he had to hide and watch, eventually he would find Felix Avila. Then—

Mig was long in coming, and when he rode back up the slope, it was behind his father. They swung to the ground and the boy put down a white cloth.

"The new deputy came here, from Dog Canyon," Miguel Chacon told Pony. "He had lost your trail and *someone* in that posse thought that you might have turned to me for help. It was sad, but I could tell him nothing. I could not remember, even, when I had last seen you, it had been so many months. I think he may not have believed everything I said, but—he rode away. The boy tells me that you killed Horton; and that you could have killed those two *ladrones,* Shea and Rosen, but would not."

"And now I am going to kill Felix Avila," Pony said, nodding. "I will find him and give him a pistol in his hand—then kill him. Afterward, I ride for Mexico, I think."

"Avila?" Chacon cried. "But—but did you not hear what I heard? Avila died two days past. He tried to ride a stallion and it threw him and his foot hung in the stirrup. You cannot kill twice."

Pony glared at him. But, after a moment, he shrugged. If Avila had died violently, it seemed as if judgment had come to him, for the lies he had told. And his death simplified the affairs of Pony Kirk. Avila had made a statement and sworn to it. But some day—when conditions were greatly changed in the Territory—Chance Fielder might feel safe in standing trial, knowing that a statement might not be admitted, where a witness could take the stand.

"Yes, he is dead," Chacon said slowly. "So, I think that your *negócios,* your business, is done as well as you can do it at this time. It will be death, if not today or tomorrow, if you stay, *amigo.* When Bully Witt learns of our last raid upon the Flying W, that, if not your killing of Horton, will make him sleep upon your trail. This new deputy is no Horton. He will follow you like a hound the wolf."

"*Es verdad,*" Pony agreed. "It is truth. I will go. Now. There is nothing to hold me here and, like you, I have a very good opinion of this new man, Couch. I will take this food and tobacco and I will go—"

He stopped, frowning. The letter had come to mind. Mentally, he repeated the phrases that girl, that distant cousin of his, had put into the mouth of old Roaring Red Roy— Only four of his line left; only two of the Kirk name. Suddenly, his hard, strained face relaxed.

"*Por dios!*" he grunted. "Miguel, I have the desire to see some of my own blood. That letter you know of, it was from a cousin of my father's. He has a horse ranch in Texas. He asks that I come to visit him. I will go there!"

"The people of a man's own blood are good," the grizzled Chacon said, nodding. "If they are good. If they are not—you know the saying of our folk: 'Better a quiet bed in cactus than lacking sleep in the house of your wife's mother.'"

"I will go to Texas. And, *amigo mio*, I thank you for all the help you have given me. To Miguelito I owe my life, from the other night at Dog Canyon. To you—"

"There is no debt! You would have done as much for me and any of mine. You gave me money for the great doctor when my woman was dying, and he kept her from dying. But one favor I will ask. Take this cub with you. He will be nothing when you are gone. For he wishes to be such as you are—a friend of his friends, death to his enemies, open of hand, afraid of nothing that walks or runs or flies— Take him, *amigo*. He will come back, one day, a man!"

"But it is not good for a boy to ride with any outlaw! I think that such riding might shape him so that he could never be the *ranchero* that you would have him. Even now, if Witt knew how much he has helped me—"

"But, I think he does know. Or he will know, soon. The *diablito* has not told you, but after we took those steers, he was chased by some of the posse which caught you at

Dog Canyon. And he must lead them in a looping trail and lie above them and fire at them. He says he hit one of those rascals from the Flag Saloon. The posse knows him." ·

"All right!" Pony surrendered. "I will take him and try to keep him from harm. Tell your mother and your small sisters *adiós*, Mig. Then we will ride. Tonight we sleep in the old place on Wolf Peak, above the Nacho road."

"I have told them," Mig said, grinning. "I knew that you would take me, when you were sure that I must hide or ride."

He nodded to his father, mounted the sorrel, and gathered up the reins. Pony and Chacon shook hands when Pony sat the big black. Then Mig led the way up the hill and from the crest waved cheerfully to his father. He was grinning, and Pony, looking at him, grinned, also. He guessed that it was thought of riding a new road, into a strange country, that affected Mig. But now that he had turned his back on the Territory, he found himself in much the same mood.

"What kind of outfit, I wonder, is old Cousin Roaring Red Roy running?" he asked himself. "And what kind of people are Constance Hall and Floyd Milton? Red Roy I can sort of see; Dad told me enough about the hell-raising old *lobo* to give a picture. But the others— What is it, *muchacho?*"

"What manner of place is this Texas?" Mig repeated. "I have listened to you men of Texas so much that almost I have believed it no less than a part of heaven, different from all other land beneath sun and moon, where every man is twelve feet tall and every woman is beautiful!"

Pony laughed. They were over the ridge, now, facing a land that seemed empty of man.

"Perhaps all that is not true; not altogether true. But
—once a *Tejano*, always and forever a *Tejano!* We men
of Texas gave to all this country the cow business; taking
our herds away to the northward, even across the *frontera*
into the country called Canada. I—have explained this,
a time or two, to men of Idaho and Montana and Wyo-
ming and Canada, as to vaqueros of California. But you
will see! I say only that some of the best men and some
of the worst men I have ever met were Texans."

Darkness found them upon Wolf Peak, as Pony had
planned. They camped and ate the beef and beans and
tortillas brought from Chacon's and slept until dawn in
a shallow cave which had sheltered Pony and Pat a score
of times. After breakfast they rode cautiously through
pines, paralleling the Nacho road. For Pony could not
forget the skillful trailing of that deputy, Couch. Now
that he was going, he wanted no more fighting in the
Territory.

In late afternoon they came out of the timber and began a descent to the comparative flatness of a bit of
plains watered by the Ojo's tributary, the Culebra. Down
there was an ancient *rancho*, the Hacienda Miramar, a
Spanish grant to the Tinocos. Pony knew Don Joaquin
Tinoco very well. As Chance Fielder the rancher he had
bought stock from Don Joaquin; and Chance Fielder the
outlaw had eaten and slept a good many times in Tinoco
line camps. But Mig voiced his thoughts of the moment.

"He is a great man, Don Joaquin," the boy said slowly,
staring downslope at the checkered fields of Miramar.
"And a good man, too, we think, remembering always
that since the day of Oñate, and before, the Tinocos have
been *caballeros*, scorning to cheat or steal or betray. Except, my father says, perhaps in a large manner worthy
of grandees— But—with all the Territory humming
against you, *amo*, more than ever before, I am wondering

if we dare trust Don Joaquin too far!"

"His son, young Joaquin, *is* close to the governor at Faith, and wishes to be closer," Pony admitted, grinning. "I think we will not strain good Don Joaquin's liking, my son! We will look at Miramar and, if Don Joaquin is alone, we will eat with him. But if he has visitors, important men like sheriffs or marshals or deputies, we will not go pushing rudely in, to interfere with Don Joaquin's hospitality to them. And we will explain that we go north, to see the Rowdy River and the Diamond. We go immediately, we will say. So Don Joaquin will understand that it is not worth while to send any word of our stay on Miramar to—anyone."

He laughed and Mig grinned, watching him.

"That is good!" the boy said suddenly. "That you laugh again, I mean. You look like the man who used to ride up to our corral in—before the troubles came. Laugh again, *amo!* I like to hear that sound."

They came to the flat and forded the Culebra, to ride along the *acequias,* the ditches that brought water to Miramar's fields from the river. There was a straggling collection of 'dobe houses, the quarters of Don Joaquin's vaqueros and laborers, behind the great house. Here a slim youngster putting on the *chivarrias,* the leather leggings of the Mexican rider, looked curiously from one to the other with eyes as dark and alert as a wolf's.

Don Joaquin, he told Pony, was in the big house. On Miramar was none but Mirámar's folk.

Pony thanked him and rode on to the patio entrance. He left Mig with the horses and clicked down the tiled passage to the open square around which the house was built. Don Joaquin had settled his considerable bulk in a great rawhide-laced chair. He was smoking peacefully until a turning of big head showed him Pony within two yards. Then he straightened with a jerk, and the cigarette fell to the tiles.

"Amor de dios!" he whispered. "I—I— Don Chance! This is the last place in the world that you should have come. Only yesterday, the sheriff and three men were here, with questions, questions, questions! They asked me this and that; they asked my people this and that. Always about you. Other posses search north and east and south— everywhere! The sheriff may come back this way. He said that might be—or not."

He stopped, panting. There was no mistaking his nervousness. Sweat stood on his brown forehead and the thick hand he gestured with was trembling.

"I thank you for the word. Now, I will not risk his coming back and finding me here—nor anything else that might make trouble between you and the law. We will eat with you, beg a little food to take with us—there is a boy with me—and go on. I think, now that you tell me of this new hunt, the Rowdy River will be safer than anywhere else."

"It will be! Put it behind you, Don Chance. Ride on to the ranches along the Diamond River. The sheriff has heard that you—he believes that you—stole steers from his pasture and sold them. I, of course, know nothing of this. I would not believe such a tale. But he believes it! So he hunts you and, this time, he says it will be to the death. I think he went toward Jupiter again."

He got up laboriously and waved his thick arm around.

"It is your house! But—but I think that you will never be safe from death, in the Territory. Colorado, California, Texas, Mexico—anywhere will be better. One day these troubles will pass; the country will be quiet. Then all things may be arranged to clear you of the charges written against you. But now— Come with me, Don Chance. What Miramar can give is yours—food, tobacco, cartridges —And I hope that you will leave the Territory far behind with all the speed that lies in your horse's heels!"

"I go, as I said," Pony told him calmly. "And I hope that none tries to stop me."

He grinned reassuringly at Don Joaquin, but the *ranchero* was too badly shaken to notice. Bully Witt, Pony thought, had evidently acted here like—Bully Witt.

CHAPTER VI

"I hit Bully Witt"

PONY LAUGHED as they rode away from Miramar. There was no doubting the sincerity of Don Joaquin's good-bys. He wanted only to see their backs and that for the last time. They had been fed at his own table; in the saddlebags were cooked food and .44 cartridges and tobacco. Don Joaquin had fairly crammed the *alforjas* with whatever he saw in the storeroom.

"And so we ride as toward the Rowdy," Pony told Mig. "Until we are out of sight of his people. Then we will twist about. Tomorrow, Nacho! And then we can say *adiós!* to the Territory, *muchacho!*"

They slept in a canyon and Mig roused Pony before daylight. When they had eaten in darkness, making no fire, Mig went to saddle his horse without stopping for a cigarette. He said that he felt something. But what that something was—

"I do not know," he confessed. "But it is bad. Let us go, *amo!* I do not like to be caged in a canyon such as this. Not unless I know where the other people are. Let us go!"

Pony laughed, but went to saddle Dan. They were gathering up the reins, ready to start, when Mig caught Pony's arm and whispered tensely. Pony nodded. He had heard that clink of horseshoe on rock, somewhere off to the right. He slipped the carbine from its scabbard and waited, but there was no more sound in the darkness.

"It might have been a stray horse of Don Joaquin's," he told Mig. "We are to the side of them. So we go on to Nacho. I think that we will not see them."

They came out of the canyon and turned to the right. Nacho, last town of the Territory, lay that way.

Pony thought that nobody in the little *plazita* knew him. He had been there but once in all his time of wandering about the Territory. They rode for a dozen miles before the sun rose. Then at trot, lope; trot, lope. All that day they saw nobody except a few lean, tanned, and silent cowboys and Mexican *pastores* herding goats or sheep on the ridges, gaunt, wild figures with each a dog at his heels and a pouch of smooth stones for the inevitable sling. In late afternoon they saw Nacho below them and there was nothing to be seen through Pony's glasses to alarm them.

"Thirty miles from here and we will be gone from Bully Witt's reach," he told Mig as he lowered the binoculars. "I think we are safe to ride through the place; the country on each side is rough. We gain time by using the road."

There were no more than a dozen 'dobes in the village. A few horses stood under cottonwoods or mulberries, along the fronts of the houses. They rode looking left and right, Mig with rifle across his arm, Pony with his carbine scabbarded. Then a man came from what seemed to be a saloon, a long 'dobe with four horses standing half asleep before it. He stared at them, scratching his red-stubbled face, nodded slightly, then walked slowly to the corner of the 'dobe and went around it.

Pony watched him go, but only because watchfulness was ingrained in him, had become second nature during a year on the dodge. For the man was a most ordinary sort of figure, shabby in old gray hat and faded flannel shirt and waist overalls rammed into rusty boots. And, too, he had not seemed interested in the newcomers to Nacho.

But when he saw Mig's inquiring lift of brows, on impulse Pony spun Dan and turned at the near corner of the 'dobe, to ride along its wall and look along the backs of the buildings on this side of the road. And there was his man, not walking, now, but running with head down and elbows held close to his side, as if racing with someone.

Pony turned back to the road and to Mig he said quickly, "Keep going, boy! Ride faster than I do. Go straight on out of Nacho. Something funny's here. I won't have you mixing in. If—anything happens, you go back home to your father. If anybody stops you, asks you anything, you just met me on the way. You don't know me from Adam's off-ox—the white-faced one!"

"But—" Mig began, scowling. "But—"

"Go!" Pony said, slipping into Spanish. "I will not have you beside me. Whatever this may be, it will be something for men, not children. Now—go!"

Sulkily, Mig touched his sorrel with a rowel and left Pony to continue at the walk between Nacho's 'dobes. Men were here and there, in doorways, on the hard-packed ground which served as sidewalks. Mig rode at the trot. At the far end of Nacho he turned in the saddle to wave and Pony jerked left hand up in answer. Then the boy disappeared, going around some building.

Pony, lounging in the saddle like any weary man thinking of a place to eat and drink and rest, wondered why the man had pretended lack of interest in him, then rushed away as if to carry an urgent message. It seemed to him unlikely that Bully Witt could be here in Nacho. The sheriff had left Miramar pointing toward Jupiter, according to Don Joaquin's account. Nor was there any sign here on the street of sheriff or posse.

"Of course, word might've been sent to look out for me," he admitted, eyes shuttling left and right, ears strained to hear any sound behind him. "And if that fellow's one of the lookouts, he might've run to tell the constable or deputy—"

Then Bully Witt came from a doorway as if hurled out, with three or four men behind him. He had a pistol in each hand and his big body was slightly stooped, his feet set apart. The men backing him also had drawn guns.

Scoundrel that he was, partner of those other thieves, Shea and Rosen, Bully Witt had one quality which made many in the Territory forgive him his sins. He was a bulldog in a fight, and Pat Curran, who had known the sheriff far longer than Pony, had always speculated on the comparative speed on the draw of Bully Witt and Pony Kirk.

Pony did three things flashingly, so rapidly that they seemed almost simultaneous. He whipped the ready Colt from his holster, fired at Witt only a split-second after Witt had loosed two shots that were very close, then spun Dan and sent him rocketing across the road to the wide doorway of a store.

Behind him the possemen were shooting. He heard the sinister whine of lead past his ears; saw the bullets knock dust from the 'dobe front of the store. But Witt, he thought, was not shooting. He had seen the sheriff drop his right-hand gun and jerk the wounded arm like a man stung by a wasp, then bend to the pistol as if forgetting that his extended left hand already held a Colt.

Pony lay over the saddle horn and spurred Dan straight at that open door. Inside the store, he turned and emptied his pistol at the possemen, now running into the street after him. They scattered and ran back as his lead sang around them. Clerks and customers in the store jumped or dived for the shelter of counters or stacked merchandise. Dan walked the length of the store and Pony ducked again to clear the lintel of the back door. He reholstered the empty Colt.

He jumped Dan into a gallop and raced along the backs of this row of buildings. Hoofs clattered behind him and he reached for his carbine as he turned. But it was Mig, holding his rifle high like an Indian, the gleam of teeth splitting his dark face in a warrior grin. Pony swore and got out his Winchester. With Mig's sorrel at Dan's heels, he left Nacho and the hollow rattle of shots that told—Pony thought—of the posse cautiously pounding the front of that store.

He slowed a little and when Mig was at his stirrup he looked up at the low sun and grinned.

"It won't be hard," he yelled, "to keep ahead till dark. I hit Bully Witt. Hope I broke his damn arm. But you never can tell. Maybe I just skinned his knuckles. Anyway, we've got a start And, come dark, we'll show 'em a wolf trail—a whole damn tangle of wolf trail. Thought I told you to hightail it! Not to mix in."

"But I did go!" Mig yelled back, over the drumming of hoofs. "You said nothing of not coming back if I heard shooting. And when the shooting began, naturally, I wished to know what it meant. Anyone would have wished to know! So—I came back, and when I saw them shooting at you, I forgot, *amo!* I shot at them once."

"Bet you never went a bit farther'n around one 'dobe and right back!" Pony charged. "Just hunting a chance to unlimber that one-bark yellow-belly. Hit anybody?"

"I *killed* nobody! I had but the one shot, so I kept it for what seemed a certain target. But I had no luck. This old Remington shoots never the same way twice. One time it carries to the right, the next time to the left. So,

when I aimed carefully at the belly of a fat man behind
Bully Witt the bullet struck a man five feet away—in the
leg. I could have cried!"

Pony, looking at that woebegone face, burst into a
whoop of amusement. Mig scowled for an instant, then
grinned.

"If I had sighted *your* carbine, *amo,* that fat man would
now be yelling away his life, louder than ever he yelled
over the Flag whisky that Bully Witt serves free to such as
he and his kind. I need a new gun."

"And a new gun we'll buy you," Pony promised. "The
minute we land in Texas, Mig, at some store where we
can outfit, we'll both jump into the middle of new clothes
and things. When we hit that Two Bench spread, over
behind Vasko, we'll be cowboy dudes. We'll scatter some
of the money we lifted off of Bully Witt to do the paying,
too!"

"One comes!" Mig said quickly, leaning a little, turning his head wolfishly. He had ears like any wild thing.
"One horse, ridden by a man who is not hurrying."

"I hear—now. There is no need to turn. If we have
heard him, he has heard us. And I think that we are not
afraid of one man—even a Texas man!"

They went on through gray light, keeping to the lope.
A man topped a ridge a hundred yards or less away. One
glance at the black, telescoped hat, the general shape of
the rider, and Pony grunted, "Arizona!" to himself.

They pulled in, and the cowboy's shrewd, restless dark
eyes flashed from one to the other, then came to rest on
Pony's blank face.

"Hi," he said tonelessly. "Been to Nacho? I'm off Ewbanks's Rafter E, on the Culebra nawth fawk. Heading
for Nacho. Our noble sher'f there? One of his posses is
eating the boss out of house and home. I swear, I never
seen a finer bunch of chuck-line special dep'ties. If they

could just hold a eating contest with this Chance Fielder they're supposed to be hunting, the boy'd be the same as hung, this minute."

Pony studied the bronzed, good-humored face without reply, for a half minute.

"Rafter E," he said at last. "The word has got to me that Ewbanks is a good, straight man."

"And he don't team it with Bully Witt too well, either," the cowboy added, nodding. "Now, some on the spread, I won't answer for. But the most part of us in the bunk-house. if we was to meet up with this Fielder, I bet you we'd even beg him out of a cigarette."

He put out his hand toward the dangling tag of Pony's tobacco sack and Pony held out the *Seal of North Carolina*. The cowboy went on talking, almost as to himself, while he made his cigarette.

"Yes, sir, a grand bunch of saloon dep'ties. But they say Bully Witt's out to loop this Fielder; got three-four posses combing the country. They aim to squat across the road by the Rafter E, in case he heads that way. If he was to ride along this road, now, he'd run right into a first-class bushwhacking. But, if he was to come from Nacho—even with somebody on his trail—and turn over yonder to about the white pillar, he'd find himself in right rocky country. Man couldn't trail a herd of elephants through that *malpais*—and this ain't what you'd call right *good* elephant country. Then he'd bear for three peaks in a row—Three Fingers, we call 'em. He'd ride past them and—one posse'd still be eating the Rafter E into a new page on the family mawtgage."

"I bet this Chance Fielder would appreciate knowing all that—if he was up this way," Pony said gravely, understanding. "I reckon he turned north, though, hitting for the Rowdy and the Diamond, after he had his li'l run-in with Bully Witt at Nacho a while back. He wouldn't take this road. So you won't meet him. Reckon you won't see a soul, unless it's somebody out of Nacho thinking he rode this way."

"That's so," the cowboy agreed, blowing smoke. "Certainly is a lonesome road, when you ride clean from the Rafter E to Nacho and never see a soul; can't even find a *pastor* to beg a cigarette from. Well, I can't set here a-talking to myself. Somebody might come along and think I turned sheepherder in my old age."

He looked placidly at the second button on Pony's shirt—as if there were no button, no shirt. He gathered up his rawhide reins and the buckskin horse he rode swung forward in running-walk. They watched him go, Pony grinning. To them carried his cheerful voice, a pleasant baritone.

> "I love not Colorado,
>   Where the faro table grows,
>   And down the desperado
>   The rippling bourbon flows;
>
> "Sweet poker-haunted Kansas
>   In vain allures the eye;
>   Nevada rough has charms enough
>   But its blandishments I fly—"

"I think," Pony told Mig drawlingly, "that we'll just let the Rafter E *get* devoured out of house and home. It'd be a shame to yank Witt's bold guerrillas up from table, just to have buttonholes stitched in 'em. We'll hit for the *malpais* and the Three Fingers.

> "Shall Arizona woo me—
>   Where the sweet Apache bides?
>   Or New Mexico, where natives grow
>   With arrow-proof insides?

"Nay, 'tis where the grizzlies wander
And the lowly Diggers roam,
Where the grim Chinese from the squatter flees,
That I'll make my humble home!"

CHAPTER VII

"I'll have to buttonhole you"

VASKO MAIN STREET opened before them, two weeks later, as a shallow canyon, drenched with fall sunlight, the canyon walls—buildings of frame or brick, for the most part one story high with square false fronts upon which signs were painted. Pony sat Dan and viewed the county seat critically through narrowed lids, from the courthouse on his left, a smallish yellow brick building with boxlike cupola and tin figure of Justice, to what seemed to be the public corral at the far end of the street. Vasko, he thought, looked to be a drowsy little town.

He grunted to Mig and they went, with the horses walking, along the dusty street, Pony looking left and right curiously. Upon a building ahead of him he saw the sign *H. L. McCune, Lawyer—Abstracts,* and it occurred to him that he might easily learn the road to the 2 Bench from the lawyer. He wanted to ask as few questions here as might be. Two quiet weeks were too unusual to do other than make him uneasy and watchful. And, he reminded himself, there were such things as reward notices, to travel far and meet a wanted man.

On his right was a large store with wooden awnings over plank-floored porch. Here two young Mexicans sat with legginged legs thrust out before them. Between them was a can—of peaches, Pony guessed. They looked neither up nor down but only sideways—each watchful of the size of the other's grab at the can.

In the thin shadow of the Criterion Saloon hitchrack a man sprawled, mouth open, snoring so loudly that he could be heard for thirty yards, and with the forehoof of a cow pony almost against his bulbous red nose.

The Mexicans, the sleeping drunk, were for the moment the only signs of human life on Vasko's street.

Then a squat, gray-haired woman stepped from a doorway just ahead and to the right of them. She shaded her eyes against the westering sun and spoke over her shoulder to someone still in the small building which bore the sign *Quaid's Racket Store*.

"I can't see a thing of him; not a smidgin of sign of him, honey," she called. "Can't even see the buggy. But if ever a man *was* to git somewheres he was supposed to be, nigher'n the *day* he was supposed to git there—"

A girl came out of the racket store to stand beside her and also stare along the street, a slim figure in tailored tweed suit.

Young Mig gaped at her and to Pony muttered, "*Amo,* this is one who looks like the pictures I have seen in a *diario,* a newspaper! Is she, then, of this your Texas? Or from some great city like New York?"

"*Quien sabe?*" Pony answered in the same low tone. "But I think that she is not a girl of Vasko. I have seen her like upon the streets in Dallas and Kansas City and San Francisco and Chicago. The clothes she wears—but more, much more, *muchacho,* the way she has of wearing them."

"Not a soul in sight," the older woman said now. "You could believe the whole blame town was sound asleep. Just that trifling, worthless Pink Snake Casselberry under the Criterion hitchrack, a-snoring fit to shake every window in Vasko. Must be some pilgrim in town! Pink Snake can't mooch drinks off the home folks no more. Well, honey, nothing to do but set down and wait till he comes, I reckon. He—"

She turned then, as if hearing for the first time the soft, slow fall of the horses' hoofs, to stare at Pony and Mig. The slim girl turned, also. Pony met their eyes with blank face, uninterested manner. But Mig straightened in the big-horned saddle. He was very proud of himself, barbered and rigged from head to foot as he was in new clothes—gray Boss Stetson, short blanket jacket over blue flannel shirt, pants of fine, dark-blue woolen, tucked neatly into new boots. Only his bone-handled .44 Colt was out of sight, with holster and belt in a saddle bag. But the new Winchester carbine was in its sleek, new scabbard and Mig was—and realized it—the very model of a *gran vaquero*.

She's certainly pretty, Pony thought, studying the smooth oval of her face, the wide, dusky eyes that watched him so intently. *About the prettiest girl I ever saw, I do believe. And, if she's Texas, she's been other places. Not a country girl in the state'd know how to handle those clothes and put that li'l hat on just that way.*

Then his mouth tightened. In her fashion, Berta Schwartz had been as lovely as this aristocratic vision, certainly as lovely in the eyes of poor Pat Curran. And because she was the beauty of all the Ojo country, with men hanging around to do anything she asked, Berta had turned from one man to another, playing with their lives—

"It's the way of pretty girls, I reckon," Pony told himself grimly, now. "They get spoiled. They think they're too damn important. And you take hell's own chance when you put your trust in any of 'em. What's this one want to stare at me like that for? Cowboy must be some kind of circus animal to her. But the old woman's about as bad—and if she's Mrs. Quaid she certainly has looked at enough leather-pounders to take off the edge of her curiousness."

He straightened a little in the saddle. Like Mig, he was newly outfitted from black hat to tan boots, his yellow hair trimmed, his bronzed face shaved except for small mustache.

Except in the most casual fashion, he had never owned much interest in women, or attached importance to anything they said or did. The ten years of his wandering life just behind him, between the ages of sixteen and twenty-six, had been spent chiefly with men. Women were generally of two kinds only, in the cowboys' opinion. Pony had gone by the wives and daughters of cowmen almost without looking at them. At the end of a job, spree-minded, he had danced with such girls as were found in the honkytonks of thirty cowtowns, made light and care-less love to them—and gone on without a backward look. Now, it did not occur to him that any woman might look at him with interest—except for what she might get from him.

But his ears were quite good. So across the thirty feet that separated him from the women, he heard the older one's murmur of talk.

"Looky, child! You said you never seen a gunman. If *that* ain't one my name ain't Lucretia Quaid! Looky how that hand hangs close to where he'd wear his pistol if he wasn't in a town! I seen too many in my day, not to know the real A-Number-One, top-notch, Simon-pure quill. And his face! That boy ain't over twenty-five or twenty-six, but he's seen trouble, honey, plenty trouble a-coming at him through the smoke. I tell you, Connie, I know the signs!"

Pony felt that he was reddening furiously. Inwardly, he snarled. So he was an exhibit, to be pointed out by fat old women to girls who wanted to see a gunman, as they might want to see an outlaw wolf or a man-killing tiger! But when he looked at Mig, after they had passed the Quaid store, the boy was grinning and fairly swaggering in the saddle.

"Por dios!" Mig grunted. "That señora has eyes in her head. She knows a man when he rides past her, *amo!*"

"Ahhh!" Pony growled at him. "She—and that girl—"

Then he thought of the name Mrs. Quaid had used, in addressing the girl. "Connie." And Connie was evidently a stranger, both to Vasko and to—gunmen.

"Connie," Pony said to himself, frowning. "What was it Roaring Red Roy said in the letter—or had said for him? Constance Hall is on the Two Bench, already— I— wonder! Could *that* be my de-ar fourteenth cousin back there? Be Constance Hall? Cousin Roy didn't say where she was from—"

He caught himself as he was about to turn and stare at the girl; stiffened in the saddle. And the sudden thought that came was troubling. If that girl should be Constance Hall, and he went on to the 2 Bench, he would have to meet her, day in and day out, for so long as he stayed on the place. He had been rather looking forward to meeting the others of his people. It had not occurred to him that one distant cousin might be a girl like that one, standing so calmly sure of herself, studying him as if he were some interesting sort of wild animal.

"Mig," he said savagely, "we have ridden a long way, *no es verdad?* From the Territory to this Vasko. And do you know why we have come so far, and to this place? You don't, my son! So, I'll tell you! We came here so's to leave for some other place. I have changed what passes for my mind. We'll find us a place to eat, sample Vasko red-eye, then pull out. Yes, sir, boy! There's heaps and heaps of country you never have put eyes on. Maybe some between here and the Canadian line that even I never saw. We'll bodaciously take our foot in our hand and wrap our hair in a braid and we'll take out. We—"

Vasko main street, tomb-still, virtually empty, suddenly gave the effect of exploding about the strangers in its middle. It was not a single eruption, but three outbursts that came almost simultaneously in a single block.

With terrific crash and bang of swinging doors flapped back, a tight knot of men came reeling out of the Criterion Saloon. Not quite one knot, Pony saw in the next instant. For a tall man separated himself from the others, swinging a heavy chair at the others, who surged toward him. He was like a jumping jack, sliding to right and left away from their charges and flailing with the chair at their heads.

Out of the saddle shop adjoining Lawyer McCune's office—across the street from the Criterion—a stocky man came like one jumping from a cliff, head forward, arms swinging stiffly forward. His hat fell off as he clumped down on the hard-packed earth of the sidewalk, but he did not halt to pick it up. He whirled and began to run desperately fast, if awkwardly because of high heels, straight toward Pony and Mig.

He had taken a half-dozen strides when another man ran out of the saddle shop, a wisp of a black little man. This one stopped as soon as he reached the street. He had a pistol in his left hand and he lifted it, to fire bent-armed, without seeming to aim, two fast shots after the running man. Dust jumped from the runner's brown duck jumper like a little puff of smoke. He staggered with impact of the striking bullet, his knees buckled and he fell face downward, pulled himself jerkily forward, tried to get up, then sagged and sprawled there, motionless.

In the doorway of the lawyer's office a wide-shouldered, gray-haired man was framed now, looking out. The little killer seemed not to see him. He was staring at the moveless figure beyond him. The broad man of lawyerish appearance kept his bare, gray head within the frame of his own door and watched both Pony and the black little man.

Pony, also, stared at the man who had been shot. But above the clamor of those fighting before the Criterion lifted, now, the dull sound of a shot, and he turned automatically, but still leaning, still holding his pistol, hidden in the *alforja*.

The battle between the tall, gray man of the chair and those who tried to reach him still swayed back and forth. But out of the Criterion behind them came a cowboy, backing through the swinging doors. He bent far over as Pony looked at him and hugged his stomach with both arms. He turned a little and his side face showed, convulsed agonizedly. Then he sat down upon the sidewalk and drooped until head almost touched legs. He fell over and his arms dropped away from his body.

"Well!" Pony said vaguely. "Well! And it looked like *such* a quiet town, this Vasko. And maybe it is—some days!"

He lifted his reins; Mig followed his example, but scowling uncertainly and keeping a hand upon the stock of his carbine. As Dan began to move, the little man on the sidewalk before the saddle shop looked up, turning on Pony a short, square face as vicious as a sidewinder rattlesnake's, with its low and wrinkled forehead, narrow, murky eyes, snub nose, and gash-thin mouth. His hand jerked.

Instinctively, Pony had leaned back to put his hand into the saddlebag holding his Colt when the first shot had been fired at the running man. Now, he straightened as the little killer fired at him, bringing out his gun cocked.

"Why, you o'nary son of a dog!" he drawled. "I'll have

to buttonhole you!"

His movements were as fast as his speech was slow. He shot twice, very rapidly, at the little man. It was this one's red shirt that showed puffs of dust now. But neither bullet hit in the center of the chest. Pony had loosed those shots more to disconcert him, throw him off balance and make him miss, than to kill him.

Before he could fire a third time, his target jumped backward and inside the door of the saddle shop. Pony drove the star-rowels into black Dan and followed, to the very doorway. But when he leaned there, gun thrust forward, the narrow room with its trestle of new saddles and row of shelving seemed empty. He looked warily along the shop. Then the pound of hoofs behind the place told him that his man had run. He shrugged and spun Dan about to face Mig, who had his Winchester out, now, and was looking everywhere for a target.

Before the Criterion the man who had been shot in the stomach moved weakly. And the tall, gray chair swinger was in the middle of the milling half dozen, swinging only a thick leg of the chair. As Pony looked that way there was a muffled shot somewhere in the press of bodies. A man came out, like a blob of mud flung from a spinning wheel. He went to hands and knees with a harsh, wordless sound that somehow cut through the noises around him, the panting, groaning, under-breath cursing, of the fighters.

Pony and Mig rode slowly over to the Criterion and sat looking at the battle. Up and down like a piston the gray man's club swung; he seemed tireless, invincible, holding his own against six or eight men. But on the edge of the group a man's hand jerked up to his shirt, came away again with a long knife. He began to thrust through the other fighters and Pony moved on impulse.

He rammed the rowels to Dan and sent the big horse

up on the sidewalk. The pistol he had rammed into his waistband came out. He leaned to swing it.

"You're a—noble bunch of—barroom champions!" he addressed them in biting drawl. "Nine-ten of you to one old man—but you got to—try to shoot him—or knife him. Why, I'd guarantee—to show an eight-year-old orphan—a female orphan—how to run a damn corralful—of the likes of you—clean out into the—mesquite! You—"

Scientifically, he cracked heads. Nor did he need more than one deft blow to a head. Men dropped, the first three or four without turning, without realizing that they were attacked from behind. Before the bloody-faced and gasping old man's club only a thin quartette stood. One of these had the knife. The gray man swung viciously at this one's arm and there was the dull snap of a bone, then the man's shrill howl of agony. He fell.

Pony's pistol smashed another and another as they whirled. The fourth man dropped with the bang of the chair leg upon his skull, rolled over, and scrambled up to run. Pony looked at the panting oldster, head on one side.

"Well," he drawled, "I reckon that sort of settles the cat-hop. Good thing, too; you haven't got much left of that chair you started out with. Better ram what's left into your pocket. When you land home you can whittle the ends round and it'll be just about the right size for a barn door button!"

For sixty seconds, perhaps, Vasko seemed to stand moveless, like a man drawing breath, with three dead or dying men sprawled in as many places on the street. Then, out of doorways or windows—or from those other places where they had concealed themselves to watch—the townsfolk came swarming.

The tall, gray old man, with those who littered the sidewalk about him, drew the crowd. Pony and Mig found

themselves ringed about by staring men. As he turned a
slow head to look, Pony saw the squat Mrs. Quaid and
the girl Connie, coming up to the edge of those who
packed the space before the Criterion. Somebody grunted
tensely, in the crowd, "Sheriff! Comes John Sanford, just
a-helling it!"

CHAPTER VIII

"So he begun rustling"

SHERIFF SANFORD WAS A HUGE MAN and he rode a big
horse. Now he spurred furiously along the street, legs
jerking as he roweled the bay, buttonless vest flapping,
showing, hiding, the badge he wore. The crowd gave
back with the thunder of the galloping hoofs and the big
sheriff rode to the edge of the Criterion sidewalk and
flung himself out of the saddle. One look around, a glance
at the still figure nearest him, and he lifted grim black
eyes to the old man with the club.

"Whut's all this, Roy?" he demanded. "Is—is Horace
Palm dead?"

"Damn if I know," Red Roy Kirk answered calmly.
"Damn if I give a hoot, either."

He turned his unswollen eye upon the sheriff. Pony,
watching with some amusement this battling ancient who
was his distant relative, thought that Roaring Red Roy's
eye resembled most a glittering blue marble. Red Roy
shrugged.

"Good reddance if Palm really is dead. Me, I would've
settled him with one lick of my chair, he hadn't been so
damn careful to keep behind the other scoun'els. Glad
to do it, too!"

The sheriff moved ponderously over to the prone figure, bent for a swift and practiced look and shake, then straightened. His square, dark face showed no emotion.

"Yeh, he's plumb dead," he told Red Roy.

He seemed, Pony thought, to take the fate of this black-stubbled and unpleasant-faced Palm as calmly as did the 2 Bench owner. He looked around.

"Looks like the slug plowed a furrow through his heart," Sheriff Sanford grunted. "Who done it? Who was it shot him? And why did it happen? What's all this about?"

Some of those knocked down by Red Roy and Pony were getting up now. The sheriff waved them over to stand against the Criterion's wall. Nobody saw fit to answer Sanford's questions and he turned scowling eyes from man to man.

"Did you do it?" he growled abruptly, staring at Pony.

"Not lately," Pony said evenly. "My notion is, it was a friend of his in the crowd, here. Tried to shoot him"—he indicated Red Roy Kirk—"and hit Palm. The whole lousy crew of imitation fighters"—now, he let his eyes go contemptuously to those who had recovered consciousness; looked at each in turn—"was out to comb the old boy. I heard a shot and Palm pinwheeled out of the bunch. Then another one pulled a knife and started. So I took cards."

But for all the indifference he kept in tone and face, he was wishing events had not so crowded into his face here, forcing this prominence. There was always the possibility that from over in the Territory reward notices had gone out of Bully Witt's office; that such as this huge, efficient-seeming sheriff of Vasko had his description—and black Dan's. Even though Bully Witt knew him only as Chance Fielder, while now he was using his real name; even though the original Bar C brand on Dan's shoulder had become a skillfully hair-branded Box O; still, a sheriff of

John Sanford's apparent caliber might find him to fit a printed description carefully pored over and memorized.

"Huh!" the sheriff grunted, his tone half doubtful, half suspicious. "For a stranger, seems to me you got a gun out right quick."

"Well," Pony told him gravely, "when I'm home, I'm not a stranger. That kind of tangles me up, account I got a poor memory, when I'm traveling."

From across the street a strong voice was calling Red Roy Kirk's name. The old man turned. In the doorway of the saddle shop stood the wide-shouldered man of lawyerish appearance, making beckoning motions.

"Come over here quick!" he called. "Big Otto Ozment is dying in the shop. He's calling for you, Roy. Hurry! He'll be gone in a few minutes."

"Big Otto!" Sheriff Sanford yelled in his turn, whirling. "Who shot him, Mac?"

"A little, dark man. Don't know who he is. Chased him out of the shop and shot him down. Come on! I've got the doctor, but he'll be cashing in his checks in a minute. I think he's got something to tell you, Roy."

"Shack!" the sheriff called fiercely, to a gangling, uncertain-looking young cowboy wearing a star, who had just clumped up and stood staring vacantly around. "Take charge here. I don't want ary one of this bunch to leave here till I come back. *Sabe?* You let one slip off and I'll bodaciously rip the trifling hide off you and bat you dizzy with it!"

He indicated the groggy men against the Criterion wall and two who still sprawled unconscious on the ground, where they had fallen in front of Red Roy Kirk. Then he ran after Red Roy, Pony, and Mig, who had started across the dusty street to the saddler's—followed by some of the curious.

Beside that cowboy shot down by the black little man,

on the floor of the shop, a white-haired man kneeled with a shabby black bag open. He looked up at Red Roy and the sheriff, as they, with Pony just behind, stopped before him.

"About gone," he said. "But I've given him a shot; his last strength is gathering, now. He wants to tell you something. Better be quick about it."

To Pony, this enormously wide Big Otto Ozment seemed already dead. His eyes were half closed, his mouth sagging, his breathing too light to move the shirt on his great chest. Red Roy Kirk scowled down at him, then went to his knees and touched the drawn face with hand surprisingly gentle.

"Otto!" he called shakily. "Otto! It's me, Roy Kirk. You want to tell me something?"

"Yeh," Ozment whispered, without so much as a flicker of eyelids. "Me and Ambrosius Quell—come to town—hunting you. I met Ike Isbell—in here—he picked a row—I knowed he had a gun—aimed to use it—run outside to git mine—my *alforja*—he shot me—back—"

Red Roy leaned closer to the cowboy. His battered, bloody face was twisted anxiously.

"Yeh? Yeh?" he demanded. "But, did you and Ambrosius find out anything? Otto! Otto! What did you and Ambrosius find out? Otto!"

Ozment was like a dead man, eyes glinting palely between his lids, mouth unmoving.

"Otto!" Red Roy called, in the voice which had given him the nickname "Roaring" among relatives and acquaintances both. "Did you and Ambrosius find out anything?"

"Plenty!" came the very ghost of a whisper from Ozment. "Last bunch of hawses was stole by—stole by—"

There was a long, breathless pause that seemed to last interminably. Then the sagging lids lifted and Ozment's mouth widened in a grin. Very naturally he looked up at Red Roy.

"You see?" he said, like one who had finished a full explanation. "He was gambling. Always losing. We knowed it. Had to git money. So he begun rustling. My notion is, that Ike Isbell—"

"Who was gambling? Who stole the horses? What did Ike Isbell have to do with it? You mean Ike Isbell got hard up, account he was losing at gambling, and stole Two Bench horses? Otto! Otto! Talk, boy! Talk!"

But that surge of energy was almost gone. Otto Ozment, who with Ambrosius Quell had discovered something about stolen horses, was far from the affairs of Red Roy Kirk and the 2 Bench, now, his mind wiped clean of consideration of gentry riding with "long" ropes and "hungry" loops and "flexible" running irons– or anything else that those around him knew. His eyes were still open. His smile was almost ludicrously wide, with something of amazement in it.

"Peggy!" he called in an excited tone. "Peggy! The li'l scoun'el bit my finger! He's got a tooth!"

And that was the last speech of Big Otto Ozment, a Bench rider. The doctor stood, when he had put a tiny mirror before Ozment's mouth. Red Roy got up, frowning, and looked vacantly about. When he faced the sheriff his head jerked.

"Ambrosius Quell!" he roared. "John, you heard him. He says him and Ambrosius found out who stole that last bunch of my horses. I sent the two of 'em out, to hunt sign of them damn thieves. And, looks like, they got the trail! Where's Ambrosius, though? Anybody see him?"

"I never," Sheriff Sanford grunted. "I was coming into town when I heard the racket. I never seen Quell."

"Did you, Mac?" Red Roy asked the lawyer. "You see him?"

"No. I just happened to see this Isbell, if that's his name, shoot Ozment—and this cowboy"—he nodded at Pony—"shoot Isbell and run him into the shop here. I carried Ozment in here and stopped the doctor. That's all I know."

"You shot at Isbell?" the sheriff said to Pony. "You certainly do ride right into the middle of things, for a stranger!"

"I'm downright sorry," Pony told him evenly. "I really am. If you want me to, I'll stand on your courthouse steps and beg the town's pardon for ramming into Vasko's private affairs, instead of yelling for some native to come save my life. But, you see, I was riding along, peaceful as a parson, when your damn street just come unraveled in my face. This Isbell shot him—Ozment. Then he shot at me. I would have buttonholed him, except I had to reach clean back to my *alforja* to find my hardware. I burned him twice, anyhow."

He turned from the sheriff to Red Roy.

"If *you* don't mind a stranger talking, in this Vasko that's the sheriff's private, posted range, it's my private notion that you won't find out a bit more from your man Quell than you got out of Ozment. Or even as much. I never did claim to tell fortunes from cards, or read coffee grounds. But if I'm any kind of guesser, Quell's lying dead among that bunch you bucked in front of the Criterion. If you hadn't had your back to the saloon, you would've seen him drop. If they hadn't shoved you out of the Criterion, likely Quell would've got to you with the word he had. Of course, I do'no Quell, do'no anything about your affairs. What I'm saying is just my guess."

The sheriff made the shop door in two long strides and stared across to the Criterion and the group gathered there.

"Shack! Shack Rolison!" he bellowed. "Is Ambrosius Quell over there?"

"Yeh. Dead as Pontius Pilate," the deputy's flat drawl answered. "Somebody shot him. We just noticed him."

"My—suffering—sacred—sainted— Three in one afternoon!" the sheriff cried. "It's like the old times! It's too damn much like the old times! It—It—"

He charged out, and Red Roy went after him. Pony and the doctor and McCune the lawyer followed more slowly. When they came to the Criterion, only one figure lay upon the ground. And as Pony had guessed, it was the second 2 Bench cowboy, Ambrosius Quell. He was dead with three buckshot wounds.

Sheriff Sanford went inside, taking the sullen men who had been guarded by Shack Rolison. These only answered official questions with denials of any knowledge of Quell's death. They had fought with Red Roy Kirk because he began a row in the saloon. They were very vague about the causes of that row.

The bartender seemed to know hardly more. He was a shaky figure behind the long bar, waving bottles and glasses and towel without much apparent thought of what he set before his customers.

"I don't know much more'n you know, Sheriff!" he cried earnestly. "There was a line here, drinking. Some body started a fight and I started away! They kind of rolled outside, Kirk and them others. I got behind some barrels yonder. And after they was all on the sidewalk, I seen Quell run by me and head for the front door. Then I heard the bar shotgun bellering and I peeped out and Quell was backing into the swing doors a-hugging his belly all doubled up like he had a cramp. Somebody was *just* going out that side door over there. I never got but the one glimpse at him. The shotgun was lying on the floor in front of the bar."

"Then what'd you do?" Sheriff Sanford demanded.

"Do? Me? I went right back down behind them barrels! And I never come out till everything was quiet everywhere. Go on! Turn up your nose if you want to! I maybe ain't never been a he-ro, yet. But I certainly ain't never been killed yet, either! I let every man kill his own damn snakes."

"What started the row?" Sanford asked Red Roy. "Looks like the Two Bench kind of hubbed hell, today."

"I don't rightly know about it all," Red Roy grunted. "I was having a drink, here. Horace Palm come along and tromped on my feet. Then he ask' me what the hell I thought I was, blocking up his pathway."

He shrugged lean shoulders and a corner of his wide, grim mouth lifted sardonically.

"It kind of unbalanced me for a minute. Horace never was the kind of critter I'd expect to come hunting trouble with me! I reckon I took time to look behind him and try to see if a lot more Palms had moved into Vasko and he had 'em all a-backing him up. While I was unbalanced and looking, Horace hit me. Right square in the nose; come mighty near to hurting me! So I started in on him easy, aiming to kind of warm up gradual—and make him last, too. Damn if somebody out of that bunch of illegitimates, yonder, never hit me behind the ear! So I turned round and I settled that one and somebody else hit me and—I do'no much about what happened."

"Put-up job! Whole thing was put-up, looks like!" the sheriff growled. "The row with you, killing Ozment and Quell. Reckon it was a good thing for you, Roy, this cowboy came along. Well, I got plenty work to do, looks like. And nobody but that trifling, o'nary Shack Rolison to give a hand. You staying in town awhile?"

"Nah. I got to gether up my young cousin and drive her home. I want to see Floyd Milton. Might be that Otto

and Ambrosius come by the house and told Floyd whatever it was they aimed to tell me here in town, about
them stolen horses. Now, John, you take care of funerals
for the boys, will you? Give 'em whatever Vasko can fur-
nish and I'll foot the bill. We'll all come in for the bury-
ing, but right now I want to see Floyd Milton."

Pony found the sheriff staring inquiringly at him. He
shrugged and met the grim eyes indifferently.

"My notion is to keep on going, the way I was heading
when all this started," Pony said. "West, somewhere. You
know more about all this than I do. All I messed with
was shooting at Isbell and helping Kirk a li'l bit. If you
think I have got to stand up and tell some coroner what
he'll know by the time I stand up before him—"

He waited, but the sheriff only stared, turned, and went
out of the Criterion, moving toward Mig and the horses.

CHAPTER IX

"Dumpty Downes got killed"

THE CROWD HAD GONE from before the Criterion, with
moving of Ambrosius Quell's body. Pony saw Mig and
beckoned him. Toward him along the sidewalk came Mrs.
Quaid and the girl Connie—his cousin, Constance Hall,
he reminded himself. He ignored the women.

Red Roy Kirk was behind him and roaring reassurances
to the girl. Then he tapped Pony on the arm.

"Son," he said earnestly, "I don't want that you should
think I don't appreciate you ramming in to help me. And
that shot you took at Isbell, I appreciate *that* lots more!
If it happens it did settle his hash, I'll be plumb tickled.
Now, you told the sheriff you aimed to head out. Why'n't
you come out and throw your roll under a Two Bench

bunk? I got a fine crew—and now I'm short two good boys. I—"

Mrs. Quaid and Connie Hall stared at him. Pony shook his head inexorably.

"Thanks. My ramming into your war was mostly accident, as you can see. And I still want to roll up the dust. Maybe this country's too sudden for me!"

"For you?" Red Roy roared. "Too sudden for—*you?*"

Mrs. Quaid made a snorting noise. Connie Hall's dark eyes were narrowed as she stared fixedly. Then interruption came.

"Where you from, stranger?" Sheriff Sanford demanded. His voice was slow, grim as his eyes. "Which way you come in?"

Pony turned very slowly and looked at the sheriff with great weariness. He shook his head.

"Just as soon as I can arrange it, I'll be able to tell anybody that asks me I'm from Vasko. The *from-er* the farther and the better. But, right now, from Montana."

"On a Texas tree—" Sanford drawled, looking at Dan and the plain saddle, where Mig had paused two yards away. "Me, I always seen and heard about rimfire kaks and dally men up in that country. It's Texas uses the double-barrel hull and's hard-tie with a rope."

"My notion, too," Pony admitted calmly. "But—Sheriff, you wouldn't mind even a Montana man changing his way and his rig? I don't quite *sabe* you. You're sort of hard to read, for a country boy. Is it because I rode into town when some of the home-towners started shooting, that you're so interested in me? Or—just on some kind of general principles I don't know of?"

Dan was close enough, now, for a quick step and swing into the saddle. So much, Pony saw from the corner of an eye. But he continued to face Sheriff Sanford and stare hard into his eyes. For Sanford's right thumb was hooked in his shell belt, just over the sagging butt of his pistol. Pony got out tobacco and papers, poured the yellow flakes into a brown paper, but did not go on with the rolling of his cigarette.

"I reckon I'm kind of unsettled," the sheriff grunted. "I had so much on my hands today. I'd like you around for the inquest, but— Well, if you want to push on, I reckon you can."

Pony nodded without show of feeling or interest. He accepted his reins from Mig and caught a stirrup; swung up. Out of the Criterion the bartender came and he appeared to be a man quitting work for the day. Pony took advantage of the turn of everybody to the man of drinks. He sent Dan away and with Mig trailing moved at the walk along the street.

He did not look back, but Mig rode chin-on-shoulder, reporting the events behind.

"They talk to the sheriff," he told Pony. "They talk very much, waving their hands. But I think they do not care, now, what *we* do. Ho! This Texas is what I have heard it called! So quiet, so sleepy, the street. Then— boom! Boom! Boom!"

"I thought for a minute that big star packer had notions about me," Pony grunted, as much to himself as to the boy. "He looks like an officer with a head on him, Mig'ito. And I don't think I'd choose him for a war."

They quickened pace when the town was hidden by a twist of the road, sending the horses on at the trot. A mile was behind them, and perhaps half another, when Mig twisted in the saddle, saying that someone followed. Pony turned to watch.

"Buggy," he said—needlessly. "My seventy-seventh cousin and that pretty girl, Constance Hall, who's another 'way-off cousin. They're heading for home. She certainly is a looker! Green as grass about this country—

this kind of country. That's why she stared at me so, when that Mrs. Quaid said 'gunman.' I wish she didn't make me think about Berta Schwartz, so—"

He drew in smoke and let it trickle upward from his nostrils, kneeing Dan over to the edge of the road to give Roy Kirk's racing buggy ample room to pass. Not even when the hoofbeats of the buggy team were at Dan's very heels did he turn. Then the grim voice of Sheriff Sanford sounded and he looked sidelong. The sheriff, gun drawn and at his side, sat his big horse just behind the buggy that held Roaring Red Roy Kirk and the girl.

"Just—a—minute," Sanford commanded. Then a slow grin appeared on his hard face and he added, "Montana!"

"Yeh?" Pony drawled. He flipped away the stub of his cigarette and got the makings from his pocket—as he had done in Vasko when facing the sheriff before. "What's it, now?"

His palm was full of tobacco. He replaced the sack.

"You come into town from the east or west?"

"East. Past the Daniels Ford crossroad. Why?"

Incuriously, he watched the sheriff—and perfectly understood the officer's small frown. For if he and Mig had *not* left the road, skirting Daniels Ford to come back to the Vasko road, they would have been seen at Daniels Ford—riding straight from the Territory. But he thought that nobody within Sanford's bailiwick had seen them coming from the west.

"Been around Nacho? Been in the Territory?" Sanford demanded, while Kirk and the girl sat silently watching the pair of them. "Uh—since Montana, I mean!"

"I've decided not to go to the Territory," Pony answered calmly, pretending to misunderstand. "Thought about it some. But I'm going to work north. Take it easy. May be a year before I hit Montana again."

"This boy Mex'?" Sanford asked, staring at Mig.

"Apache. Found him wandering around and he looked like a good boy. So I let him trail along. He wants to see the northern ranges."

"Talk Apache," Sanford ordered Mig, looking from one to the other. "Let's hear what it sounds like."

It seemed to Pony that Red Roy Kirk stiffened slightly and waited as for something expected. But Mig was talking in the singsong, Chinese-like Apache tongue, saying that he was an orphan and that the cowboy beside him was kind. Sanford listened with blank face. Then Mig looked the sheriff in the eyes and added another sentence.

"Shut up!" Sanford snarled at him. "I'll show you— both of you—whether my head's empty or not!"

"You mean —you *sabe* his lingo?" Pony grunted, in real surprise. "Well!"

"He was over in Arizony, years back; around the forts and the Indians," Red Roy Kirk explained, grinning. "Well, John? I take it he really is Apache. So—you satisfied?"

"Nah!" the sheriff replied flatly. "How do I know this man never come from the Territory? There's been a tough killer over there, raising Cain for a year. Reward out on him. And this fellow comes near enough to this Chance Fielder's description to hold. If he ain't Fielder; if he ain't the man they want over at Ojo— Well, we can always turn him loose!"

He grinned and began to lift his pistol. Pony's hand moved more rapidly, as he touched Dan with a rowel. He threw his handful of tobacco into the sheriff's face, then leaned and slapped from Sanford's grasp the drawn pistol. With no more than backlash of the motion, he pulled his own Colt and sat comfortably, covering the big man.

Mig had been only behind Pony in producing a gun. Importantly, he waved it at Red Roy Kirk. He was grinning ferociously, yelling commands in his broken English.

Red Roy squirmed uneasily; yelled in his turn.

"Turn that blame' cutter away! This ain't a thing in my life! You' going to shoot somebody accidental! You—"

Sanford was pawing at his streaming eyes and snarling. From the buggy carried the sudden sound of Connie Hall's laughter. Pony clucked reprovingly at the sheriff.

"Now, now! You ain't killed. Tobacco stings for a minute, but it's nothing to having a glass of whisky in your eyes. *I* remember one time in Henrietta a man slammed a pint of whisky in my face and I would've swore the saloon'd caught fire. Take it easy, Sanford. You're really a mightily lucky man!"

He grunted to Mig and the boy leaned from the saddle to scoop up the sheriff's pistol. Sanford got the last tobacco out of reddened eyes and glared at Pony, who faced him calmly.

"I said—you're lucky! You're about as full of questions as any two men ought to be—and fuller of suspicion than a dozen! I'll be plain with you. I don't like every man I run into asking a lot of questions—to say nothing of having him throw down on me with a plowhandle. I could have killed you—and all the rest of your family. But I didn't want to. All I want is to go on peaceable and mind my own business."

"You can't git away with this!" Sanford said angrily. "I happen to be sheriff and unless you *do* kill me you' just heading straight into more trouble than your clothes'll stand."

"I'm not going to kill you. And I don't expect to have trouble, either. I'm a quiet man. I rode into Vasko and all I did was what any man would do. It seems to me you're more interested in collecting a reward on this Fielder man you're hunting than you are in trailing that Isbell murderer. Why is that? Your county pay you for looping rewards or handling its affairs? Not that it's anything much to me!"

"A'right! If you're not Chance Fielder, what is this name of yours, that you've been so shy of telling?"

"John Kirk—more often Pony Kirk. You ask' me where I was from and I told you truth—Montana. But I was Texas long before the northern ranges ever saw me."

"John Kirk!" the girl cried, staring. "Why— Then you must have got Cousin Roy's—"

"I got his letter; the one you wrote for him," Pony admitted without pleasure. "You wrote it about six months back, but a cowboy's not like a railroad man, about getting places in a hurry. And—after I got to Vasko I didn't mean to stay."

"You see, Mr. Sanford?" Connie Hall cried, turning to the sheriff. "This is John Kirk, Cousin Roy's distant cousin—as I'm his cousin and Floyd Milton's his cousin. I wrote a letter to John, there; to the Eight Lazy Eight ranch at Landusky."

Red Roy Kirk was staring Pony up and down. Now he nodded, looking at the sheriff.

"Yeh, that's right. Connie wrote the letter for me. I ask' John to come to the Two Bench for a visit. Close to six months back. But, like he says, Landusky's a long way and a cowboy takes time to drift."

"A'right," Sanford surrendered. "I reckon if he's John Kirk off the Eight Lazy Eight he ain't this Chance Fielder that's been killing and robbing in the Territory. And if he's a bodaciously sudden hairpin, he ain't a bit different from the rest of you crazy Kirks. Never knowed but one, Roy, until now. And he'd have to rouse out before day to come up with you! A'right, John Pony Montana Texas Kirk. Put away the cutter and gi' me mine. I won't hold a grudge."

Mig passed over the dusty pistol, grinning. Sanford blew upon it and shoved it back into the holster.

"Got to be heading back," he said. "Want to git after Ike Isbell. So long."

"If you do find out who killed that o'nary Horace Palm, hand him ten dollars and charge it to me," Roy Kirk called after him. "No! Make it twenty. That was a fine job he done!"

CHAPTER X

"Hell popping on One End Creek"

ALL OF THEM WATCHED the huge figure going away. Pony drew a long, but inaudible, breath of relief. He felt almost at ease again, almost willing to be pleasant and "kinsfolkish" as he expressed it to himself. Mig was very straight and important in his saddle, like a man sure of his large part in the sheriff's vanquishing. Pony looked at the boy and grinned faintly.

Then Red Roy Kirk and Constance Hall turned to survey him. The old man's shrewd eyes were narrowed. Up and down Pony he looked, a corner of his hard mouth lifted. The girl seemed to own equal curiosity, but it was not shown in Red Roy's open fashion. She bent dark head a trifle and studied Pony from under her brows.

"*Uh-huuuh!*" Red Roy said to himself at last. Then his head turned to look once more after Sheriff Sanford. "When'd you leave the Territory, son?" he asked softly.

"Thought you heard what I told John Law," Pony said evenly.

"Yeh, I did. I heard you tell him— Well, ne' mind! Ne' mind! I reckon your back trail's a good deal your own private business."

"I've entertained some such notion about it," Pony assured him flatly. "But about Sanford, yonder— I do'no if I ought to feel complimented or just what, about his handing me a gun-fighter rep all ready to fit me cheap like a pair of Justin boots off the shelf. This is a sort of puzzling country. You have had plenty of gun-fighting, today; and I have seen some men that *I* would size for gun slingers if I met 'em in church. But does your sheriff bother about 'em? No! He chooses me to spend his time on! Why? Because I'm a stranger, or because I look like what he thinks a gun slick ought to look like? It has got me bogged down, Cousin Roy."

"*I* don't think you look like a killer!" Constance Hall thrust in abruptly, raising her head to look at him levelly. "And—gun fighters are usually killers, aren't they? The sheriff is just—I suppose he's shaken by all the terrible affair in town, John. He couldn't take you—as young as you are and—and as nice-looking as you are!—for a swaggering killer. I don't know much about Texas, but *I* know better than that."

Red Roy's eyes went sidelong to her without movement of his head. Young Mig stared fascinatedly at her flushed, pretty, earnest face. Pony studied his saddle horn.

"Well, now, I certainly do thank you for coming to cheer me up this way," he told her gratefully. "But it still leaves me a bogged-down man. I think I had better light a shuck out of here—*pronto!* That man's likely to study and dream awhile and rise up certain that I'm Jesse James. You know, there's been a good deal of talk that it wasn't Jesse, but a man that looked like him, killed by Bob Ford. Or he might think about the tale that Bill Longley really didn't get hanged that time in Giddings, but was let escape. Of course, Longley was dark as an Indian and over six foot high, but what's that to a hard-working sheriff?"

Red Roy was chanting softly to himself, as if alone and pondering something:

"Down in the canebrake, close to the mill,
There lives a yaller gal, her name is Nancy Till.
She knowed I loved her—she knowed it long;
I gwine to serenade her and I sing her this song:

"Come, love, come! The boat lies low;
She lies high and dry on the O-hi-o-o;
Come, love, come! Won't you come along with me?
I'll take you down to Tenn-es-see-e-e-e—

"Don't figure on lighting a shuck right yet, boy!" he grunted suddenly, like a man making up his mind. "Come on out to the ranch with us and let's get acquainted, the four of us."

"No," Pony said slowly. "I don't think I'd better. Thanks for asking me—when I was in Landusky and now. But I think—"

"Nonsense!" Constance stopped him impatiently. "You came all the way back to Texas because of Cousin Roy's invitation. Now, you act as if Sheriff Sanford's growling is dangerous! What in the world could he do, even if he were inclined to do something? He could even persist in his thought that you're this terrible Chance Fielder from the Territory and it wouldn't mean anything! Why, if he sent for an officer from the Territory, that officer would only have to take one look at you!"

"Yeh," Pony conceded, with the impulse to laugh, "you're absolutely right about that part. A deputy from the Territory would only need one look at me— I see what you mean."

"Come on out!" Red Roy said heartily. "Your name's been in the pot a long time, boy! Like Connie told you in her letter, out of the straight line from old John Kirk that first come over from Scotland, I just trace us four— Connie and Floyd Milton and you and me. I— Well, I been right lonesome since Ma died. A man's own blood somehow pulls at him like strangers or even good friends can't do. I—"

He stopped in embarrassed fashion and Pony looked at him with softening of his set face.

The old boy's not used to showing his feelings, he thought. *But they're there and, por dios! They're pleasant to know about, for a man as lone as I am.*

But he thought of Sheriff Sanford and his determination to ride on was not weakened by the something like affection he began to feel for this grim and lonely man. If he stayed on the 2 Bench, someone from the Territory might ride into Vasko and stir up Sanford's suspicions and make them more than mere suspicions. If the big sheriff decided to capture him, the next clash between them might easily end with Sanford the winner. Riding away from Vasko—away from Texas—seemed the sensible thing. Then Red Roy began to talk again.

"I got Floyd Milton down from Cleveland where he was clerking in a bank. Then Connie come from California. Floyd's turning into a right tolerable hand, for a boy that never straddled a horse before he hit the Two Bench; and his head for figures has helped a lot with my books. Connie's been bossing the house. I couldn't get on your track for a while; you been drifting like a tumbleweed, seems like. Then Dumpty Downes started riding for me and he said he'd rode with you on the Fence and you headed for the Eight Lazy Eight—"

"Dumpty Downes!" Pony grunted, staring. "You don't mean to tell me that li'l sawed-off, hammered-down bundle of dynamite is around here? Well, I would certainly like to see Dumpty and ask how-come he didn't marry the widow-woman with her livery stable and live in town, the way he said he was going to! Dumpty Downes—"

"Look! Cousin Roy! Look yonder!" Connie interrupted

suddenly, pointing to the left. "Isn't that Anker Wing? It looks like his big black!"

Out of an arroyo a rider had popped as if hurled upward. He was heading for the road on which they had stopped and with sight of the group he turned his lathered horse slightly and quirted him that way.

"Yeh, that's Anker," Red Roy Kirk muttered. "But what's he so much in a hurry about? He—"

The cowboy came up to them and jerked his mount back to its haunches. He was swarthy and hook-nosed.

"Hell a-popping on One End Creek, boss! South Fork. Floyd Milton sent me to tell you. Him and Dumpty Downes, they was over thataway this morning, to take a look at the menathy.* They run into Clubfoot's outfit. Floyd says there was plenty lead flying. Floyd got nicked in the arm. Dumpty Downes was shot two-three times in the back as he was running away with Floyd. He's dead, Dumpty is. Floyd ain't really hurt."

"Clubfoot!" Red Roy snarled. "He—He—"

Then he bent swiftly to gather the reins. One long end flicked out and cracked sharply. The team jumped and the buggy shot ahead with Connie holding tight to the seat.

Now the swarthy Anker Wing stared curiously at Pony, who looked at him, ticketed him for typical cowboy, then glanced at Mig and shrugged.

"It's either catch up or get left clean behind," he said to them both. To Anker Wing he added, "I'm another Kirk—last of the roundup, I reckon."

The three of them spurred after Roy Kirk's racing buggy and came up with it, to ride abreast until the 2 Bench big gate was reached. That was seven or eight

---

*"Menathy"—Anglo-American corruption of Spanish mañada, a stallion's harem of mares (with colts, if any).

miles out and another two miles of range stretched between the gate and Red Roy's rambling cut-stone house.

Anker Wing rode up to the team's head when they all came into the graveled driveway and Red Roy pulled up short. Connie got out and sighed as with relief. The old man was on the ground before her—and apparently without thought of her. He went lurching toward the long veranda which extended across the entire front of his house. A tall young man came to meet him. Anker Wing led the buggy out of sight.

"What's all this, Floyd?" Red Roy began bellowing instantly at the young man. "Downes killed—you hit— Say! How about that menathy?"

Pony sat black Dan with hands crossed upon the saddle horn before him. Floyd Milton, he thought, had reached out and taken Texas to his heart—the gaudier aspects of Texas. Pony surveyed one by one the snowy beaver hat—a fifty-dollar Stetson—the blue silk neckerchief, the white silk shirt, the tailored fawn-colored trousers, and inlaid alligator boots. Floyd Milton, Pony thought, had certainly dressed himself as expensively as any dude-cowboy could manage. His shell belt and holster were beautifully hand-stamped and trimmed with gold and silver like the pearl-handled double-action Colt he wore. His spurs were gold-trimmed and little golden bells tinkled on them as he walked. Even his hatband was a golden rattlesnake with a string of red stones for rattles.

"*Carajo!*" Mig breathed, staring enviously at this magnificence. "Your cousin? Then—how different cousins may be!"

Pony grunted. He was listening to the quick exchange of question and answer between Red Roy and Floyd Milton and studying the young man's olive-skinned face as it set in grim lines.

"So," Floyd Milton said at last, "if Clubfoot was with

the rustlers, I couldn't identify him. I incline to think he wasn't with that half dozen we met, or it might have been worse—for me, I mean. They would have made a clean sweep and you'd have found two of us dead on the range as you've found others."

"And they lifted the menatha on you!" Red Roy snarled. "Stole the best stallion, best bunch of mares I raised in my life. They— The damn slinking, bushwhacking scoun'els!"

"As I said," Floyd Milton told him evenly, "they had the *mañada* before Downes and I rode down into the creek. I saw the last of the mares topping out on the far side as this bunch came swarming at us. There was nothing to do but spur down the creek; we couldn't climb the bank again with them shooting at us. As it was, they chased us two miles or more along the creek before anything like cover showed. And Downes was killed as he tried to get behind a big boulder. I stumbled over him and was burned on the arm."

Pony looked at the girl suddenly. She stood watching Milton fascinatedly and—admiringly, Pony thought. As Milton moved his left arm slightly, she shook her head and tightened her mouth. Pony grinned. She had evidently caught the remark about stumbling over the fallen Dumpty Downes, as he had caught it. Dumpty had been ahead, that meant; Milton had brought up the rear—heroically or otherwise. But it was plain that she thought him passing over a brave retreat with casual mention of it.

"How'd you make it, after that?" Red Roy demanded.

"By pure luck! The luck of Vic Tait being close enough to hear the shooting as Clubfoot's killers began to rain bullets on that boulder. Vic came up to see what the trouble might be and he had a good position over them. His fire drove them back far enough to let me do some shooting. Between us, I believe we hit a couple of them, but not badly enough to keep them from riding away. If only we could get to them! With something like an even chance, the kind of men in *your* bunkhouse, Cousin Roy, wouldn't be worried by any of that gang!"

"I'll come up with 'em," Red Roy assured him raspingly. "If it takes every penny I can raise on the Two Bench and every minute of my time from here on out, I'll show this sneaking, killing, would-be king rustler something about trouble. I—"

"You can count on me to the end of it," Milton said quietly. "We've got to stop him, Cousin Roy. So we will stop him. And I owe him for—this! Well, it's too late to do anything today. Shall we ride out the first thing in the morning and see what kind of trail they left?"

"Reckon," Red Roy agreed grudgingly. "No use making camp out there on One End Creek when we can sleep comfortable in the house and make about as much speed by going out tomorrow early. Oh! This here's the last of our bunch, Floyd—John Kirk, my cousin's boy you know about. He finally got to Vasko."

Pony pushed Dan closer and swung down. As he stretched himself and stepped toward Red Roy and Milton and the girl, the old bullet wound in his right foot twinged and he limped slightly. Milton looked down at that foot and frowned, then looked up at Pony's face and across at Red Roy.

But he shook hands with Pony and said without tone that he was glad to see him on the 2 Bench.

"He certainly rode into Vasko just in time to find all sorts of excitement," Connie told Milton. "A terrible series of killings, right there on the street! The most mysterious sort, too. Cousin Roy hasn't had time to tell you—"

"Come on up and set down," Red Roy grunted. "Now it's all over, I reckon I'm a li'l bit tired. It was Big Otto and Ambrosius Quell, Floyd. Two mighty good men!"

Pony turned to call an order to Mig—to put their horses in the corral, their saddles in the shed. Mig nodded and rode down the driveway toward the back of the house. There were huge cypress chairs on the veranda. Red Roy settled himself in a rocker and fumbled for tobacco and papers. Connie came quickly to his side and took the Durham sack and book of wheatstraws. Deftly, she rolled the old man a cigarette and struck a match for him. He drew in smoke, staring out across the wide range as if he saw something invisible to the rest of them. Pony dropped down on the edge of the veranda with back against a post. Connie perched on a wide chair arm just above him. Milton lounged against a post, with a thin cigar in his fingers.

Red Roy began to tell of the killings in Vasko. He described them bitterly in detail, and Pony understood, he thought, how loss of two hand-picked men hurt the 2 Bench owner—hurt his pride and his rough affection for men who served him well.

"Two mighty good men," he said several times. "Right now, I needed 'em awful bad. Awful bad. The Two Bench is in good shape. I ain't owed a dollar in years. But if this stealing ain't stopped—*pronto!*—I ain't going to be able to say that. We lost over five thousand dollars' worth of stock already and looks like we're going to lose more if that gang has its way. I been through plenty tough spots in my day in this country, same as the other old-timers. I tell you, you young fellows today don't know how tough things can get. I seen some trouble through the smoke like you don't hardly see now— What's the matter, Connie?"

"Oh—nothing," the girl said quickly. "I was just thinking. That's twice I've heard the expression 'trouble through the smoke.' Mrs. Quaid used it."

She looked covertly at Pony, and he kept his face blank. But he had been doing that, looking respectfully at Red Roy whose experiences, Pony thought modestly had hardly been tougher, smokier, than Bully Witt and the Territory had furnished him almost daily for a year

"Well, ne' mind all my history! What I'm driving at is if I have got to take down my other gun and start wearing it—and using it!—to get to live quiet like we been living á long while until six months or so ago, then down she comes!"

"What was it Big Otto said before he died?" Milton asked, squinting against the smoke of his cigar.

And when Red Roy repeated accurately the fragmentary statement of Big Otto, he shook his dark, handsome head.

" 'He was gambling. Always losing. We knew it. Had to get money. So he began rustling. My notion is, that Ike Isbell—' It's maddening, to be told that much, without a clue to his real meaning. Is it Ike Isbell who is stealing Two Bench stock? Or does Ike know something about the stealing? To come so close to having the answer—or what Big Otto considered the answer—and yet have nothing! It's plain that Otto and Ambrosius had discovered something. I was over on One End Creek, so they decided that their discovery was urgent enough to justify a ride to town to tell you. If only I had been here at the house! By the way, who is Ike Isbell? Oh, I know he's a tramp cowboy. But has anyone more information than that, about him? Who are his friends and associates around here? It seems to me that we have got to answer that question and some more questions. For I do believe that this gang works with full knowledge of the land's lay."

"I do'no about Isbell," Red Roy said absently. "Tramp cowboy. That's all I know about him."

"Well, I don't like to suspect our neighbors," Milton told him grimly, "but we've got to look at every possibility and, personally, I'm about ready to suspect anybody!"

Pony relighted his dead cigarette. It occurred to him that he was very much the outsider here. That, of course, was natural. Floyd Milton had been a good while on the 2 Bench and by Red Roy's account was actively helping with the management. He knew these affairs in detail; to another Red Roy must explain them all. But— he found the troubles of the 2 Bench interesting. It was just such conditions which had brought him to the Territory—and to several other troubled regions, before that. For all his youth, he was a veteran range detective.

"Five thousand dollars' worth of stock is just plenty to lose," he put in now. "Plenty! Who are these neighbors you can think about, even if you don't come right down to suspecting 'em of dabbing a loop on your stuff, whole-sale?"

"Nate Azle's got the Ladder U on my west line," Red Roy grunted. "Ben Britt's Seventy-Seven outfit lies to the south. My other neighbors I couldn't suspicion, no more'n they'd suspicion me."

"This One End Creek you've been talking about; how did that get a name so—one-ended?"

"It starts up northwest of the house, here. Runs south-east and dives straight down into the ground on the west side of the Spear Hills. Never does come up again—in our part of the country. Queer kind of creek. Queer kind of country, for that matter! The Spear Hills are awful rough and rugged. Man and boy, I been around here forty year and there's places in the Spears—plenty places —I never did see. No sense to busting your neck or your horse's legs, scrambling around there. Nothing in the Spears, anyhow. So we don't use 'em much."

"And you have got the Seventy-Seven and Ladder U

outfits to think about. Just them. Been having trouble with those spreads?"

"No. Not what you'd call trouble. Seven-eight year back, me and Nate Azle fell out over a poker session in town. I—kind of wrecked Nate. Never hurt him bad, but he was laid up two-three weeks. He ain't spoke to me since. This Seventy-Seven spread of Britt's is a newish lay out and it looks hardcase to me. I do'no exactly what I do think, about Nate Azle. But I wouldn't trust Britt— or his hands—behind me!"

Pony whistled tunelessly. Milton and the girl were watching him. Red Roy's mind seemed to be on something else.

"Well," Pony drawled, "to a common kind of cowboy, it does look like a simple business—up to a point. Either the Seventy-Seven and Ladder U, one of 'em or both of 'em together, have been chewing at your range, or there's an independent gang of long ropers headquartering close by. Might even be holing up in these Spear Hills. I don't see any more. Even another end to your One End Creek wouldn't seem to help a lot!"

Floyd Milton laughed.

"Yes, a very simple business. And as you describe it, practically solved. All we need is knowledge of what part, if any, the Seventy-Seven and Ladder U have played, a little important information about the independent gang, if such exists—"

"The trail of the stuff run off hasn't told anything?" Pony asked—in almost humble tone. "The direction of it?"

"We've lost bunches of stock, north, south, east, and west of the house," Milton explained impatiently. "Always, we've found this clubfoot track somewhere about the scene of a theft. The trails we've cut have never led us very far. As Cousin Roy told you, the range is rugged.

It could swallow an army and there would be no sign of it. Well—there's the supper gong!"

CHAPTER XI

"They're hunting killers"

·WHATEVER IT HAD BEEN in the life of Red Roy's wife, the dining-room of the 2 Bench house was like none Pony had ever seen on a Texas ranch. He wondered if Connie had brought her California ideas with her and persuaded the lank, grim Red Roy to let the long, dusky room be lightened with cream plaster and the table shine with snowy linen and bright silver and glassware and thin china. There was even a Mexican waiter in white jacket, to serve them.

"Different from wolfing straight beef or venison under a juniper, with one eye on the sky line," he told himself ·with grim humor. "It looks newish, all of it, that room they gave me and this downstairs part. Reckon she made the house over. More country show place than cow outfit."

But he liked it. No hotel in Dallas or San Antonio could have bettered that meal, even though every vegetable came from a can. Pony watched Red Roy. The old man ate like one concerned more with his food than with the way it came to him. But he accepted the service of the Mexican as if grown accustomed to Eastern ways, whether approving them or not.

Some of these days, Pony thought, *when I annex me an outfit of my own, I think I'll have it done like this. Not a bit of sense to living like a wolf just because you're away from town. This layout proves it.*

Then he had to laugh inwardly at the picture of Pony

Kirk settling himself quietly to ranch it. Bully Witt and Rosen and Shea and various other tall figures in the Territory would see that he kept on the move, if they managed nothing more. And that thought brought another, very naturally.

I ought to be moving, right now, he reflected. *That big Sanford sheriff keeps running in my mind. If Bully Witt gets a tolerable idea that I headed for Texas, he'll send so many reward notices this way the country'll think a paperhangers' convention has landed in its lap.*

He listened to the low, curt talk of Red Roy and Milton. They seemed not to be thinking of him. Occasionally Connie spoke in his direction, but usually it was to ask some question about his life and the work he had done, and he had to reply so carefully and with so much consideration of what he said that his answers were slow, almost hesitant. The girl gave him up at last. She watched Red Roy and Floyd Milton instead of talking.

As they drank their coffee, Milton surprised Pony by looking straight at him for almost the first time since the beginning of supper and speaking in a friendly, almost a sympathetic, tone, about Pony's injured foot.

"I noticed your limp," he said. "Is it just a temporary injury, or is the foot badly hurt?"

"Got it scratched some while back," Pony answered evasively. "It's not bad. Most of the time I don't know it's tender. But a long spell in the saddle sort of stiffens it and after I get on the ground it hurts. So I favor it. Walk with it held stiff, you know. Then the stiffness wears off and I'm all right again."

Milton got up, smiling at Connie. Red Roy stood, also. He looked at Pony and nodded abruptly.

"See you tomorrow, John," he grunted. "Floyd and me have got some things to go over, tonight."

Connie and Pony left the dining-room together. But

she went upstairs and he drifted out to look for Mig. The boy was waiting for him on the veranda. He had eaten in the bunkhouse with three cowboys, he said. He liked the 2 Bench very much. It was even better than Don Joaquin Tinoco's Hacienda Miramar, he told Pony cheerfully. The bunkhouse was a finer place than Don Joaquin's *casa grande*.

"Look carefully at it," Pony advised him. "For I do not believe that we stay here long. That big sheriff is not one to easily give up a thought he has owned. He had reason to think me Chance Fielder. More reason, it seems to me, than he said. So he will go on wondering if, in some way, I cannot be Chance Fielder. He will do something to make himself sure. You will sleep in the bunkhouse, Mig'ito. I have a room here."

Mig disappeared silently on his explorations, and Pony sat smoking. Then Connie came out and took the big chair just above him. Pony was not pleased to see her. He had been thinking of Dumpty Downes and the days when they had ridden together. His thoughts were grim. For Dumpty had been a good man, one of the best, a better man in many ways than gay Pat Curran. And Dumpty had died with thieves' lead in his back.

They don't raise 'em better than Dumpty was, Pony was musing when the girl sat down. *I never knew a man whiter or gamer. And here I am, right straddle of the fence; ought to be piling up the dust behind me; feel like staying right here to do what he'd have done for me—slam some lead at whoever killed him.*

"I can't get over what happened in town," Connie said slowly. "I didn't know Quell except to see him go about his work. But Otto was such a good-natured bear of a man; rough and strong, but so gentle with children; the Mexican youngsters on the place worshiped him. And now—he's dead! They're dead, he and Quell. Cousin Roy was almost killed. Dumpty Downes was killed and Cousin Floyd barely escaped— It's terrible, John! And there seems no end of it in sight."

"*Es vida,*" he grunted, not much impressed by her tone of trouble. "That's life. You go along and do the best you can by the rules you hang to. Then something pops up and throws you and you can't see rhyme or reason to it."

"You said you're often called 'Pony,'" she said after a moment. "Why is that? It's a nickname, isn't it?"

"I was working on a Devil's River spread one time. New to the country. The boss sent me up on the Pecos to rep for us—you know, to represent his brand in a big cow work and see that our stuff was tallied for him. On the way I hit a store-saloon and there was a tough gang there, some of the Fray boys that were suspected of having a hand in rustling and train robberies and a lot of things, including some killings. Well—we had trouble and I got worked over from ears to tin cup, you might say. When I waked up, the Frays had gone and they'd stripped me—saddle horse, pack horse and outfit, my saddle and my guns long and short—everything was gone. They'd left me a dogified Mexican pony and a blanket and surcingle. Oh, yeh! And one of those kid's water pistols like you buy in the store with Cracker-Jack for a nickel."

"It was that pony that gave you the nickname?"

"Yeh. In a way. The storekeeper could hardly keep from laughing about it. I was bunged up like a man that'd missed his bulldogging hold. Both eyes about shut, face all skinned up, one arm strained. He asked me what I thought I'd do— That was when I was sort of describing the Frays and their line from Adam on down. I said I'd ride that pony until I got back my own and a li'l bit more from the Frays.

" 'Kirk,' he said to me. 'Yeh. *Pony* Kirk.' Well, I caught up with the Frays and I did get back my own and a li'l bit more. But the name he handed me stuck and it spread from Devil's River, because wherever I worked somebody would drift in to call me that. I'm as used to it now as to John."

"Dumpty didn't tell me that. In fact, he didn't say much about you, except that you'd ridden together. But when Cousin Roy was talking to him about you, Dumpty said, *'That gun bulldogger!'* I couldn't tell whether he meant it as a compliment, or not."

"Probably just some of his hurrahing. Old Dumpty— I have been sitting here thinking about him and wishing I could stay to come up with the men who rubbed him out."

"But—you are staying! I was just thinking that you'd come at a good time, that Cousin Roy's idea, getting all of his own around him, was almost providential. Everybody on the place has ridden himself almost to a shadow, hunting for this clubfooted murderer and thief. You've been a cowboy all your life. You can help Cousin Roy a great deal, because you know what to look for and—"

"The stealing's been going on for six months or more?"

He thought that he could keep his distance from her and yet learn certain things that he wanted to know. He would have preferred a long talk with Red Roy, but since his cousin had quite plainly put him out of whatever council was going on, Connie was the only one who could tell him anything.

"Yes, about six months. It's the most maddening, mysterious thing! Horses and cattle disappear and always there's this track of a malformed foot or the imprint of a dragging foot, like a mocking trademark, or signature, somewhere about the scene of each crime. But no trail that can be followed for more than a mile or so."

Pony grunted with some scorn.

"Six months of it; several expensive robberies; but just dead men to show for it!" he drawled. "Just Ozment and Quell really getting onto something—and nobody will ever know how much they really found out. I did guess that they believed they'd located the robbers, the boss of the gang, anyway."

"Oh!" she said acidly. "You think that Cousin Roy and Floyd and the rest are incompetent, because they haven't stopped all this, in six months."

"Seems queer," he admitted. "You don't want me to say I think the stock's been carried off in a balloon?"

"I suppose *you* would have had it all cleared up, by now! The robbers arrested; the stock recovered; Quell and Ozment and Downes still alive! It's just too bad that you didn't get here six months ago."

Pony laughed placidly. He felt oddly more at ease with her because of the waspish outburst. She sounded so young, so very young, loyal to those she liked, resentful of an outsider's criticism of them, ignorant of the things every cowboy knew by instinct about this country.

"But you're safe to imply that *you* could do so much better! Because you're not going to stay. Your infallibility can't be tested—"

"Whoa! Don't throw the dictionary at a saddle tramp! I don't know what that is, that I'm supposed to have. But it sounds dangerous. Keep your language down below a coarse sight out of *McGuffey's Fifth Reader* and I'll make out to understand you, with a few smoke signs and some hand talk. But that in—*infallibility*— Not guilty! I never done it!"

"I just thought of a simple way in which you can leave early, since you're not fond of our company, and still help Cousin Roy tremendously! Just get up early tomorrow and ride around for an hour or so, then tell him who the thieves are and how to catch them!"

"I just thought of something, too. Maybe not so simple. Floyd Milton hasn't got much use for me. Why?"

"What makes you think that? Why wouldn't he like you? He was terribly worried, today. That made him pre-occupied. Though for that matter neither he nor Cousin Roy has been natural, normal, since this trouble began. Just because he didn't fall on your neck when you appeared is no sign that he dislikes you, Pony. Remember, he'd been shot at, wounded—"

"That might have affected him, all right," he agreed. "I don't want·you to think I expected him, or anybody else, to—fall on my neck. After all, we're nothing to each other but strangers that happen to be mightily distant kin. But I still don't think he likes me."

"And I think you're wrong—and unreasonable! But, are you absolutely determined to leave us quickly? You won't stay and give us the benefit of your enormous ability in tracking down thieves and murderers—and doubtless your vast stores of experience? Please stay, Pony! Surely, you can't refuse a girl's request. Every cowboy I've seen—"

"I could make a living, refusing girls' requests! Here's one cowboy that's never had much time for women. If I do give my special imitation of mind-changing, it'll be because of Dumpty Downes. I'd like to heel this gang and pay off for him. And—I still say it oughtn't to be too hard!"

"Do you think you could do it in—say, a week?" she asked anxiously. "And what methods do you favor? If it's tea leaves, I'll speak to the cook tonight. Or you can have coffee grounds. I hope you don't use slates, though; there's only one on the place. But, surely a week's enough? I'll mark my calendar—"

Mig appeared at the veranda as silently as he had gone, his sudden materializing jerking a gasp from Connie.

"Does she have Spanish?" he whispered. "Try her, *amo!*"

Pony snapped the question and Connie said in surprised tone that she did not understand.

"*Bueno,* then," Mig said in natural voice. "I hid—what was in your *alforjas* where it will be safe and yet easy to take up again. Beyond the corrals are rocks in a pile. That which Jink Lowrey gave you is beneath two of those rocks. I came back, then, to look at this fine house. Through a window I saw the old man and that other, your cousin. As I passed that window I heard them speak of the stolen horses and the men who died. *Amo!* This man Downes was a *buen amigo?*"

"He was my very good friend. As much my friend as was Don Patricio. Why do you ask?"

"*Pues,* in this room with table and papers where they sit, I heard his name. The young cousin told the old man of his belief that your friend, Downes, was in some way connected with the thieves. He said that he has no proof, but for a good while he has been suspicious of Downes. He feels that the two men killed today in town had learned that Downes was one of the thieves. They spoke sometimes in voices set so low that I could not hear all the talk. But the old man seemed to think as the young man thinks, at the last."

"*No es posible!*" Pony snarled. "Uh-uh! That cannot be true of Downes. I knew him well. I rode with him, ate with him, slept with him, talked of all things with him, drank and danced and gambled and fought with him. He could not change entirely, *muchacho.* If he had for some reason turned rustler, even, he would not have robbed the man whose pay he took. No! Downes was never thief and traitor both. *Nunca! Jamás!*"

He had a large impulse to go face Floyd Milton and give him the lie, direct. Then he relaxed and faced Mig.

"Did the young man tell my other cousin why Downes was killed, if one of the thieves? It seems to me that he should have explained this strange thing; that the old man should have asked him to explain it."

"The *viejo* asked him that question," Mig said quickly. "It was in my mind, also, as I listened to him. And he said, that it seemed to him that Downes was mistaken for one of the honest riders of this ranch. For— What was the name? Vic Tait! The thieves believed that Downes was Tait."

Connie had been leaning forward, looking at the two faces palely lighted by the moon. Now she said eagerly, "Did the boy discover something? Something about the robbers? About Clubfoot?"

"No. And I can't see why all of you talk about a Clubfoot gang. It makes it sound terrible, all right. Gives you a neat, easy handle for the rustlers. But just because a clubfoot track shows around where stock's stolen is no proof that the boss of the thieves is the man who made the track. That might have been put there by one of the gang and the puniest one. Or it might even be just a stall, —you know, a print made to make people hunt for a clubfooted man when no such man *is*."

"True! True!" she mocked him. "On the other hand, it may just as reasonably be that we're right; that a clubfooted man *is* leader of this gang. I take it that Cousin Roy and—and others judge by the position of the track the place the maker of it occupies in the thieves' ranks."

"Well, anyway, Mig'ito here hasn't looped the thieves. I do reckon that we'll have to do that ourselves."

"And in a week! You did say you could catch the thieves within a week, didn't you?"

"I did not," he drawled calmly. "You can maybe rawhide a lot of men into jumping without looking, for you're the kind that gets under a man's skin, being sarcastic. But I'm not one of 'em. I didn't say I'd catch any thieves—not in a week or any other time. Right now, all I've got to say is—"

"Yes? What have you got to say?"

"I'm going to turn in. Tomorrow *ought* to be another day."

CHAPTER XII

"I won't ride off"

BREAKFAST, IN SPITE of the cheerful room and the brightness of the table, was a meal begun almost in silence among the four of them and becoming more and more grim as it progressed. For Red Roy was in a humor that seemed close to the point of exploding in fury. He said nothing at all to Pony, Floyd Milton, or Connie; he answered the Mexican waiter's hesitant questions with curt snarls.

Floyd Milton had come to the table in another outfit but one as expensive as that Pony had seen on him the day before. His shirt was blue, like Pony's. But there the resemblance ended; Pony wore coarse, clean chambray, while Floyd's shirt was of heavy silk. His *chaparejos* were batwings made of chrome leather, faced with brown calf-skin and spotted with Mexican silver coins of varied size. Pony conceded that his cousin made as splendid a figure of the Riding Man as one could hope to find in Texas.

Connie came into the dining-room wearing a house dress of some figured stuff that perfectly matched her dusky hair and eyes and clear ivory skin. She was prettier, even, than he had thought. For the night had taken away some of the strain he had seen in her; she looked·

younger.

He observed Floyd's stare at her and how his eyes lighted when she smiled at him—her head a little back, her eyes narrowed provocatively. Inwardly, he said that between Floyd and Connie was certainly more than mere cousinly regard. Much more! And it was only natural, he admitted. They had been together here for long enough to become well acquainted. Either was unusually attractive.

They made him feel more than ever the outsider. He looked at Red Roy Kirk with sympathy and understanding. He and the old man were of the same kind, creatures as native to this land as the thorny mesquite or the distant sky-lined lobo wolves. Neither Floyd nor Connie could ever be more than foreigners here. The faint tie of blood did not make them like Red Roy—as *he* was like the gaunt, grim old man. Moved by the thought, he asked Red Roy what he intended to do after breakfast.

"Why— Well," Red Roy answered slowly, poking at his big steak with a fork, "I reckon me and Floyd will see what we can find out about this business of yesterday— losing the menathy and him being shot at and Downes being killed. We buried Downes there where he was dropped. That is, a couple of the peons went out early today and he ought to be buried by now. He never had any kin, he told me. Reckon it was as good as we could do for him, to bury him right there."

Pony continued to stare at him, wondering why he was so hesitant in his speech and why he talked almost as if he elaborated on the subject of Dumpty Downes's burial to avoid talking of something else.

"I reckon," Pony agreed. "It's the cowboy's lot. Plenty of 'em have been put in the ground they shot over, between here and the Canada line. And Dumpty told me the same thing, about not having kinfolks anywhere.

About the exploring around— Well, I thought maybe you wanted me to do something; that boy that's with me is good' at trailing. I'm not exactly a slouch at it, myself. Anything I can do I'm certainly willing to do."

"Why"—again Red Roy pushed at the steak on his plate and seemed to hesitate—"I reckon Floyd and me'll be enough to do whatever's needful. We— Well, we aim to ride over to where he was shot at and—and kind of look around, you see. Hunt a trail and— Ought to be some kind of sign som'r's I can figure out. And if I stumble onto one it might tell just a whole lot. That menathy can't sprout wings and leave the creek without my seeing something."

Pony stared at him very steadily, in honest curiosity. Red Roy looked up sidelong at him, then down at his plate.

"No need of more'n Floyd and me," he said hurriedly. "I tell you what, John; you just make yourself at home around the place. You know, just ramble around and kind of look over things and kind of get the hang of the Two Bench. Likely, we'll be back early, in time for supper, anyhow."

Pony continued to regard the old man fixedly. He wondered what had caused the embarrassment that showed so plainly in Red Roy; why Red Roy's manner toward him had changed overnight; why he was virtually being told that his presence was not wanted at the place where, if anywhere, he might be helpful. But there was no further remark from Red Roy to give a clue to his attitude.

He looked Floyd Milton's way. But that young man was looking at his meal. From his expression it could have been believed that he had heard none of the talk; that neither Pony nor Red Roy existed for him, at that moment. When a moment later he looked up, it was to face Connie and speak to her about a buckskin horse she had wanted.

"I had him put in the corral for you, yesterday," he told her. "Vic Tait's ridden him pretty carefully. Vic says he's perfectly safe for you, Connie. And he's got a mouth like velvet. Not like that black."

"I'm glad of that," she answered—but in a vague tone, as if her thoughts were not altogether upon the subject. "I don't need any more runaways, to complete my education. When Blackie got the bit between his teeth last week and began to imitate a bird and just sail over arroyos instead of troubling to climb down into them and climb out, I wondered how I'd look with a bunch of lilies in my hand at the funeral."

"The buckskin can travel, but he's gentle and easily handled. You've got to remember to ride loose-reined, though. I had the same trouble, learning to neck-rein these Texas horses. Well, Cousin Roy? I'm ready, if you are."

Red Roy nodded and mumbled and shoved back his chair. He lifted his sleeve mechanically toward his mouth, seemed to remember the napkin which had dropped from his lap, stooped and snatched it up, scrubbed his mouth with it, and let it fall. He went out of the dining-room without a word to any of them, straight-backed, seeming to drop his years as he went at short, rocking step.

"I'll see you both later," Floyd told Pony and Connie, before he followed. "We'll certainly be back for supper."

"I don't understand it!" Connie burst out, when the rap of their heels had died away. "Why didn't Cousin Roy ask you to go with them? I don't understand it at all!"

Pony was staring at the wall, only half-conscious of her presence and not in the least interested in the girl. He had been asking himself the same question put by her, in a half-dozen ways. And in him was rising slow anger at the way he had been dismissed from the affairs of the Two Bench.

I didn't know, myself, whether I wanted to mix into his business, he was thinking, *but I certainly did want to make up my mind about it, for myself. You could think I was ten years old and likely to be a drag on grown-up men, the way Red Roy sounded. And after my taking cards in town, to save the old wolf's hide, you'd think he could see I'm not exactly a shrinking violet in a row. But he's showing me, now, that Cousin Floyd from Cleveland is a better man in his eyes than Pony Kirk from Texas. Without throwing just a lot of bouquets at myself, I do believe that if I was going to hire a man out of the pair of us, for this kind of situation, it wouldn't be a pilgrim like Floyd I'd choose.*

He looked toward the girl, who was waiting for his answer with elbows on the table before her, leaning a little and studying him quite frankly.

"Do'no," he said quietly. "Except from what Red Roy told me. Which certainly wasn't much."

He was debating it all, Red Roy's coolness toward him, his own sensible course. If he got up, now, to saddle black Dan and take Miguelito, he could put behind him the small puzzle of the 2 Bench and his kin. The idea was attractive. Red Roy seemed to have changed his mind about at least one of his relatives and Pony told himself grimly that he had never been a man to stay where he was at all unwelcome. Then he thought of Dumpty Downes, buried on the range where he had been killed by the thieves; and of the black, vicious little man who had shot at him before Lawyer McCune's door.

Ike Isbell typified for him, at the moment, the thieves who had raided the 2 Bench and murdered Dumpty Downes. He was ugly enough, in Pony's memory, to rouse antipathy for the rustlers; he became a sort of gathering-point for all Pony's mixed anger, a symbol of the whole gang.

And he's loose, somewhere, Pony thought. *One of the gang, sure's shooting. I won't ride off, just yet. I'll stay long enough to look around for Mr. Isbell and hold some discussion with him about shooting at me. It might be that finding him will find some of the bunch that killed Dumpty. But I don't need to headquarter here, to hunt his trail. Red Roy and Floyd can work by 'emselves the way they look like they want to work. I'll go to town and around. I'll follow any trail I cut and they can do the same with their findings.*

"Mrs. Quaid called you a gunman!" Connie broke into his thoughts abruptly. Her eyes widened, then narrowed calculatingly. "I've been so shaken by all the things happening, the—the killings, I haven't really been thinking, I guess. Or I have used only a part of my mind. I wonder if Cousin Roy hasn't been doing much the same thing."

She shook her head as if the action could clear it.

"She said something about knowing you for a gunman, a—a 'real A-Number-One, top-notch' gunman. She spoke of the way you rode when you came into Vasko, with your hand swinging mechanically close to where your pistol would be when you wore it openly. She—"

"I noticed her," Pony admitted carefully. "Heavy-set, grayish woman, standing with you in front of a store. Uh-huh. I could tell she was the excitable kind, given up to wild notions. You mustn't believe all folks tell you, down here."

"I don't!" she assured him, smiling faintly. "At this very minute, I'm remembering that I mustn't. I can't understand Cousin Roy forgetting the way you saved him and ran off the man Isbell, and how Sheriff Sanford looked at you, and how you treated him as if he had been a little boy—and a clumsy little boy, at that. I should think that, going after thieves and killers as he and Floyd intended, they'd particularly want a—well—a man like you, to help."

"Well, he didn't," Pony said calmly. "Now, I think I'll take some of his advice and ride around and look the range over. Mig and his eyes'll be worth a lot; maybe a whole lot."

"You *are* very skilled with weapons, aren't you?" she persisted. "Isn't that what Dumpty Downes meant, when he called you a gun bulldogger? I'm sure it was! Floyd is a very good shot, I think. He has learned since he came down here. He's a good rider, too, and certainly he's brave. But he's so good-natured. Usually, he likes everybody; trusts everybody. I can't imagine him as the trailer of desperate thieves."

"Don't be fooled," Pony grunted. "There's plenty of iron in Cousin Floyd's back. Plenty. He won't be a cowboy in a thousand years; didn't start soon enough, the way most of us did. There'll always be a good showing of pilgrim—Easterner—in him, no matter how much the dude-cowboy he looks. But that's not for lack of toughness inside. I've seen several like him, in my day and my travels. I'm still wondering why he dislikes me, the way he really does dislike me."

"You keep harping on that! And I'm certain that you're mistaking worry for coldness of manner. He feels much responsibility for the Two Bench management. You see, Pony, the real reason for Cousin Roy's rather strange decision to get all the Kirk clan here is not the reason he gives. It's not that he's lonely without his own kin around him—not altogether. He won't admit that he isn't just as competent as he was twenty years ago, but secretly he has come to understand it. I know that he realizes how old he is, and concedes that he should be making any plans he wants to see fulfilled. He is amazingly proud of the Kirk blood, the Kirk name. He wants us here so that, when he does go, we'll be ready to step into his place and divide this property between us."

She hesitated while Pony watched frowningly.

"I— He— You didn't answer his letter. We know, now, why you didn't. But your lack of interest—as he considered it—hurt him greatly. For you, alone, have the name. So he made a will and divided the Two Bench between Floyd and me. Of course, now he'll change that and make you an heir, too, receiving an equal part of the property. He—"

"Oh!" Pony's tone was very expressive, as his grin was sardonic—"so that's why Cousin Floyd could kind of hold himself in when it came to saying his howdies to me. I drift in and maybe bring about a three-way cut instead of just a halving between you two. It does look plain to me, now, as the Fencerail brand that takes up all of a cow and a calf."

"That's not so!" she flared, standing. "Floyd Milton is the soul of fairness, of generosity. Never at any time has he said a word to indicate that he didn't actually want the last Kirk to come and share with us. Never!"

"You know," Pony drawled indulgently, getting up to smile at her, "you're just about as young and innocent as —as you are pretty. And I'm telling you that's just plenty! I believe that you believe every word of that. I believe that you're actually glad to see me here; that you're more than willing to take a third instead of a half. And I'd be a funny kind of critter if I didn't like you a lot for being that kind of girl. And I do like you a lot—more than I thought I'd ever like any girl again."

She flushed, then laughed and shook her head.

"Ah, dear me! I do believe that I've uncovered a

blighted heart! That's the secret! It's not a gory record
such as Sheriff Sanford suspects, that makes you so se-
cretive. It's a wrecked love that made you resolve never-
never-never to like a girl again, but to always be un-
pleasant toward girls, and to smile only when you can't
help it. I must tell the sheriff."

"I may not be back for supper. Expect me when you
see me at the door. If Cousin Roy happens to remember
about my getting here yesterday and asks, you can tell
him I'm looking around and sort of storing up landmarks and—faces."

He went past her and out of the house. Miguelito was
on the corral bars admiring the half-dozen big half-blood
geldings inside. He grinned at Pony and indicated a four-
teen-hand buckskin that stood just below his perch.

"If your gray cousin is willing, I will trade my horse
for that one," he said humorously. "Once my father
owned such a *caballo* which he had from Mexico because
the man who had ridden it needed it no longer after
they fought, he and my father. I do not believe that even
your Dan could best that one, *amo.*"

"It is the horse of the señorita, my cousin. Now, we go
like that bear of the song, which climbed the mountain
to see what might be seen on the other side. And—we ride
our own horses, my son. I do not wish to push into any
of the *negócios,* the business, of my cousin's ranch. We
will trouble him as little as may be."

"*Bien,*" Mig said gloomily. "But I wish that Bully Witt
or Johnson had raised such horses as these of the Two
Bench, in our Territory. A man could have—*arranged*
then to own one."

Pony whistled to Dan and the big black came over
obediently to the gate. Mig got their saddles and bridles
and roped his stocky bay. They were done saddling when
Connie came up behind them.

"Why don't you let your horses rest and ride Cousin Roy's?" she asked Pony. "That bay with the starred forehead is called one of the finest horses in the country. The chestnut is almost as good, Cousin Roy says. And I'm sure he would want—"

"They look awful snorty, them horses," Pony told her solemnly. "Now, Dan, he's a regular old grandma's buggy horse. I know he won't pitch with me, not even on a frosty morning. A cowboy can't be too careful. You know why cowboys hardly ever get old? They don't live long enough! So any li'l thing we can do to kind of drag out the tally, why, we ought to do. I will stick to Dan and Mig will keep his goat."

"You—wouldn't *hurrah* me?" she demanded, suddenly frowning at him. "You aren't taking your own horses because you intend to ride on away from us? Somehow, I'm not at all sure of you, Pony. It would be strange, if a man could just toss away the third of a big property like this, because of an instant's irritation, but I believe you're quite capable of it. As for leaving your affectionate relatives—"

"You're right! I'm not thinking about a third or any other part of the Two Bench. I have never in my life been bodaciously handed something in a paper sack. There never was any prospect of that happening to me. So I reckon I'm just not in the habit of expecting presents, or hanging around trying to be a nice boy so somebody'll leave me something when he dies. The Two Bench means not one li'l bitty thing to me!"

"Nor your cousins, either?" she asked him sadly. "Don't tell me that you don't care for us as—as we might care for you! Why, you said that you like me better than you expected ever to like any girl again. And I believed you! Now, I suppose I'll have a hurt heart—like yours—and my life will be spoiled—like yours—"

Pony took his Winchester from Mig and rammed it into the carbine scabbard.

"Don't leave us, Pony!" Connie cried, putting out her hands imploringly "Don't ride into my life just to ride out again. Stay and I'll promise not to hurt your poor broken heart—not to ask you to smile, even—"

"I can't be changing in my old age," he said in tone as sad as her own. "I can feel sorry for you, same as I have for thousands of others including my seventeen sorrowing wives. But when it comes time for me to ride I'll have to go, same as always, no matter how it grieves you. But that's not this morning. I won't ride off—not yet."

Mig swung into his big-horned saddle and Pony mounted, to twist Dan so that he looked down into the girl's pretty face. She was in every way the most attractive girl he had ever met and, meeting her eyes, he could wish— Then he caught himself sardonically.

Tonto! Nitwit! he told himself mentally. *You have read a book about the big, handsome cowboy marrying the lovely schoolma'am. What you and the other fool cowboys didn't read, though, was the book for grown-ups about the married life they had, people as different as day and night penned up in the same house year after year, one of 'em eating with a knife and the other eating with a fork!*

"You will be back for supper, then?" she asked.

"I'll be back, anyhow," Pony assured her.

CHAPTER XIII

"I can tell plenty!"

A HALF MILE OUT OF VASKO Pony left the disappointed Mig in a hollow of the low hills. From this point the boy could see the road from the county seat and, with Pony's glasses, could easily make out the faces of riders on the road below and to the right of him.

"I don't think I'll have a bit of trouble," Pony assured him. "But you'll be a lot more help here, *jovenito*, than you ever could be at my elbow. Just consider! I come helling out of town and you see me. You can drop a slug or maybe six between me and the army—whatever army it is—on my trail. So I get a chance to pile up the dust."

"If that is the way it is, then I will stay," Mig said grudgingly. "But if it is because you expect trouble and think I am not yet man enough to take half of that trouble—"

"Oh, no! Not a bit of it!" Pony cried as indignantly as he could manage. "You're my back coverer, Mig. But remember—no shooting *at* anybody, even if they're chasing me. I don't want any notches on our guns in this country. I'll take almost anything before I'll shoot and you've got to do the same."

When he rode into the main street of Vasko, it was as quiet as on the day before. Piously, Pony hoped that its drowsy stillness would not again be exploded by a battle. He was passing the racket store of that Mrs. Quaid who had labeled him a gunman when the lady herself hailed him and, all unwillingly, he wheeled Dan and stopped.

"Well! You' back right quick," Mrs. Quaid remarked pleasantly, arms on hips, elbows out, gray head on one side as she studied him. "So you're the last of the Kirks. Huuuh! Must have been different kind of country your pa settled in, to what Roaring Red Roy's folks picked out. Uh-huh! Not high and slabby like him, you ain't. But a sight handsomer."

"My pa was as tall as Red Roy," Pony said humbly. "But it was a hard year, the one I was born in. Everything got kind of dogified and puny. I was awful delicate;

hard to raise. But they took the trouble account I was sweet-natured as well as pretty."

"Yeh! I seen some of that sweet nature of yours working right here! Gonzales County— You see, I know all about you. I heard Roy talk about his kinfolks by the hour, the last hundred year or so. Some right salty young roosters have come from Gonzales. Well, I do think Roy had a good notion, when he decided to git all you children on the Two Bench. I ain't so took with that Floyd Milton; he's a mite too uppity for me and some more plain folks. But I reckon that's only natural, him being a clerk in a bank back in Cleveland. And that Connie, she's as sweet a girl as anybody ever met. And now, you—"

She surveyed him critically again, abruptly smiled.

"You'll do! You seen plenty for your years. Can't fool me, son. But, like I told that big bulldog, John Sanford, that ain't a speck of reason to believe you got to be *anybody* listed on his dodgers, much less that cold-blooded murderer Fielder from the Territory. Say! Who showed you that tobacco-throwing trick, anyhow? Well, ne' mind! Ne' mind! What was I saying? Oh, yeh! About John Sanford. He's a one-cluck kind of chicken. Always was. When Quaid was sheriff here—rest his soul!—and he hired John Sanford for deputy, he told me the first week, he says, that Sanford'd fight a buzz saw, but you got to take him right up to it and prove to him it really is a buzz saw, and after that, even if you was to have proved to him a windmill was a buzz saw, it wouldn't make a bit of difference to Sanford. Uh-huh! That windmill'd always be a buzz saw to him."

She beamed, and Pony cleared his throat and gathered up the reins again.

"And how's the Two Bench going? Nothing new on that scoun'elly Clubfoot? I swan! It was too bad, Roy losing two good men like Ozment and Quell, right when he needed 'em most."

Reluctantly, Pony told her of Dumpty Downes's death and she clucked furiously.

"Dumpty! That—that hits me like the boy was my own kin! He was the nicest boy! Always stopped by to talk—"

There were tears in her eyes and she dabbed at them with her sleeve. But suddenly she looked hard at Pony.

"And how come," she demanded metallically, "you ain't riding with Roy to trail that gang? It does look like to me your third-interest in the Two Bench ought to kind of rouse up some interest in you. Even if you don't worry about a Two Bench man being rubbed out by a gang of sneaking killers, while he was riding Two Bench range, you might figure that every head of stock run off is a lick at your pocket."

"Oh, Cousin Roy seemed to think that he'd do better without a stranger tracking up the place," Pony said vaguely. "But"—now he gathered the reins and Dan lifted his head—"Dumpty Downes was my side partner for some time. I never had a better friend in my life. See you some more, Mrs. Quaid."

He rode on to the little sheriff's office and dismounted. But the shabby room was empty and the iron door of the two-cell jail swung open. He looked curiously around at the reward notices on the wall and with sight of a new one bearing the name *Chance Fielder* under the caption *$1000 Reward,* he grinned one-sidedly. He was reading it when that gangling, uncertain-looking cowboy-deputy, Shack Rolison, loafed in with a dusty, but otherwise neat, cowboy.

"Howdy, Kirk," Shack Rolison greeted him, in his flat, weary drawl. "If you happen to be hunting the sheriff, he's gone to Leon Creek on a tale Isbell headed that way."

"I just happened to be in town," Pony said carelessly.

"Thought I'd drop by and see Sanford; tell him about the latest on Clubfoot."

Once more he told of the *mañada* vanishing, of Dumpty's death, and Floyd Milton's escape. Shack Rolison settled in the sheriff's great chair, all but sitting on his shoulder blades with long legs pushed out storklike upon Sanford's desk.

"Sheriff'll paw the ground and snort, when he hears about that," he prophesied gloomily, at the end. "Wonder if I ought to light a shuck out to see about it. No-o, reckon not. Old Roaring Red Roy, he don't like me; I quit him to take on with the sheriff. He was firing me, anyhow, when I quit, but he took it ugly, all same. Besides, the sheriff told me particular to ride herd on town while he was gone. We'll let him and Roy make medicine when they git together next."

The cowboy who had come in with him had stood listening intently to Pony. He was short, stocky, with a square, tanned face smooth and young and cheerful, and large, almost girlish, blue eyes. Shack seemed to remember him at last. He waggled a limp hand without shifting position.

"That's Lyde Upshur, Kirk," he drawled. "Says he's a top hand with hawses. But he's from som'r's up the other side Red River in the Cherokee country so maybe what he really is is just good with Injun ponies. But he heard about Roy Kirk's Two Bench *caballos* and drifted this way aiming to hit Roy up for a job. Reckon, after all I told him and this last one you just unloaded, he'll change his mind."

Pony grinned and nodded to Upshur. Young as the cowboy seemed, he had about him the unmistakable air of competence. Now, he grinned easily at them both.

"Oh, I reckon not," he assured Shack. "Can't be worse around the Two Bench than it's been plenty times in the

Strip. If the Two Bench'll take me on, I'll give it a whack. And I am good with horses, stallions especially."

Pony decided that he liked Upshur, and he nodded and told him cordially, "Then I wouldn't be a bit surprised, even if I don't know a thing about Cousin Roy's business, if he handed you a job. He's bound to be short three men."

Then he turned back to Shack and began to talk with the deputy about the thefts of 2 Bench stock. Shack discussed them freely, but it was apparent that he knew little more of the circumstances than Floyd Milton and Red Roy. Ike Isbell he had seen around town a few times, but the dark little man was only a drifting cowboy to him.

"He never seemed to me to hang out anywheres special, or with anybody special. Sheriff tried to git a line on him yesterday after the shooting, but he never. Looks like Isbell just come from nowhere and stayed nowhere when he wasn't in town and went right back when you chased him off the street."

They smoked silently for a time. Pony, staring fixedly straight ahead with thumb hooked mechanically in his shirt over the Colt hidden in his waistband, wondered what he might expect to find here in Vasko.

Somebody's bound to know something more about him, he thought irritably. *The bartenders—or maybe he had a girl—or one of the men at the livery corral—*

"You going back out to the Two Bench, tonight?" Upshur interrupted his puzzling. "If you are—"

"I do'no. Nothing to do out there, for me, with Red Roy combing the range. Maybe I'll stay in town tonight and go out tomorrow. 'Long as I'm here I might as well see if I can pick up a feather or two this Isbell may have dropped in town. But when I'm ready I'll tell you and we can make it a pair out. Unless you want to head right out."

"I can wait for you. No use going out if the Big Auger's away. I'll buy the drinks, now."

"Can't take you up," Shack drawled sadly. "Sheriff made me promise not to even smell a cork while he was gone. I wish I wasn't so damn set on keeping promises. But like you noticed, he's a awful big man and lots of times it ain't a word and a blow with him—it's the other way around."

Pony and Upshur went up the street together, after Shack had promised to put Dan in the corral behind the jail.

"That's certainly a horse of yours," Upshur said admiringly. "What's that Box O—Montana outfit? Sheriff told us this morning you'd rode up there."

"Idaho," Pony told him—quite truthfully. He had thought of that fact with some amusement, when altering the Bar C on Dan's shoulder. "Yeh, he's really got four legs."

"And they all touch the ground! How'd you like Idaho and Montana? I never did land beyond Kansas City and that was just taking up some steers and coming right back. When I started out six months ago I thought I'd hit for Texas account the climate would suit my clothes and my disposition better. But, one day, I think I'll give the northern ranges a whirl."

They were talking range differences when at the door of the Criterion a shambling and bleary-eyed man stopped them. Pony recognized the town drunk, named by Mrs. Quaid, Pink Snake Casselberry, who had snored under the hitchrack on the eve of yesterday's battle. He looked coldly at the man.

"You're Red Roy Kirk's cousin," Casselberry mumbled. "I seen you yesterday in the fighting. I was drunk, then. But not too drunk I couldn't hear some things and see some things. I heard some questions being asked and

—funny—"

He stopped short, with a kind of shrewdness in red face and bleary eyes, wagging a trembling forefinger.

"Awful funny, because—the questions was about something I seen and looks like nobody else seen. If you'll buy me a few drinks, I—"

He shifted position lurchingly, but quickly. He looked past Pony at the moveless swing doors of the Criterion, then twisted his head to stare left and right.

"I don't mean, exactly, buy me drinks. Gi' me a dollar to stop the shakes I got. Then I'll talk trade with you— what I know that the Two Bench would like to know."

Pony stared hard at him, then looked frowningly at Upshur. The stocky cowboy shrugged as their eyes met.

"I'm just a stranger here," he grunted. "But if what the Two Bench wants to know is what a man'd guess it wants to know—"

"I can tell plenty!" Casselberry said earnestly. "Quell got shot right in there, yesterday, remember!"

"Don't try that on me," Pony told him scornfully. "You didn't see him shot. I saw you, snoring like a pig under the hitchrack, before the rows ever broke out. Then, when Roy Kirk came helling out here, you got up—I remember that—and you began to stumble away and when Isbell shot Ozment over yonder you picked up plenty speed. I saw you, without paying much attention. Now, what's it you know, that's so valuable? That's worth even one drink?"

Three men, town folk by the look of them, shouldered out of the Criterion and glanced at the two cowboys, then at Casselberry. They went on and one of the three said something about "Pink Snake" and "strangers" and laughed. After they were out of hearing, Casselberry leaned closer to Pony.

"I ain't going to tell you—exactly—what I know. But

you figure it like this. You know Isbell shot Ozment. But who shot Quell? Barkeep says *he* do'no; everybody else that's been asked says *they* do'no."

"But you do know?" Pony drawled incredulously. "You saw the man run out of the side of the Criterion, here. But you didn't tell the sheriff when he asked you. Ahh!"

"He never ask' me. Did I see who 'twas? Why—I can't remember! I got the shakes that bad I can't remember nothing. If I did or if I didn't. Well—see you some more, maybe."

He seemed to feel himself master of the situation, now. In spite of his shakes—and he was jerking and shivering like an epileptic—there was confidence in his red face.

"I think you'll see us, right now!" Pony disagreed, putting out a steely hand to clamp on the man's trembling arm. "If you saw the man who killed Quell, you're telling about it. Right here and right now!"

"I never seen a thing! And nobody's going to *make* me say I seen something. And if you was to manhandle me—well, the way I'd tell anything I did tell, nobody could make out head from tail. Le' me go! You won't hand over a month's drinks, so you can go to hell! I ain't talking!"

Pony hesitated, then shrugged. Looking at Upshur he met that young man's lifted brows.

"I'll cure your shakes, then, with a dollar," Pony surrendered. "And if you can tell me the name of the man you saw running out of the Criterion, I'll hand over the month's drink money. But if you lie to me—"

"I ain't going to lie," Casselberry assured him, almost whispering. "But I got to do it my way. I got my skin to consider. Gi' me the dollar! I'll straighten up. Not here, but down the line where *agua'diente's* cheap. At dinnertime, when everybody's eating, you come down to the Luna. Down yonder. Go out back to the corral. I'll meet you there. That's the only way I can do it—and see day-light tomorrow. If it was knowed in Vasko that I seen what I seen—"

He tried to snap his fingers. Pony slipped a dollar into his hand, and Casselberry lurched off.

CHAPTER XIV

"How long would I live?"

WHEN THEY STOOD ALONE in the door, Pony and Upshur looked at each other, then again at Casselberry's hurry-ing back.

"Ah, well, it's only a dollar," Pony said sardonically. "And from what I hear, Pink Snake's sort of entitled to one bite out of every stranger. Funny, though—I wouldn't have given him credit for figuring out what I might want to know, that he could claim to know, worth the price of drinks."

"If he did happen to see something—Quell's killer run-ning out of the side of the place, which is something nobody else admits seeing," Upshur answered thought-fully, "I reckon you and Kirk would figure his month's drinks low pay. I was around with Shack Rolison and Sanford early this morning and I heard 'em talking to the barkeep in here and to some others. *Somebody* killed Quell with the house shotgun, but that's all Sanford found out."

A big man came through the swing doors and looked with unwinking light eyes at each of them, with a sort of hawklike deliberation, before going slowly down the street. He was in saddle-warped overalls and hickory shirt and he smelled of sweat and horse. There were touches of gray in his shaggy hair and the stubble of beard on his harsh face, but he looked hard and fit. Mechanically. Pony noted the bulge of a pistol under the faded shirt. beneath the left arm.

"Well," he told Upshur, "we have still got those drinks to buy. So you heard the bartender's tale in here."

"Yeh," Upshur replied, grinning faintly. "I wanted to ask Sanford about the country; about the Two Bench and so on. I had to talk kind of in between his examining."

They found a small line at the bar and turned in near the door where they stood alone.

"Sanford's mind don't let him handle too many different things at once," Upshur went on. "I reckon yesterday crowded him plenty. He had this handful of business in town to puzzle over. Then he was wondering if you mightn't be a bad man from the Territory name' Fields. And I wanted to hear about what kind of outfit the Two Bench might be."

The bartender moved their way, bringing bottle and glasses. Pony nodded blankly to Upshur and spoke in an absent way.

"Yeh. He told me he was looking for a flame-snorting murderer. I think he called him Fielder, though, not Fields. Must be a reward on this Jesse James that Sanford's after; I figured that when he all but busted out crying when he found out who I really am and where I come from and why I headed for Vasko anyhow."

He nodded to the bartender and that worthy shook his head and sighed cavernously.

"I'm tuckered out," he confessed. "I ain't one of them gladiating folks like you read about. I like peace and quietness. It was bad enough to have the killings right in my lap, yesterday, but on top of that John Sanford's been hounding me about who it might have been killed Quell and what I maybe did see without knowing I seen it. Ask' me over and over again the same questions. I swear!

If I wasn't set against it I believe I'd take to drinking myself!"

He poured their drinks and went on complaining while they emptied the glasses and had a second round. Upshur yawned and said that he wanted to buy some supplies.

"Going to be here awhile?" he asked Pony. "Then I'll see you and—if you want me—trail along at dinnertime."

He disappeared through the swing doors and Pony considered the death of Quell and the disappearance of the man who had killed him here. It seemed plain enough to him that Quell and Ozment had discovered something about the thieves—and that Isbell and at least one other man had known of their discovery, and moved quickly and efficiently to shut the punchers' mouths. He could hardly doubt that the fight in here, started by the dead Horace Palm with Red Roy, had been part of the same move to keep Red Roy from meeting and talking with Quell and Ozment. Which might or might not mean that Palm had been one of the rustlers. He might only have been hired by a rustler.

"Yeh, yeh," Pony said vaguely to the bartender. "You heard the shotgun and you peeped out from behind your barrels and Quell had been hit and somebody was leaving by the side door—just a cowboyish-looking back was all you saw; just one glimpse of that much. But—it certainly wasn't Isbell, was it? You'd have noticed his red shirt."

"Yeh, I'd have noticed a red shirt. But this was blue—could have been that shirt you're wearing, right now. And he had on overalls. Anyhow, it seems to me like he had on overalls. But, like I told the sheriff, I couldn't swear to anything but a blue shirt. And Isbell had on a red one."

"Funny about Isbell," Pony drawled meditatively. "He was around town a good deal. Enough for about everybody to know him by name and looks. But that's all! Nobody can say who he hung out with or where he holed up when he was away from town."

"That's so," the bartender admitted, frowning. "Leastways, I don't think of anybody special he sided. Horace Palm and some of the town tinhorns might've knowed. But Horace is dead and the others won't talk—them that can talk since they run into Red Roy's chair and your six-shooter. Isbell broke some horses around Daniels Ford, I remember. Then he hung out in Elleon west of here, but not for long."

There was the sound of wheels outside, then high-pitched women's voices. Pony and the bartender both turned mechanically to look over the swing doors of the Criterion to the long, shabby 'dobe building opposite. Brilliant-blue letters made a sign along the peeling plaster of the front of that building. Pony read the sign for the first time—*Terpsichore Palace*. The bartender grinned slightly as three vividly rouged girls got out of a trap and stood talking loudly to the driver.

"Delrio Dolly's place," he explained. "She named it that Tearp-see-shore when she opened up. Says it means all kinds of dancing and she certainly did make it mean that from the start. Got a bunch of right good-looking gals, Dolly has. See that redhead? That's the one Ambrosius Quell was stuck on. Beatrice, her name is. She plays the piano a lot. She used to play 'I'm Only a Bird in a Gilded Cage' for Quell and he'd hang over the piano and buy drinks for the house 'long's he had a nickel. Yeh, he was certainly sunk on her."

"She takes his killing pretty easy," Pony remarked dryly. "Well, a dance-hall girl can't drive dead horses."

He considered Beatrice for a while, then straightened and told the bartender that he was going to drift. He went out and looked at the door of the dance-hall bar.

The Palace was quiet, now, the girls gone in, their trap driven away. Pony crossed the street and looked inside Delrio Dolly's place.

Along the wall to his left ran a once-ornate bar, scarred and sprung by years of rough usage. Small tables were set close to each other around the other walls of the big, barnlike room. Just now, only a gray Mexican with a broom and a yellow-skinned, unhealthy-seeming young man behind the bar polishing glasses were in the place.

As Pony moved toward the bar the yellow-faced bartender lifted his narrow eyes as high as Pony's chin and mumbled a greeting. Pony asked for whisky and rang a twenty on the bar. As if the sound of the gold piece were a signal, two girls put their heads through a door down and behind the bar and looked at the customer. One was a faded blonde with fat face and piggy blue eyes. But the other was Beatrice the redhead. At her Pony stared admiringly, then bashfully.

"I— She—" he stammered in the bartender's direction. "You—reckon the lady with the *orburn* hair would— I mean I'd like to buy her a drink."

A corner of the bartender's loose mouth lifted contemptuously. Without turning his head he called "Bee!" and the redhead came into the room, smiling mechanically, her walk an exaggerated swaying.

"I—I'm Pony Kirk. I reckon you know my cousin that owns the Two Bench," he said nervously. "I'm a stranger in Vasko."

She put him quickly at ease, steered him to a table, and sat with arms folded upon it, long green eyes roving up and down Pony while she smiled and talked. The whisky she poured out and gulped down was not her "usual," she was quick to tell him. But, after yesterday—

"I reckon it don't hit you like that, though! Say, that was slick leather-slapping, the way you filled your hand

and cut down on Ike Isbell. Wonder you didn't cut him clean in two! But you come plenty close for Mis' Isbell's mean li'l boy, Ike! He stirred up the dust pulling his horns in. I happened to see it all. The bunch of us was looking out, watching Roaring Red Roy and Horace Palm and them others. One minute you never had a thing in your hand, next minute you was dusting Isbell. It was plenty slick, Pony. I told Kane, yonder—the barkeep—I been around a lot—for a girl, you understand—and I never saw a faster draw. You're staying in town—I hope."

He nodded and refilled her glass, then his own.

"You get jolted bad enough," he told her sagely, "and you can fill your hand faster'n you ever thought you could. Me, I was right hobbled, being new and not knowing a soul in the whole bunch, Isbell or Quell or Ozment or even my own cousin! But Isbell looked like shooting at me, so—I cut loose on him. I reckon"—he grinned weakly at her—"I'm just slow around girls."

"You'll do! And don't try to tell me you ain't had plenty lady friends! They don't get to your age, good-looking and—free-spending as *you* are, without some girl telling 'em so. What about Isbell, though? Anybody find him after he hit the trail out? Somebody was saying the sheriff rode off hunting him."

"If he was found I never heard about it. Maybe he kept on going, clean out of the country. That'd be his play, unless he had a lot of backing. The Two Bench was all painted up for war when I left the house this morning. Got their tomahawks all sharp for a scalp hunt. Seems like they thought a lot of Ozment and Quell."

"Ozment I never knew. But Quell—ah, he wasn't so much of a muchness," she said carelessly, lifting her glass and putting it down empty. "Ah, but I needed that! Just like so much water, today. After all the smoking, I was about to pieces last night. You mightn't believe it, but

I'm nothing but a bunch of nerves. All auburns are like that. Look at my hand! But I was saying, about Ambrosius—nothing but a thickhead leather pounder. They says to his mother, I bet you, when Ambrosius was born, that he was going to have curly hair and a grin and learn to dance real good and never would make more'n forty a month and cakes. But he liked me a lot—"

While she had still another drink and very smoothly examined him after a practiced routine, about his past, his finances, his plans, and he answered in the fashion of a prosperous and bashful young cowboy, Pony studied her.

From their table he could look out into the street and across at the Criterion. If she had been standing in the doorway of the Terpsichore as Quell staggered, dying, through the Criterion's swing doors and his murderer had run from the Criterion's side door, she might very well have seen that blue-shirted man of whom the bartender had spoken.

She was smiling most cordially at him now. Her face showed haggard lines beneath its rouge and the green eyes were slightly swollen. She said that she had poured down drinks until her gizzard nearly floated, but could not forget the deaths of Ozment and Quell. Pony was sympathetic. He asked casually who had killed Quell.

"Nobody seems to know," she answered as casually.

"You happen to be looking across there when Quell ran out? See him, I mean?"

"I thought I recognized him, kind of through the crowd that was fighting Red Roy. But there was so much happening—men running back and forth, out of the Criterion side door and popping into stores—you couldn't be certain of much."

"Out of the Criterion side door?" Pony repeated innocently. "Who would that have been? The bartender said—"

He stopped, frowning. But she yawned and looked at the bottle and said that she guessed another *little* one wouldn't hurt her and it might help. Pony poured it for her, filling the glass to the rim. He tried prompting her once more.

"I thought nobody was in the Criterion but Quell and the bartender," he said easily.

"And the man that killed Quell, of course," she reminded him. "The one who *might* have run out the side door. Say, do you dance? If you don't, I can learn you easy. I can tell by looking at you it'd be easy—and I'd like it. I like the way you treat a girl, Pony. In fact"—she stopped and put her head on one side to smile at him—"I like just everything about you that I know of, except one thing. That's an awful bad habit you got, boy, of asking the kind of questions that'd get somebody killed. Most anybody."

"I—wonder," he drawled, "if you'd like something about me you don't know much about yet—a couple of twenties slid into your lap under the table. Nobody would ever know that you told me the name of just one man, a fella in a blue shirt that popped out of the Criterion side door."

She looked levelly at him, green eyes infinitely wise, sardonic. The red head was shaken slowly, very emphatically.

"Suppose I saw that fella. Suppose I recognized him— Suppose I *could* tell you his name—and told you. How long would I live?"

"Funny," he said slowly, staring at her with real curiosity. "Why don't you take the—fifty dollars and tell me just any old name, Hezekiah Hoogenstrooper from the 'Leven Lazy X-on-a-Barn; any old thing?"

"Maybe I would've, yesterday," she confessed. "But I

ain't over the killings, I reckon. If I could tell you the man's real name— You know, I like you! You had me fooled some at first. The way you acted like a even-thick-headeder puncher than Ambrosius. Now, you had to drop that, to try to pump me about that fella. You ain't fooling me a li'l bit, Pony Kirk! No more than I'm fooling you. And—I like you plenty, the way I size you. I won't lie to you to grab fifty dollars. I—"

She was looking past him, toward that wall beyond the end of the bar. Her eyes narrowed and she swallowed with a sticky sound. Then she was smiling at him again. But he shifted in his chair so that his back was covered by the wall against which the table rested; so that he could see what had startled her. She got up, stretching, yawning, groaning. She said that she was worn out; she was going to flop for a while.

That big, cold-eyed, shabby man who had passed Pony and Upshur in the door of the Criterion with deliberate stare was standing at the end of the bar, a little out from it. He was staring at Beatrice or Pony with blank fixity of light eyes.

"I'll be looking for you, tonight," Beatrice told Pony in a careless tone. "Learn you to dance, cowboy!"

He nodded. The big, staring man with the ominous pistol bulge under left arm, looked at Beatrice. It seemed to Pony that the girl went so as to keep two long yards from the man when passing him. But he did not move; transferred his hawklike stare to Pony when she had gone by and neared a door in the wall.

Pony stood, but left hat and bottle on the table. He crossed to the street door and looked up and down the quiet length of the street. Beyond loitering figures he saw two men standing. One, he was pretty sure, was Upshur. As he watched, Upshur shoved the other man violently and turned away.

About time to go to the Luna, he thought. *Looks like Upshur's got there and's waiting for me. If Beatrice saw that man run out of the Criterion, whether she knows he killed Quell or is just guessing he's the one, it may be that Pink Snake Casselberry did see the same thing. Both of 'em seem scared to talk. But Pink Snake can get over his scare, if he's paid and if he thinks he'll be safe afterward.*

He turned back to the big room. The shabby man had not moved. Pony thought with grim humor that he could believe the man's eyes had not blinked. He went over to the table to get his hat and the bottle. When he stood beside the table the rap of boot heels suddenly broke the hush of the room. He pivoted deliberately. The big man was coming toward him. The bartender Kane was hunched, looking at him. From the doorway in the far wall Beatrice was watching, a clawing hand over her mouth as if to hold back a scream.

CHAPTER XV

"Jean Elam killed Quell?"

PONY HAD BEEN in far too many tight places, not to be sensitive to what he called the "feeling of murder." That atmosphere was here now. Why this cold-eyed man intended to kill him, he could not be sure—except that he guessed his talk with Beatrice was behind it. The girl's manner indicated that. If his questions about Quell's murderer had brought this attack, then this man was either the killer or one of the rustlers he wanted to find.

He sagged a little and watched the man approach, ignoring both the bartender and the girl, keeping his face blank. The man's hand swung loosely at his sides. If he intended drawing that hidden pistol, he had as long a draw to make as Pony had. But he stopped a yard away, his back to the bar, merely looking Pony in the eye.

"Hear you're a Kirk," he said. He had a vague accent, but Pony could not place it. "Seems like you are. Coming into the country and trying to ram your nose into things same way that old son of a dog, Roy Kirk, has done all *his* life."

Pony moved his left hand flashingly, to catch the quart bottle and whip it out underhand. It caught the man on the forehead and broke, spattering his face with whisky, staggering him. Pony heard Beatrice scream, but he was jumping, whipping out his pistol, when he heard the sound. For over the bar the yellow-faced Kane had raised a sawed-off shotgun and the flick of movement had caught Pony's eye.

The heavy detonation of the Greener seemed to rock the stagnant air of the room. A charge of buckshot splintered the table beside which Pony had been standing a split second before. The shabby man staggered again, as when the bottle had struck him. Then he turned so that he faced the bar. He was making jerky little movements with his right hand, over the bulge of his pistol. He took a long, careful step, now, toward the bar. Pony, Colt out and lifting to cover the bartender, was puzzled—but not to the point of hesitating.

"I reckon—" the man began mumbling, then stopped.

He was suddenly all joints. He collapsed on the floor, falling forward to lie still. Pony's slug had gone toward the bartender, who had begun to duck as soon as his shot was fired. It was a miss, and the scrambling noise behind the bar told of the yellow-faced Kane going fast toward the open door at the end of the bar. Pony ran that way, but when he leaned over the bar to get a second shot, Kane was gone into the gloom of the room beyond.

To Pony's right was the door in which Beatrice had

stood. The girl had disappeared and he ran through the door into a dusky passage, off which opened a half-dozen doors. Somewhere ahead of him he heard the scrape of a foot and lifted his Colt uncertainly. He had no way of knowing whether that person moving was Beatrice or another girl or the man he wanted. He listened, heard the sound again, and took a silver dollar from his pocket. He threw it against the wall of the hallway, in the direction of that sound. Instantly, there was the roar of the shotgun. Buckshot tore into the plank partition beyond Pony.

He was too eager, that wielder of the shotgun, the yellow-faced bartender. After the shot, he paused only for about the time Pony calculated necessary for slipping two more shells into his gun. Pony groaned artistically and into the dusk of the hall came the bartender, popping out of a room like that in which Pony stood. The shotgun was held at hip level; he leaned tensely forward, head shuttling left and right.

Grimly, Pony shot him twice, as fast as he could thumb back the hammer of his Colt. The bartender fell sideways against the wall and dropped his weapon. It bellowed thunderously but the charge of both barrels only hammered into the floor—and Pony had exposed no more than his gun arm and the side of his face. He waited, the smoke acrid in nose and eyes, squinting as the bartender began to slide down the wall, muttering.

"The place," Kane said in a low, troubled voice, "it's a-going round and round. I ought not to have—"

Then he crumpled on the floor and was quiet. Pony looked steadily at him, without particular emotion. When he was sure that Kane's stillness was not a trick, he came out and looked around, then at Kane again.

"You're right," he said flatly, as if Kane could hear. "You ought not to have picked up a load as heavy as this.

Rolling drunks you could handle, maybe. But killing—"

There was stamping and loud talk in the big dance hall behind him. Then a high-pitched call.

"Come out of that, you! Come a-reaching!"

He went back by the way he had come, to the door at the end of the bar. There he stopped and ejected the empty shells from his pistol and replaced them.

"Who's that?" he demanded, when the command was repeated. "This is Kirk. I'm coming out. I dropped Kane."

"This is Shack Rolison, Kirk. Come on out."

Pony scowled and moved his shoulders uncomfortably. He had a crawling sensation between his shoulder blades, almost a shiver. What would Shack Rolison do? It was not likely that Sheriff Sanford had left with his deputy any statement of friendly feeling for John "Pony" Kirk. And what he had seen of Rolison, added to what he had heard, made the deputy loom now as an uncertain quantity.

But he went out as if to meet a friend—and Upshur was standing at Rolison's elbow, his square, bronzed face very grim, his eyes a trifle narrowed.

"All right, Kirk," Rolison said calmly. "Come on and spin the yarn. You downed Kane Gravis, huh? All right— how-come it? What'd you pick a fight with Jean Elam for?"

He had a short shotgun like that of Kane Gravis's. He held it close up to his belt and Pony saw that the hammers were back. This was not the shiftless, dull man he had seen before. Even as he looked at Rolison he could wonder if Sheriff Sanford had made the same mistake about his deputy.

"Beatrice!" Pony called, instead of answering Rolison. "Oh, Beatrice! Come out here a minute, will you?"

The girl, spots of rouge glaring on her paper-white

cheeks, appeared draggingly in the door through which she had left the room. She looked at the street wall, keeping her chin lifted—as if forcing her eyes away from the sprawling figure on the floor. There were men in the street door of the Terpsichore, now, but they stayed outside, gaping in.

"Tell Rolison what happened," Pony ordered her quietly. "I have got an idea that you won't mind telling it—now—just the way it happened."

She looked flashingly at him, hesitated, then shrugged.

"You got him wrong, Shack," she said almost in a whisper. "He never killed Jean Elam. That was Kane—by mistake. Kane cut loose at Kirk, but he hit Jean. Then Kane ran afid—and—"

"And he took another shot at me out back," Pony supplied.

"But—what'd Kane want to rub you out for?" Shack grunted in a new tone, very plainly surprised. "What'd you rowed with him about?"

Pony considered his answer carefully. Those quiet men in the street, listening—any of them might be rustlers, allies of Kane Gravis and Jean Elam. He knew far too little of these people to talk loosely. He was not sure what he thought of Shack Rolison, for that matter. Then Beatrice cut in and saved him the effort of evasion. She spoke wearily.

"Pony never rowed with Kane! Jean Elam was on the prod and when he saw me sitting with Pony that started him off. Jean liked me plenty! I reckon he mistook Pony for a shorthorn. Anyway, after I started out, Jean begun to curse the Kirks, and Pony he slammed that bottle into Jean's face, and Kane— Well, him and Jean was awful good friends and maybe he thought Pony meant to kill Jean. And he could've killed him, easy. Or maybe Kane wasn't lying this morning when he told me he was going

to cut the next rowdy cowboy in two that raised his voice
in here. Kane, you know, he never liked cowboys a li'l bit."

"But Kane was shooting the shotgun. Jean was hit just
once, by one slug," Rolison objected coldly.

"Right on both counts—if there's just one slug in him,"
Pony agreed. "Most of the slugs went into the table after
I jumped. But one hit Elam. One was plenty!"

A paunchy, bareheaded little man came into the dance
hall as if pushed. Now, the onlookers crowded in, behind
this shabby and shaky old man. Rolison still held his
cocked shotgun, but he looked at the little figure inquiringly.

"Reckon you got to hold the inquest, Judge," he
drawled.

"Inquest! Inquest!" the justice stammered. He looked
at Elam and looked away, swallowing. "I tell you, I got
enough of this killing business. I don't like guns and
dead men and I don't care who hears me say so. I heard
enough from this boy and that girl to tell what happened
—specially when I knew Jean Elam and that trifling Kane
Gravis like I did. What she says they did is exactly what
they *would* have done, in my mind. But—"

His shaky forefinger stabbed out at Beatrice, then at
Pony.

"You swear what you said is the truth? And you?"

"It's the truth. I'd swear it anywhere," Beatrice answered earnestly.

"I swear to what I have said," Pony said in his turn.
"But—Kane Gravis is in the hall back there. He tried
another shot at me before I cut down on him. Hadn't you
better see—"

"It's all the same case! I don't want to see him. It's my
verdict that Jean Elam and Kane Gravis came to their
death by gunshot wounds, Gravis killing Elam by accident, Kirk killing Gravis by intent but rightly—and I

hope Vasko can manage to get along without any more shooting!"

Pony looked at Rolison. Stiffness went out of the deputy. He let down the hammers of his shotgun carefully. He was the slouching, uncertain-seeming cowboy again and it was hard to realize that he had ever been anything else. He grinned amiably.

"Reckon you' in the clear, fella. And I'm glad of it. What you aim to do, now?"

Pony went over to Beatrice and faced her gravely.

"Thanks," he said in a low voice. "I appreciate that and—maybe I can pay it back. I'll be seeing you."

"Funny," she whispered, watching the room, "that was all truth but— You know what I mean. You can kind of move truth around if you got to. Sure! I'll be seeing you. But not tonight. Me nor you either will feel like dancing!"

She turned into the darkness behind her and Pony, moving deftly past and around those men who wanted to talk of the killing, went back to Rolison and Upshur. Two Mexicans had appeared from somewhere, to carry Elam out.

The three of them got out of the Terpsichore and on the street Rolison looked at Pony.

"Let's drift down to the office a minute," he drawled. "That kind of knotted me, not knowing but what I had to put the cuffs on you—or cut you off pocket-high if you fought. I'm going to take that promise I made the sheriff and stick it in a drawer for long enough to have a big drink out of his private bottle he thinks I don't know where he hid. You all need one, too!"

When they were in the sheriff's office with the bottle of rye between them on the desk, lowered by three drinks, Rolison regarded Pony sleepily.

"You don't have to say a word if you don't want to. You have been washed clean and white by Judge Zink.

But I would like to know—and I bet you Lyde Upshur, there, he feels the same—what really did happen and take place. With Elam."

Pony studied him, without effort at concealment. Rolison pushed the bottle to him

"Take a drink—and know your friends!" he counseled. "When you come to think about it, Pony, I never shot you! I just wondered about you. And I'll do you the compliment to say I really do'no if I could've shot you—and not got killed!"

Pony took the drink and grinned in his turn. For the first time in weeks—since gay Pat Curran's death—he felt that he stood beside friends. Grimness fell away from him like something dropped.

"Well," he said weightily, "it was like— You know the tale of Samson and Delilah?"

"Learned that in Sunday school, ninety year back! Samson whacked off Delilah's hair and made him mad, so he handed her over to Goliath and then David rode up—"

"I reckon," Pony told Upshur, "I had better just tell this straight, before Shack really comes unraveled! I was pumping Beatrice—she was friendly with Ambrosius Quell —to see what I could find out about who killed Quell. Either Elam heard something or he guessed what I was after. She saw him and got scared and left me. He and Kane Gravis had decided to rub me out before I ever saw him. Must have! Elam was sober. But he talked like a kid cowboy that'd been slapped in the ear with a bartender's towel. He wasn't trying to pick a row with me. He was just stalling to keep my mind off Kane Gravis, who had the shotgun, to give Gravis a shot at me. So— who was Jean Elam? For I'm pretty certain *he* killed Quell!"

"Jean Elam killed Quell? But—what for? Elam was foreman of Nate Azle's Ladder U outfit! And I'll swear

Nate's honest as the day is long. What'd a Ladder U man want to kill Quell about, then? The man who killed Ambrosius was stopping him from telling Red Roy something he found out about the rustlers. You can't dodge that! So—how does the Ladder U fit in?"

"Now you tell me and I'll tell you!" Pony grunted. "I have been around a li'l bit. I have seen the elephant and heard the owl. But this whole business about and around One End Creek has got me pawing the bits. One End Creek— Huh! She's deep and she's wide and she's got a current like the Pecos on a high lonesome, it does look like to me. And here I am, just a trifling tramp cowboy, trying to wade her without owning even a pair of galoshes!"

"Your trail's hard to follow," Rolison said slowly. "I wonder what you' talking about."

"I wish I knew, myself," Pony confessed sadly. "I do!"

He looked at Upshur and thought that Pink Snake Casselberry was in the stocky cowboy's mind, as in his. As he began casual-seeming excuses for leaving Rolison, a gaunt giant came to the street door and stooped to thrust his head inside.

He shifted the stub of his cigarette to the side of thin mouth and said tonelessly, "Shack, that pore, trifling Pink Snake's down back of the shed behind the Luna. Somebody shoved a foot of knife into him a couple times and he's dead. Nobody around the Luna knows a thing about the killing. Thought you'd want to know."

When he was gone, Shack Rolison groaned.

"What I ever took this job for! Jean Elam and Kane Gravis—now Casselberry! You all want to come along while I see about it?"

"Uh-uh!" Pony answered promptly. "I only speak of my own feelings, Mr. Rolison, but I do think Upshur and Yours Leavingly have got just one mind between us. I think we're going to eat and leave you. I know I am! Back on the Two Bench is where I want to be. This town of yours is too rich for me."

"I kind of thought I'd use around awhile—maybe buck the tiger at the Criterion and such-like foolishness," Upshur said uncertainly. "Wouldn't you like to kind of take in the sights, too? No telling when us country boys'll have a chance to look at a big place like this, next."

"I wouldn't feel safe! No, you take your flyer if you want to. Come on out when it's over. I'm going as soon as I eat."

"Then I'll side you. Probably be dollars in my pocket at that, to go. We'll let Rolison chase his murderer."

They ate and got their horses. When they rode out of Vasko, Upshur looked thoughtfully at Pony.

"So it was Elam—or one of his hired knives," he grunted. "I *wondered* if he didn't overhear the talk with Casselberry at the Criterion door. He came out right in the middle of it and he did look interested."

"I think it was Elam, all right. I think he killed Quell, killed Casselberry, and meant to kill me. He just slipped."

CHAPTER XVI

"You shot that man"

THEY WERE HALFWAY to that hollow of the hills where Mig had waited, when Pony thought of the moment before Jean Elam's attack on him.

"You had a li'l trouble in Vasko, yourself, didn't you?" he asked. "Down toward the Mex' end of the street."

"Trouble?" Upshur said frowningly. "What d'you mean?"

"Just before the Terpsichore sort of exploded in my

whiskers, I looked down the street and saw you push a man clear off the sidewalk," Pony explained.

"Oh, that! I had forgot it. Just a drink-begging Mexican. Hit me up for a drink while I was looking around, waiting for you. I didn't like his looks a little bit. After looking around Vasko and hearing all I heard, maybe I wasn't too polite to drunks that didn't seem exactly common drunks. So I—kind of shoved him when he talked rough."

"Might just as well have been some kind of racket," Pony told him. "I don't know who, in Vasko, sides with this bunch of thieves and killers. Isbell and that Horace Palm somebody shot by accident and Elam and Gravis, I put the brand on. And if that many happened to be in town, it would be surprising if some more didn't use around there. And you'd been walking with me, remember. I tell you, Lyde, this is a mixed-up business for strangers like you and me. You want to watch the sky line, if Red Roy sets you riding for him. I'm sort of lone-wolfing it. It's like this—"

He described the 2 Bench briefly, speaking without much detail of Red Roy and Floyd Milton and Connie Hall.

"It's reasonable enough," he concluded, "that they don't want to take time to explain everything to me. But this Dumpty Downes was a good friend of mine and— Well, I sort of stick by my friends and hang and rattle with 'em when they're in trouble. I—"

He laughed, looking ahead toward the place where Mig should be.

"Don't mind me, if I brag a li'l about how I'll back up a man I like. I'm like a woman Dumpty and I used to know in Del Rio, that was slinging hash there. She was about four-foot-nine and six foot thick. Must've weighed around three hundred. She was cross-eyed and some of her teeth had quit her long before. She had smallpox scars all over her face. But she paid a lot of money for her shoes and always got red ones. For she had a li'l bitsy foot. Well—I haven't got a lot to brag about, so I have to put red shoes on what I do own and keep 'em out in sight."

"I—would have guessed you owned that habit," Upshur said quietly. "I am downright interested in all this Two Bench trouble. I hope the old man lets me ride for him. And I'd like to side you while you're looking around. You don't expect the sheriff to give you trouble, about that notion of his that you're a sight daft on some Territory town?"

"I don't much think so. He's got a handful of grief without entertaining wild notions about me. I think, too, that he's made up his mind I'm no wild-eyed killer, because I happen to be a man he can check up on through Red Roy Kirk."

He thought of the remark Connie had made, about officers from the Territory needing only to look at him to satisfy Sanford. He grinned faintly and lifted his hand in signal to Mig.

"If Sanford's still bothered about me," he drawled, "he can always have me assayed by some officer who'd know the man he's hunting. The thing is, I am not fond of jails, and if I can help it, I'm not going to board in Sanford's hotel while he goes through his motions. There's a kid that rides with me—anyway, he's been riding with me since some days back when I picked him up. Apache. You sling the lingo? Or Spanish?"

"Uh-uh," Lyde Upshur grunted, staring at Mig. "Salty boy, from his looks. Talk English?"

"Little," Pony said briefly. "Seems like a good kid. He wants to have a look at Texas and on up north. Says he's out of Mexico. I left him there when I rode into town.

Didn't know what the blame place would do this trip and it didn't seem right to drag a boy into Vasko's kind of murder."

Mig rode down the slope to them and nodded. His face was blank and he only nodded stolidly when Pony introduced Lyde Upshur. The three continued toward the 2 Bench, Mig jogging behind the men and whistling softly or listening to Upshur's questions and Pony's replies.

When well after dark they came up to the 2 Bench house, it was lighted in almost every window. Pony dismounted and Upshur swung down after him. Mig took their horses and Pony led the way up to the front veranda.

Red Roy, Floyd Milton, and Connie were waiting. Red Roy asked without much cordiality where Pony had been.

"To town," Pony answered flatly, "mingling with some of your good friends. This is Lyde Upshur, from Red River way. He came into Vasko job-hunting and I brought him out to see you."

Red Roy grunted and began a cross-examination of Upshur. Floyd Milton listened to the talk. Connie moved over to where Pony lounged against a veranda post.

"Come on into the dining-room, and I'll give you supper," she said. "He can rouse out Hung On and get something to eat with the men."

Pony hesitated, then shrugged. Red Roy was still asking Upshur questions about his experience with horses. Pony trailed the girl into the house and sat down in the dining-room. She shook a bell and the Mexican waiter appeared and went out again. Pony exhaled smoke and looked at her, where she sat with arms folded on the table across from him.

"Well? What did they find?" he asked. "Cut the trail?"

"Judging from their tempers when they came in, awhile ago, they weren't very successful," she said absently. "And you? Did you discover anything in Vasko?"

"Well, I got out of town alive and without the Law at my heels! I reckon that stands for doing something."

Red Roy came into the dining-room and sat down to look from one to the other. He jerked his head toward the door.

"I hired him," he grunted. "Seems like a good man. Glad you brought him out. Floyd's fixing to gether him some supper. Anything happen in town?"

Pony was waiting for the Mexican to put his plate before him. He straightened and looked thoughtfully at his cousin.

"You know Kane Gravis, the barkeep at Delrio Dolly's place? He killed Jean Elam."

"Why— How come? That Elam was a mean customer. Canuck from 'way up north som'r's. Worked for Nate Azle a long time. But he wasn't a quarrelsome man, in my mind. Just—tough."

Pony had begun eating his roast beef and mashed potatoes. He shrugged, wishing the girl were not there. But she leaned tensely, staring at him.

"Why—Gravis killed Elam by accident. Seems they were pretty close friends. Friendly enough, anyway, for Gravis to do a job of killing when Elam just asked him to cut loose."

"Say!" Red Roy bellowed, when Pony resumed his eating. "What the— What kind of— What you talking about, anyhow? If you know! Gravis killed Elam— They was close friends— Elam could ask Gravis to do a killing and he would—"

Pony looked steadily at the irritated face.

"I generally know what I'm talking about," he said evenly, "even if I don't go around yelling at the top of my voice. Elam told Gravis to kill me, but I jumped out of the way—"

Floyd Milton came in and the three of them listened while Pony told of the attack on him. He said nothing at all about Quell or Casselberry, in connection with the shooting; made it seem that Elam had for an unknown reason attacked.

"I be damned!" Red Roy cried at the last. "I never hear the beat of it! They just chose you—and looks like it was made up before Elam ever spoke to you account Gravis had the shotgun ready— And you rubbed out Gravis, huh? I'm glad you done it. I never did like the look of that yellow face of his. But—I can't understand it. Elam was Nate Azle's man and—I reckon if I was to be pushed, in spite of our row I'd go on the witnessing-stand and say I believe Nate's straight as a die. Yeh, I would."

"I don't understand it, either," Floyd Milton said slowly. "You—didn't know Elam, John?"

Pony shook his head and went on with his meal. Red Roy and Floyd talked—loudly and in much detail, on Red Roy's part. Connie continued to study Pony silently while he ate. When he pushed away his plate and drew his coffee cup nearer, Red Roy stood abruptly.

"Well, whatever brought it on, I'm glad it never worked out like they schemed it. We never done much, on One End Creek. Trail's mightily twisted. But we're going to keep after it. I got most of the men scattered, looking the range over. You keep on, sort of—well, looking around—"

"It won't be dangerous?" Pony asked solemnly. "I mean, if I don't get too far away from the house, where somebody can sky-line me and bust a cap blowing me out of the saddle?"

" 'Course not," Red Roy said seriously. "You'll be all right, son. You just do that; keep kind of close to the house and—and just look the place over."

He was plainly anxious to get away. Floyd Milton went

with him when he left the room. Connie had hardly moved, where she sat watching them all, but particularly studying Pony.

When he poured himself another cup of coffee she said, "This girl in the dance hall—she was pretty? I understand most of them are. It seemed to me, reading between the lines as you told about the man Elam, that he was jealous. Don't you think he was?"

"She thought he was, anyway. I reckon she does pass for a pretty girl. But—pretty hard. Looks hard, talks hard. Not much wonder. They live a hard life, those girls. You can see that; see how they would."

"You didn't find the man Isbell? He must be pretty seriously wounded, don't you think? You shot him two or three times."

"Twice. But he was twisting. From the way he jumped back into the saddle shop I don't think he was more than burned. Nobody seemed to know where he went. In fact, nobody admitted knowing much of anything about him. I was giving up the hunt—in Vasko, when this Elam-Gravis partnership decided to rub out another Kirk."

"I—just don't get used to it—quarreling, settling quarrels by shooting, killing. You—yo ushot that man, Gravis. Oh, I know you couldn't help it! I don't believe that you wanted to. I know enough about this country, now, to understand that if you hadn't killed him he would have tried again and again to kill you. But you take it so calmly! I suppose you went out after the inquest and—"

"Ate my dinner. I certainly did. It's bad business, having to wear a pistol and use it. But so long as this country is what it is, you nice people are going to be a lot better off because of people like me—not so nice—killing off human wolves. Human snakes is what I really mean. Gravis was a snake; Elam was another. Now, I think I'll ramble down to the bunkhouse and see how Lyde Upshur's making out."

Floyd Milton called her from the living-room and she
answered him while staring curiously at Pony's blank
face. She seemed about to say something else, but went
out with no further word. Pony followed and on his way
to the door saw her sitting with Floyd on the great
handmade Spanish bench before the fireplace.

Upshur had just finished eating and was making a cigarette. He grinned at Pony and indicated two cowboys
playing stud at the far end of the pine table.

"I'm a Two Bencher," he said. "Mr. Kirk decided that
with a li'l patting and trimming and first-class whittling
here and there, I may make a hand, yet. You know these
boys? Well, then, meet Mr. Tap Enlow and Mr. Dell
Cloud, old-timers on the spread. They've been telling me
all about things—telling it scary."

Pony looked at the lanky towhead, Tap Enlow, then at
the short, red-haired, and amazingly freckled Dell Cloud.
They nodded to him. In the faces of both men there was
something of forced blankness, as in blue eyes and green
there was something veiled. They were on their guard
against him and he wondered if that were because he was
Red Roy's cousin and a possible heir to the 2 Bench, or
merely the cowboy's way of waiting to see what kind of
man the stranger might be.

He nodded as colorlessly to them and Lyde Upshur
talked for all of them. Now that he was a man with a
job he showed a side that Pony had not seen, either in
Vasko or on the road out. He told of men and incidents
beyond Red River, where the mixture of white and red
men produced queer happenings. Pony knew some of the
men Upshur mentioned and he grinned in spite of himself at some of the cowboy's tales.

They played stud poker four-handed after a while and
Mig came in to watch. The boy had a bunk in a corner

and both Enlow and Cloud talked to him in friendly fashion, Enlow speaking Spanish as fluently as Pony, for he was an Arizona man from San Simon.

"You men cut any trail of this Clubfoot?" Pony asked the two of them, while they played. "From what I heard tonight, my cousins didn't have more luck than usually the Two Bench has had. Except, of course"—he shoved matches out to raise Upshur's bet—"Quell and Ozment. They must have found something."

Tap Enlow turned his cards over and shrugged. Dell Cloud saw the raise. So did Upshur. Pony exposed his hole-card to show a pair of eights.

"I thought you were high-carding," Upshur grunted. "I had a pair of fives. Cloud thought you were fishing, too; thought his ace-king high would take the pot."

"Yeh," Cloud drawled, yawning, "I thought you was fishing. Well, I think I'll turn in. We'll be out before daylight, Upshur. That'll put us in Needle Rock pasture by noon. It's pretty rough country but good range. We run quite a bunch of mares there."

He looked at Pony blankly and yawned again.

"Yeh," he said, "I certainly did think you was fishing, that time."

Pony made a cigarette and got up. He understood that neither Enlow nor Cloud intended to talk about 2 Bench affairs to him. Whatever the reason might be, there was nothing to be got here by talking.

"I could *tell* you thought I was fishing," he answered Dell directly, with one-sided jerk of the mouth. "Well— *no es importe*. I managed to win. That happens to me once in a while, playing poker and—monkeying around. See you some more."

Outside, he looked at Mig who had followed him.

"Keep eyes and ears open," he said in a low voice, using Spanish. "Something moves here that I do not compre-

hend. It may be bad or not bad. *Quien sabe?* But listen
without seeming to listen. Tomorrow, we will ride and
look."

CHAPTER XVII

"Seventy-Seven horses, maybe?"

RED-ROY AND FLOYD MILTON had ridden away when Pony
came to the breakfast table. He found the dining-room
empty, but before he had begun his meal Connie appeared. She was in riding-outfit and the dull red of her
silk shirt beneath beaded vest contrasted most satisfac-
torily, Pony admitted, with dark hair and eyes. She smiled
at him and spun around as for inspection while he stared.

"Well? How do I look?" she demanded, coming over to
the table to sit opposite him.

"Oh, there are plenty of girls native to Texas as—lovely
as you are," he said judicially.

"Well! That's not much of a compliment, no matter
how true it is! But I wasn't fishing for that; I want to
know if I could be taken for a native."

"Plenty of girls as lovely," he expanded his drawling
statement. "The thing is, I never saw one of 'em! No,
you don't look like a native. There's something about
you— The first time we saw you, Mig and I were riding
up the street in Vasko and you came out of the racket
store with Mrs. Quaid. Mig said you looked like the
pictures he'd seen in newspapers, like somebody from
New York. I reckon that's it; you may put on the same
clothes that a country girl wears, but you make 'em look
different. Those inlaid puncher boots—anybody with the
money can buy 'em or have 'em made. Same for the
whipcord breeches and all. But they suit you fine. You'll

do, Miss Hall, you'll do. As no doubt Floyd and most of the other men around have already told you."

"It may have been mentioned," she admitted solemnly, as she sat down. "Floyd, you see, doesn't go around nursing his broken heart as—as you do! He has time to say pretty things to a girl. Just in the most cousinly way, understood. When you pay a compliment, you scatter it among so many that my share is too small to mean anything."

She talked lightly while they ate and he answered absently. For he was once more puzzling the odd way in which Red Roy and now the cowboys bore themselves toward him.

"Are you going to town again?" she asked, when he had finished his breakfast. "Or is this pretty girl pretty enough to take such risks for?"

"Ambrosius Quell thought she was worth a good deal. I was told that he spent all his money on her. But she— Well, a dance-hall girl has got to own pretty tough skin, I reckon. They're always watching some man ride off. But it's not pleasing to hear one say, the minute the shooting's over that killed a man: 'He wasn't much, anyway, even when he was alive. Now, he's gone. Next!' Still—I do believe seeing him killed shook her a good deal more than she wanted to admit. No, I'm not going to town. It's a li'l bit too sudden a place for me."

Mig was at the corral when Pony came around the house. A Mexican cowboy was roping a tall buckskin. When the dust of churning hoofs had settled, Pony recognized the led horse as that one which Mig had admired, the horse of which Floyd had spoken to Connie. Mig turned with flash of teeth.

"It is a better *caballo*, even, than I had believed. But that black, there, is almost better. I wish that we might use horses of your cousin, *amo*."

"We do, today. Take the black. I will ride that chestnut. Bring our saddles, Mig'ito."

The boy was gone at the run. Pony took from the bars a short catch-rope and went into the corral. The horses milled and shouldered away from him, but he sent a loop deftly up, tossing it over the chestnut. Mig came in and as expertly roped the black.

"*Zapatazos!*" he grunted, looking over his shoulder as he led out the big half-blood. "It is easy to see why thieves hit at this ranch! If these ten are like other Two Bench horses, a man must go far and look hard to find their betters."

They saddled, and the Mexican cowboy watched, holding the reins of the buckskin. He had put upon the gelding a light silver-trimmed stock saddle of dished cantle and swelled fork, a "buster's" saddle, but of boy's or woman's size, with long-flapped carven *tapaderos* that almost touched the ground beneath the stirrups.

Pony admired the hull, then busied himself with shell belts and holsters got from an *alforja*—a saddlebag. When the belts were buckled so that they crossed to let twin holsters sag on his thighs, he fastened the toe strings from holster ends about his legs above the knees. Both bone-handled Colts went in and Mig, who knew what was coming, looked slantingly at the Two Bench vaquero, rather than at Pony.

Pony lifted both hands to shoulder level and thrust them straight out sideways. His shoulders twitched and both hands dropped with the speed of snakes racing into holes. The slap of hard palms against bone was loud. With a jerklike backlash of the flashing motion, the Colts came out with hammers back under Pony's thumbs and flicked up to level.

A dozen times he repeated the maneuver, then jerked them so that they spun in air two yards above his head, their arcs crossing, to spin downward and drop into his waist-high palms. He rolled them on his forefingers; spun them in the ancient and deadly "road agent" spin; twirled them sideways to pass each other—left-hand gun to right hand, right-hand gun to left hand—and he caught and returned, the "border shift." He drew from the waistband, front and back, from inside his shirt and out. At last he reholstered the Colts and the open-mouthed vaquero shook his head slowly and whispered, "*Maravilloso!*"

From behind Pony there came the sound of clapping hands. He turned to face Connie.

"That is amazing!" she told him gravely. "I've seen Vic Tait go through some of that practice. I thought he was wonderfully skillful, but by comparison with you— It's too bad that you weren't in the saloon, or the saddle shop, when Ambrosius Quell and Otto were attacked! Knowing them for our men, I mean. And it's stupid of Cousin Roy to treat you as if you might be hurt by our thieves and— I never dreamed that anyone could handle pistols in that magical fashion, like a juggler performing!"

"That," Mig informed her, grinning, "ees because you don' see thees *brujo*—thees—you call heem weetch—draw the pistol. One day, maybe, you see thees *patron* w'en he will have to make 'urry—fast! Then you see—nothing! Too fast to see! And w'ich hand—no different! Both hand same to shoot. Don' meess no time! *Nunca! Jamás!* He—"

"Come on! Come on!" Pony growled at the boy. "Mustn't hurrah a lady. Just because she's new in the country, you don't want to go letting that imagination of yours run unhobbled."

He passed up his split-reins over the chestnut's neck and caught a stirrup. Helped by the vaquero, Connie mounted. The buckskin reared, but she sat him easily and pushed up beside Pony.

"Which way are you heading?" he asked casually.

"Why—east, I think. Unless you want to go some other way. It's a nice country for riding, to eastward."

"I just wanted to know so I could head the other direction," he said politely. "I do want to look over this range and, the way things seem to happen on the Two Bench, I'll feel a lot better if just Mig'ito is with me."

"I can understand your feelings. But—you must allow for my feelings, too. I'd feel that I'd slighted you, if I didn't show you over the ranch. Don't worry about my being dangerous, Pony. I promised that I wouldn't hurt your poor, injured heart. I'll be just as—as *cousinly!* You don't have to smile, even, when you don't want to. Come on!"

He shrugged and followed her away from the house. But on open range he turned westward. It seemed to him that a look at what Red Roy had called a tough outfit, the 77 of Ben Britt, was the natural first step of his exploration. A look at the line between the 77 and the 2 Bench might tell a thoughtful man a good deal about the neighboring spread.

"It's a good thing that Sheriff Sanford didn't see your exhibition," Connie said after a time of easy loping across a great flat. "He might be more than ever convinced that you're a gunman. Odd! He and Mrs. Quaid both looked at you and instantly knew that you are specially skilled—with pistols, I mean. I looked at you and you seemed no more than a cowboy—a nice young man of the cowboy kind, rather handsomer than the average, of course, but—"

"Talk about slinging cripplie-compliments! You don't even tell the truth! 'Rather handsomer than the average!' Why, if they didn't call me Pony Kirk up and down the range country, they'd call me Beautiful Kirk. And"—he scowled thoughtfully—"I do believe they ought to, just because it's more fitting and suitable. Then, again, they could call me Ugly Kirk. For cowboys are animals with a horse and a misbegotten funnybone. So they call a high-pocketed man Shorty, and a fat man is Slim, and a walking beanpole is Fatty or Tubby. So if I was named Ugly, it would be the same thing as Beautiful."

"Now that we've finished with that—your not-too-clever side-stepping, where did you learn and practice all that gunplay? Cousin Roy has said that Vic Tait is a gunman; he thinks Vic is about as fast as most men get. I've heard him say so. But you make Vic seem like a beginner. Just as"—she stopped short and stared at him—"just as you made the sheriff seem a bungler! And—"

She stopped again and when Pony said nothing she rode for a half mile staring straight ahead of her, humming mechanically.

"On the road out, after the sheriff had gone, Cousin Roy said to you— Well, he asked when you'd left the Territory. It came to me, a minute ago, that the sheriff accused you of being some notorious killer from the Territory. I don't recall whether you denied it or just evaded the question. But Cousin Roy looked at you and by his question—I see it, now—he showed that he suspected you of being that outlaw! You didn't answer him, either! You told him, in effect, to mind his own affairs. What about all that, Pony?"

"Well," Pony said wearily, "if I have just got to tell you what I really think—deliver me from all this guessing and from gabbing girls!"

"Cousin Roy knows very well that you're the sort of competent man who'd be worth his weight in gold on the ranch right now. But instead of asking you to help, or even accepting your offer to help, he pushes you off to the side and goes riding on a thieves' trail with Floyd, who can't possibly be the man you are, in this country! Pony, why is that? Because of what the sheriff said? Does Cousin Roy think—"

"Does he think that I'm not really his kin, you mean?"

He shrugged easily, but the thought had not occurred to him and he turned it over mentally. Then he looked at her.

"Huh? Letter?" he answered. "The letter you wrote me? No, I didn't keep it. But Dumpty Downes told you about me— Wait a minute, though! If Red Roy is wondering if I'm not really Chance Fielder, desperado from over in the Territory, instead of John Kirk, he could believe that I just heard about this letter and that Dumpty's talk about his friend was straight, but didn't necessarily tie to me. Well—I do'no. If he says I'm not his cousin, I won't argue. I'll just go on doing what I started to do—take a crack at the men who killed Dumpty—and by doing that I'll do Red Roy a good, free job."

"You're from Gonzales County originally. Your father was Red Roy's first cousin. Pony! You Texas Kirks have kept the family traditions and, all the way from Boston to the Carolinas and down to Texas, you've somehow been Scotch and pioneer Americans at the same time. I know that from talking to Cousin Roy about himself and his father and yours. Did your mother sing to you when you were a little boy? What did she sing?"

Pony's face softened. Then he grinned and lifted the baritone which forty cow camps had known.

"Ye'll tak' the high road and I'll tak' the low road,
    But I'll be in Scotland before ye—"

She nodded, waiting, her face oddly expectant. " 'Loch Lomond,' of course! And—what else?"

"Oh, Pharaoh's hawse got drownded, got drownded, drownded;

Oh, Pharaoh's hawse got drownded, swimming in de
    Re-ed Sea!

"And then that one you hummed, awhile ago, when
you wondered about me and—Chance Fielder . . .

> "Why weep ye by the tide, ladye?
> Why weep ye by the tide?
> I'll wed ye tae my youngest son,
> And ye shall be his bride.
> And ye shall be his bride, ladye,
> Sae comely tae be seen!
> But aye she loot the tears downfa'
> For Jock o' Hazeldean."

" 'Jock o' Hazeldean!' Of course! I know you're Pony
Kirk. *I* know you're not that terrible killer, Chance
Fielder!"

"I said it before and I say it again. You're as young as
you are—pretty! I could've just heard the song—from
Pony Kirk. I might even be Pony Kirk and this Chance
Fielder, too. You know, Connie, if I break down and
start confessing, I'll have to admit that often and often,
looking at some people in this world, I do feel like start-
ing out to be a terrible wipe-outer of just cowpenfuls of
the human race."

She laughed. Apparently, the doubts she had held were
gone. She talked of a dozen things. She called Mig closer
and told him that he looked the perfect gladiator with
his pistol sagging in careful imitation of Pony's and the
little Winchester ready in the crook of his left arm. She
asked Pony a hundred questions about his life and he
answered carefully, keeping to the time before reaching
the Territory and beginning the campaign against Alec
Sells's gang. At last she lifted a hand to indicate a ridge

higher than the rolls over which they had been riding.

"Beyond that ridge—or the next one or two ridges—is the line between us and Ben Britt. Cousin Roy doesn't like the Seventy-Seven men, from owner to horse wrangler, but—I've seen a few of them and I don't see a difference between them and anybody else. Mr. Britt—I've talked to him on this line a few times and he's quite pleasant. He's young and good-looking; well educated. He told me that he was in his third year at some small college in Fort Worth when his uncle died and left him enough money to fulfill his greatest ambition—that of owning a ranch. So he looked around and finally got the Seventy-Seven a year or so ago. He has a great many plans—"

Pony grinned, and she flushed. They topped the ridge and beyond it was a tight wire fence. When they came up to it Pony swung to the ground and took a pair of pliers from his *alforja*. He drew the staples from two posts, forced down the wires and stood on them. Mig led the chestnut across carefully, riding his black.

"I'm going to explore around Mr. Handsome Britt's edges," Pony told Connie. "I wish you'd believe that you've shown me heaps and heaps and been mightily pleasant company and we'll do it again, sometime. But, right now— Well, if you'll turn that buckskin clear around and let Mig and me take our *paseo* without having to worry about you—"

"You haven't any right on the Seventy-Seven! Not in the circumstances that exist, with Cousin Roy practically calling Ben Britt a thief and Mr. Britt angry about it and— But if you can go I can go! And I will! I'll ride wherever I please!"

She jumped the buckskin forward and Pony could do nothing but hold down the wires until the gelding was across. Then he let the wires come up and took his reins from Mig.

"You had better go back," he said irritably; "you'll be a lot of trouble to me. I do'no what I'm going to run into or how it'll come."

"Then ride by yourself!" she cried angrily. "I'll do the same. But I'm not taking orders from you. You're the stranger on this place and it hardly becomes you to act as if you had authority! I can take care of myself."

She spurred her horse into a gallop and went off southeastward, to disappear quickly over a ridge. Pony shook his head with dour face. Mig grinned openly as he looked at Pony, then bent his head and coughed. Pony grinned faintly.

"A very headstrong señorita!" he drawled. "Like most pretty girls, she is used to having men give her whatever she may fancy. She cannot understand that, to me, she is not a pretty girl, but only my cousin who does not understand this land."

"*Es verdad*—that is true," Mig agreed in very solemn voice, but without meeting Pony's eyes. "She is no more to you, *amo,* than a cousin. If she were not the most lovely señorita you and I have ever seen, but most ugly, it would be the same to you. I comprehend. *Perfectamente!*"

They rode across this rolling range, each with Winchester over his arm, watching the country ahead. Very soon, they reached a well-marked trail, almost a road. Mechanically, both reined in to the side of it and stared at the hoofmarked dust. Mig dropped off and moved up and down like an eager young hound, head weaving.

"Horses," Pony grunted. "Somebody has been pushing a dozen or so along. Seventy-Seven horses, maybe? Must be, you'd think. After all, this is Seventy-Seven range and this Ben Britt is bound to have a bunch of horses. Huuuh— Heading south. Let's see. I wouldn't mind running into this good-looking Britt and seeing if his good looks softened me toward him; they've had so much effect on Connie I'm a li'l bit curious about Mister Britt! Come on, Mig. That's fresh, that trail. We'll have a looky."

His cautious study of the range was more or less automatic, result of that year on the dodge with Pat Curran. For it seemed most unlikely that any but honest men would drive stock so openly here. He would overtake the 77 cowboys and introduce himself and intimate that he had wandered over onto this range by chance. He would yarn a little with them.

"I'll let 'em educate a pilgrim," he said amusedly. "Yeh!"

CHAPTER XVIII

"Drop your gun!"

THE TRAIL LED THEM toward a range better watered; crowned with mottes of cottonwood trees, dotted with clumps of mesquite bushes so big as to be almost low trees. Rabbits jumped up before them; quail ran to right and left. But for a good while they saw neither cattle nor horses. Then Mig grunted and pointed. He had the eyes of his grandmother's people, the Apaches.

"You saw?" he asked Pony. "One man went over that ridge as we came to the comb of this one. He went not slow, not fast, I think. But—like a man riding in the drag of a horse band trotting."

Pony had not seen, but as he looked intently he could detect the thin haze of dust settling over that ridge. He reached for his glasses and when they had trotted cautiously across the swale between the ridges he dismounted and went on foot to the crest of the trampled ridge where the man had crossed. Beyond a motte of cottonwoods well ahead the dust rose; the thick trees shielded whatever animals raised that dust from his view. He drew in a great last inhalation of Durham smoke and tossed away the butt of his cigarette.

"Nothing to do, Mig'ito, but ride straight up behind 'em! We're not supposed to be afraid of anything. We're just riding from the Two Bench and have lost our way."

He swung up on the chestnut and they crossed the ridge, trotting fast down the slope toward the cottonwoods that stood, dark-green and quiet, solid-seeming from ground to sky, ahead of them.

They were still a long hundred yards from the grove when out of it a rifle began to make flat, metallic sound. Pony yelled at Mig as he spun the chestnut. The boy whirled his black. The *Hrang! Hrang! Hrang!* of close-spaced shots was echoed by the thud of lead in the ground beyond the horses' hoofs. Bent low over the horns, they raced back toward the ridge they had left. The lead sang waspishly around their ears, but they surged up the ridge and got over it untouched.

Pony got off to lift bare head and look at the cotton-woods which had sheltered the rifleman. He was coming out, now, and around the trees three more men-galloped. They had rifles or carbines across their arms. The man from the cottonwoods gesticulated excitedly.

" 'They are coming, Sister Agnes, they are coming—' " Pony said softly. "Yes, sir, all with their faih golden curls done up in braids— You can almost see the pink ribbons. Excited, Mig'ito. So I reckon we'll fold up our tents like the Arabs in the poem book and we'll silently—steal— away. For this is Britt's range and if the man feels like discouraging visitors, we have just got to discourage. We haven't got a bit of right on his side of the wire."

"I do not like to be shot without shooting back," Mig

said ferociously. "Nor do you, *amo!* I know that well. They come like children; like *tontos* empty of head! I, alone, could easily kill them all."

"Don't! We haven't the right to shoot. If I killed one of them, that tall sheriff at Vasko would have real reason to arrest me. We will ride—fast. Back to the wire."

As they mounted again and went at the gallop on their back trail, he grinned.

"Pretty poor shooting! But good enough to have us turning on a dime with nine cents change! Yeh, Mig'ito, that big John Law would be happy if I rubbed out a Seventy-Seven man. He'd naturally have him a circus day-without-peanuts, over it. These are good horses, *hombre!* I don't see those bold warriors, yet. Maybe, it's only natural, their being nervous about strangers on the range. But even at that, it does seem a li'l bit odd, the way they left one man in the cottonwoods to look back and his opening up so fast on men who might be no more than honest drifters—"

The big half-bloods covered the distance to the wire at racing gait. Mig's lighter weight gave him the advantage, for the black and the chestnut seemed evenly matched as to speed. Looking back from each ridge, Pony saw nothing of the quartet from the cottonwoods. He pulled in at the line fence.

"Well," he said sourly, "we had the ride and the exercise and the lovely fresh air, anyhow. I reckon that's all we can write down for the business. We'd better cross over—"

"But how of the señorita, your cousin?" Mig grunted, with sweep of hand toward the ground. "Her trail goes there—much in the direction those men were going. If she met them, would they harm her?"

"*Por dios!* You're right," Pony said scowlingly. "She knows Britt, but if those men don't know her, even if they are Seventy-Seven hands— And I can't swear that they're Britt's men; they might be the thieves lifting some of Britt's horses! I think we'll not cross the wire just yet, Mig."

He sent the chestnut forward on the trail left by Connie's buckskin. It was easy to follow and he tickled the big horse into a long, easy lope. Mig rode to the left of him, looking occasionally at the ground, but more often lifting fierce young face to stare ahead. He carried his Winchester straight up in his off hand, Indian-fashion.

Mile after mile they rode on Connie's trail. The girl had galloped fast for a time, then slowed to a trot, stopped to look at a statuelike formation of rock, trotted on, pulled in on a little ridge to look around—Pony could read her thoughts, almost, from the trail of the buckskin. As they went deeper into 77 range the land grew rougher. There were arroyos to cross, tiny creeks with pools of water in their beds, occasional cattle to see.

Mig topped out of an arroyo with crashing of rocks from the black's hoofs—and called instantly to Pony, pointing. Pony sent the chestnut surging up and he saw the hindquarters of a bay horse disappearing behind a mesquite bush.

The trail of Connie's buckskin pointed straight in the general direction of that mesquite and Pony, sure of this, spurred his horse that way. Instantly, he heard the distant clatter of hoofs going fast away.

The man was well-mounted; in a mile they did not see him again. Then at the edge of a long slope they pulled in to look and heard a shot to the left. A slug cut leaves from a bush twenty feet from them. A second shot came closer and they drew back a little. Pony raked the land ahead with his glasses and stiffened and grunted to Mig. For three horses were going at the hard trot a quarter mile away and the middle horse in the tight little group was Connie's buckskin. The lenses showed that she was held by the men who rode on her right and left.

Pony turned his chestnut and worked toward the man who had fired at them. But this rear guard did not wait. He spurred after the others and Pony and Mig went into the open after him, riding recklessly. He could see the man looking back; Connie and her captors were gone over a ridge. The man galloped hard for a tall cottonwood and threw himself off to shelter behind it. Pony lifted his Winchester and sent three fast shots at the big tree, then charged it, swinging the horse to right and left in zigzags as he neared the other's position.

The man fired steadily at them. Pony heard Mig yell and from the corner of his eye saw the boy's black crash down, throwing Mig ahead of him. Mig's body turned in air and he struck the ground trying to run, but stumbled and fell flat. Pony went on, riding low, carbine held like a pistol. A bullet glanced off the fork of his saddle, ricocheting through his left sleeve to burn the arm. Another hummed like an angry bee past his face and seared like flame the tip of his ear.

Then the concealed man seemed to decide that it was time to withdraw. He flung himself on the bay horse and spurred off with elbows out, leaning almost to the bay's neck. He got around a mesquite and turned to snap two shots at Pony, then galloped on.

For a mile the battle continued, with Pony shooting whenever he had a glimpse of the man, without damage to either. Pony was furious. That rear-guard action was perfectly executed. It held him back while the lead of the men with Connie was steadily lengthened.

When for the dozenth time the man halted to shoot from cover, Pony did not look for shelter from the lead. Instead, he drove the rowels into the chestnut and rode straight at the mesquite clump holding his fire, face a snarling mask, reckless of consequences, intent only on coming close enough for the shot that would kill.

Slugs sang past him as the hidden one emptied his Winchester. Then Pony was around the mesquite, facing the man's lifting pistol. He fired twice without stopping the chestnut; then as the man staggered he pulled in short and at point-blank range sent two bullets into the twisting body. He watched grimly while his target dropped. It was a smallish cowboy, as swarthy and vicious of square face as that Ike Isbell who had shot Big Otto Ozment in the back, on Vasko main street; as savage of snake-thin mouth and deep-set eyes as Isbell—but not Isbell.

"You certainly were a fighting fool!" Pony grunted, by way of epitaph. "If your shooting had been as good as your intentions, I'd be a dead man."

He caught the bay's trailing reins and knotted them on the saddle horn, then started the horse back toward Mig. If the boy had recovered from his fall, he might catch the bay.

Then Pony rode on fast, hunting Connie and the men with her. He had lost their actual trail and could only guess that they would continue in the southeasterly direction that had seemed to be their course.

He rode through bushes and crossed arroyos and came at last to an open flat a half mile or more in width. Toward the distant edge of it stood a ruinous log house, dark and quiet and somewhat sinister even in the sunlight. No horses were in sight around it, but he could not risk a ride across the open on the chance that it was empty.

He turned to the right and began to ride around the edge of the flat. He was in no mood to go slowly—even quietly. If the pound of the chestnut's hoofs were heard and there was a battle, then there would be a battle! As he went he asked himself again and again who these men could be, who had ridden away with Connie. It seemed unbelievable that they could be riders of the 77; Britt's men would hardly dare to lift a hand against a relative of Red Roy Kirk. But if they were some of the thieves from what Floyd Milton called the Clubfoot Gang, they would dare anything; a pretty girl in their outlaw hands—

"Either way," he told himself savagely, "she's in a bad fix. And so are the men who've got her!"

When he had gone clear around the flat and was behind it, he was still fifty yards from its wall. Between the dense brush and the house were clumps of low mesquite, thorny tangles impenetrable to the eye. He dismounted and let the reins trail. The chestnut was tired. He sagged and panted. Pony slid into the open and stood looking at the ruined cabin, the nearest cover.

He heard no sound, but out of a leafy screen a yard to his right a rifle barrel thrust almost into his ribs.

"Drop your gun!" a voice commanded huskily, nervously. "Drop it or—"

He twisted flashingly, slapping out at the rifle, knocking it away as it threw flame and smoke and noise—and a slug that thudded into a tree twenty feet away. With dropping of the hand he drew a Colt and leveled it. He fired without seeing his target and roused a shrill, panicky yell. The man let his rifle drop and went floundering off, his course marked by the crash and sway of brush.

Pony was down, now, sheltered from the fire of anyone in the open. He drove two more pistol bullets after the runner and drew another yell—almost a shriek, but whether of pain or fear he could not decide. Besides, a man was calling from a mesquite clump near the cabin.

"Jake! Oh, Jake! You git him?"

"Yeh! Got him!" Pony replied in the husky voice Jake had owned. "Plumb—center!"

He ran into the open, trying to keep mesquite between

him and the cabin. But his shirt was blue, the one glimpse he had got of Jake's had shown it white or gray. That hidden man would need only one look at him to know the truth. Apparently, he managed to see Pony, for the pound of his running feet came almost instantly. Pony ran straight at the cabin, but before he reached the door he heard the thudding of the man's horse. He stopped, then, pistol in hand, standing beside the doorway.

"Connie!" he called anxiously. "This is Pony!"

"Here I am!" she answered hoarsely. "I—I—"

Then as he went inside he heard the gasp of her crying. Sunshine came through the great gaps in the roof, but beyond these patches of light the big room was shadowed. He looked grimly around, seeing nothing until the girl moved in a corner and got shakily to her feet. Then he slid across to her and she fell into the curve of his arm.

CHAPTER XIX

"Some thief was careful"

PONY LOOKED DOWN at her dark head with jumbled feel-ings—most of them quite new to him. She was crying softly, jerkily, like a frightened child.

"Now, now," he said awkwardly, "you're all right. Nothing to bother you, now. Come on outside. Every-thing's all right. Come on out in the light."

He drew her gently out of the gloom and at the door set down his carbine, reholstered his pistol. She still clung to him, but she had stopped crying.

"It was awful!" she whispered. "I was never so fright-ened in my life. I never thought anything like that could happen to me. They're gone? They're really gone? You—shot them?"

"Shot at 'em is nearer the truth. I'm not so proud of my pistoleering today. Only consolation is, theirs was worse."

Now he saw how the beaded vest had been ripped so that it hung from one shoulder; a sleeve of her silk shirt was in tatters and the round arm exposed showed the red marks of fingers. When she lifted her face to him and smiled faintly, he scowled down and lifted his hand to touch the reddened cheek and its streak of blood.

"One of them slapped me; almost knocked me out of the saddle. I was trying to hold back when you—it must have been you—came in sight. I think it was the man who went out to ambush you. There were three of them; the one who ran away just now—Shorty, they called him, and Jake who saw you at the edge of the clearing and slipped into the brush to kill you, and a black, fierce little man, Chink. He stayed behind us from the start. He said he'd 'part some hair' if anybody followed. Whatever that meant."

"He was close to doing it—parting my hair with a slug," Pony told her grimly. "Best man of the three. I would even say that Chink was the only real man of the three."

"He seemed to be their leader. But when I tried to pull back, Jake slapped me. Then we came here, fast. They were awful! They just laughed when I threatened them with Cousin Roy and you—"

"With me? They wouldn't know me. How could you threaten?"

"I told them Pony Kirk, Red Roy Kirk's cousin, was within a mile of us. I said—that was when they laughed about Cousin Roy—that you were a gun bulldogger who'd seen more trouble through the smoke than a dozen of their kind could cause. I said—well, I think I just quoted everything I've ever heard anybody say about a gunman and hung it all on you. Then you came and proved it! But they told me what was going to happen to me—I'd never see the Two Bench or my gun bulldogger again and— It was horrible! But you didn't let them do it, Pony!"

She caught his arm and pressed close against him and he held her—and found it amazingly pleasant. He had never felt this exact emotion; no other girl had ever roused it. Even through his grim thought of Chink— whom he was thoroughly glad he had killed—he could wonder about his feeling toward Connie. She was like a child to be helped and protected. But also she was the prettiest, the most desirable woman he had ever known. He could admit that now. How he had ever judged her by the standards of such a cow-town belle as Berta Schwartz he could not understand now.

"We—we'd better be heading back," he said quickly, to clear his mind of such thoughts, which Pony Kirk—alias Chance Fielder—had no business harboring. "Where'd they put your buckskin? Over in the brush?"

"Yonder, I think. But I'm going with you; I won't be left alone again!"

She held to his arm as they crossed the open—Pony very alert against the return of Jake and Shorty—toward the brush where the horses had been left, beneath a big cottonwood.

Only her buckskin stood there when they came to the tree. Evidently Jake had worked through the brush to get his mount. Pony helped Connie into the saddle and led the way to where his chestnut was. When they rode out toward the cabin, she looked at him quite naturally.

"While I'm still in a very humble mood, I had better confess that I was an idiot today. I shouldn't have galloped off to show my independence. It might have caused your death—and mine. I'm sorry! I'll try to keep the lesson in mind, but I know myself well enough to fear that it won't make a perfect woman of me! But I am sorry—now;

and grateful to you."

"The trouble with you," he said weightily, "is a most common kind of thing. It's a disease that catches men and women both and lays 'em down in swaths. You can call it playing the other fellow's game, thinking you're too smart to need practice. You thought you knew a lot about the cow country—this special part of it. When the truth is, this is about as strange to you as—as Abyssinia would be." ·

He shook his head tolerantly, but grinned at her.

"This is a part of the country a lot of good folk would call lawless. But there's plenty of law here! Plenty! Some book and court law, but more of what the cowboys call the law of Old Judge Colt. Even the officers know that they have to work under both laws. Now, today, you rammed into some men and you took 'em for the kind of men you've known other places, just different in their clothes and their talk. But they are not the same kind of men! They're not even the same kind of men as average cowboys. They're renegades, and when they want something—a horse or a pretty girl or a man's scalp—they're going to get it unless they're stopped by fear or by force. Take that from Uncle Pony! It's plumb gospel."

He steered the way so as to miss the spot where Chink lay. She followed meekly where he led and when occasionally she spoke it was to elaborate upon her account of being captured. Eventually, she spoke of horses, a driven band.

"Horses!" Pony grunted, staring. "Those three were driving horses when you first saw 'em?"

"Why, yes! I thought I told you. Fifteen or twenty horses. They seemed like ordinary cowboys and I thought they must be Seventy-Seven men, so I rode out toward them. Then I knew that I hadn't ever seen any of them and they came up to me and began to ask questions. They talked in the most natural way. I told them who I am and how I happened to be on the Seventy-Seven. The little man, Chink, asked most of the questions. Jake and Shorty would look at him and put in a question or comment occasionally. At last, Chink said it was perfectly fine that I'd come along. Jake and Shorty laughed and caught my arms. Chink told them to take me along and— You know all the rest."

"Queer!" Pony said, more to himself than to her. "I would certainly like to have a look at those horses they had."

They neared the place where he and Mig had seen her between Jake and Shorty. But before they had reached it, Mig galloped out of the brush on Chink's bay. Pony lowered his carbine and yelled at the boy.

"So you caught him! I turned him back toward you, hoping that you would! How do you feel, *muchacho?*"

"That fall was nothing!" Mig boasted. "But—I *was* like a dead man for a time. Then I got up and heard this horse and caught him. I changed saddles and began to look for your trail. *Amo!* It is my belief that, today, we fought the thieves your cousins went to hunt, the men of this clubfooted one!"

"I can believe that, with ease!" Pony admitted. "But is this only a guess? Or have you seen something?"

Mig swelled importantly under their curious eyes.

"I have found the *mañada!* The stallion and the mares which were taken on the day that your young cousin and friend were shot at! They made the trail we cut and followed. They were the horses that were being driven when first that man shot at us. Two Bench mares, *amo!* They are a mile behind me, grazing toward the fence."

"No wonder they had a man covering the back trail!" Pony grunted. "I reckon your guess is good, Mig'ito; that is the *mañada* that was stolen that day. If they are Two

Bench mares, then we did fight thieves. *Bien!* We will
drive them back to the line. It seems that we got more
than fresh air and riding for our trouble, today!"

When they rode toward the grazing stallion and his
harem, Mig found a moment when he and Pony were a
little ahead of the silent girl, to whisper tensely, "You
killed the three who took her?"

"One. The man who killed your horse. A black little
wolf. He held me for a mile as a man pushes back another with his hand. Then I killed him. One other I
think I touched with my lead. The third felt the yellow
rise in his neck when he was alone. He ran away, leaving
the señorita."

"*Es vida*—that is life!" Mig condoled with him gravely.
"Wolves—snakes—of that sort are good only for killing.
But a man cannot always kill them with his first shot. We
will kill them in the end. They are wolves, but—you
know the saying: '*A carne de lobo, diente de perro*—for
wolf's flesh, dog's teeth!' "

They found the *mañada*, sultaned by a magnificent
chestnut stallion who was not too tired to show by flattened ears and rushes at them his resentment at their approach. Pony and Mig started the mares at slow, steady
pace toward the line of the 2 Bench. Looking at the
stallion, Pony thought very little about Red Roy's pleasure when the *mañada* was returned to him. Instead, he
wondered if he had not made a mistake.

"If only I could tie these thieves to some outfit!" he
told himself. "Every bit of stock-detective work I ever did
has gone just that way. Somebody's stealing stuff in a
scope of country; nearly always killing to cover up the
thefts. A detective comes in and finds this and that. But
all he picks up at first, or maybe for a long time, is pieces
of outcrop. It's tracing those back to the main body the
way a prospector works back to the mother lode that's

the work. The minute you find a line from some two-bit thief you catch or kill to the man he worked for, you've got nothing ahead but proving it. I ought to've brought that li'l wolf, Chink, in with us!"

"Men!" Mig announced abruptly. "Yonder! They have just topped that ridge. They have seen us!"

He moved his carbine suggestively while Pony studied the quartet riding close together, coming at the racing gallop, with a tall man just ahead of the group.

"I think that is Ben Britt!" Connie told Pony. "He always rides an iron-gray gelding he bought from Cousin Roy when he first came to the Seventy-Seven, with a silver-trimmed saddle."

"That's a gray and there's plenty of silver on the hull," Pony said. "Put that carbine down, Mig. That's the very man I wanted to see. He's got a few to explain."

"It's Ben Britt, all right!" Connie nodded. "And that's his foreman, Anton Jager. One of the Seventy-Seven cowboys and— Why, it's Cousin Roy's foreman, Vic Tait!"

The four riders pulled in short. Ben Britt was tall and lean, somewhere in middle twenties, with dark, daredevil face. His clothing and horse gear were as ornate as even Floyd Milton's. He jerked off his broad, white hat with sight of Connie and smiled flashingly.

"Well!" he cried. "This is a surprise, Miss Hall. A pleasant one! We saw the horses moving and wondered. Then saw you—"

Pony had looked from Britt to the very tall, very thin, man just behind him. This was a towhead with the longest, narrowest face Pony had seen in his life; with deep-set little eyes of odd reddish-brown that roved like a suspicious wolf's from Pony to Mig to the *mañada* and back again.

"Some of Clubfoot's thieves drove Cousin Roy's *mañada* over here," Connie explained. "We had ridden over onto your range. We stumbled upon the mares and Pony— This is Cousin Roy's cousin and mine, Mr. Britt, John Kirk."

Pony nodded blankly to him, turning from inspection of the 77 cowboy and the grizzled man on 2 Bench horse whom he guessed was Vic Tait, gunman-foreman of Red Roy.

"I don't know if the men were out of this Clubfoot's gang," Pony said slowly to Britt. "All this talk of a club-footed boss-thief is just hearsay with me. But some family of thieves was using the Seventy-Seven. Miss Hall found 'em before I did and they decided to take her along."

"Take her along!" Britt repeated, staring. "You mean— they tried to kidnap her?"

"You could call it that. But I wandered up with this boy and we sort of changed their minds. It wasn't too hard. They didn't seem to want to play without odds of more than three to one. So—when you rode up I was escorting the lady and the *mañada* back where they be-long. I was doing a li'l bit of wondering, too. I'm glad you came along because you know this country better than I do. Happen to know three men called Chink and Shorty and Jake?"

"I don't believe so. Did you—kill anybody?"

Pony nodded, very conscious of Connie's tense stare.

"The black li'l man called Chink. He could have been a twin to Ike Isbell, the man who murdered Otto Oz-ment in town. He's back yonder a way. I may have hit Jake. Do'no. He ran off through the brush and made it to his horse. Shorty, he just didn't play at all. As soon as he heard a loud noise coming his way, he high-tailed it."

"Pony rode into Vasko right into the fights," Connie said quickly. "How did you happen to be on the Seventy-Seven, Vic? Were you looking for the *mañada?*"

Vic Tait nodded, turning his saddle-brown face, his

round, hard, pale-blue eyes on her. He had listened to the talk without showing the slightest interest in it.

"Yeh. I was hunting the menathy, or trail of it. And I had to look at our south pasture, too, like Floyd Milton told me, to see if the horses there was all right. We kind of wondered about 'em, after the fight on One End Creek. It was certainly lucky on One End, my coming along. Else Milton would have been dead as Dumpty Downes."

"How was the stuff in the south pasture?" Pony asked him. "I didn't hear anything about that."

"All right. So I come on over to talk to Britt and see what he might've stumbled onto. Went up to the house and got him and Jager and we rode out and—here we are."

Britt had been looking with very open admiration at Connie, and Pony observed that she was conscious of the 77 owner's eyes upon her. Now, Britt turned back to Pony.

"You say you killed one of the thieves who kidnaped Miss Hall. Exactly where did you leave him?"

"I can show you. I'd like to bring him in and see if he can be recognized by somebody. Then, too, I don't doubt that the sheriff and Judge Zink will want to hold an inquest. The sheriff will, anyway. Zink is sort of fed up with dead men. I've been wondering, Mr. Britt. When the boy and I first rode onto your range we saw the dust of stock moving and we got ourselves shot at by somebody. Four men were in that bunch. I'm wondering if that could have been some of your men moving Seventy-Seven stock, or this same bunch of thieves with the *mañada*."

"Well, it could have been Seventy-Seven cowboys, all right!" Britt's teeth flashed in a cheerful grin. "If any of our hands saw you and thought you looked suspicious, or if they happened to be nervous, the chances are they'd cut down on you. We've ridden pretty loose-holstered since this Clubfoot started his depredations. I told Jager, here, to keep his eyes peeled. We can't afford to lose fine stock the way the Two Bench has been losing it. I'm a poor man! So we decided to lean a little backward on the cautious side and give the thieves some Seventy-Seven lead instead of Seventy-Seven horses. Yes, you might have run into Seventy-Seven men, but— How about it, Anton?"

"Couldn't have been," the tall, grim Jager said thoughtfully. "Not if it was inside ten mile of here. We're working 'way over west around Crater Canyon. Just happened I was at the house when Vic Tait come up, Kirk. I'd rode up from the Canyon. I reckon you run into the same bunch twicet. Not likely two bunches of rustlers'd be sneaking across Seventy-Seven range in the same day."

"That sounds reasonable," Pony agreed. "Connie, I am going to loan you the boy, here. Mig, you help drive the *mañada* and keep an eye on the señorita. Tait, I reckon you will want to shove the *mañada* back over the line and closer to the house. Red Roy thinks it's his prize bunch of mares and he ought to be mightily pleased to see 'em come back. I think they ought to be choused out of here. After all, you know, four men showed with 'em, at first. That leaves three somewhere around. They may be close, right now. If the *mañada* is left loose, they could shove it off again."

"But—where are you going, Pony?" Connie asked quickly, coming up to his stirrup. "Why can't I ride with you and go back to the house when you go? I—I'd like to do that."

Pony shook his head as he smiled at her.

"I think it'll be better this way. You see, we're going to pick up a dead man and I don't think you need to look at such sights. Too, there's always just the bare chance of finding more trouble. I'll feel better if you're safe on the way home. Mig'll take good care of you."

"Well, now—" Vic Tait began doubtfully, but stopped when Pony stared levelly, curiously, at him.

"Somebody has got to ride herd on the *mañada* and sort of keep a wing over Miss Hall," Pony said reasonably. "The sooner all of you are across the wire the better for all."

Tait shrugged and nodded. Pony watched the three ride on in the dust of the *mañada,* then looked at Britt, Jager, and the silent cowboy. He wondered what sort of man the 77's young owner might be—really. Jager and the cowboy were easily placed. He had seen dozens like them, up and down the cow country, all his life. But Britt might be this, might be that—

"Well!" he grunted, with one-sided lift of hard mouth, "I reckon it's safe for us to head back. Four of us. So, on a line with what I've seen of these thieves, they'd want at least sixteen men, to come bucking us. I ran from four of 'em today, but that was because I was afraid to shoot, being uncertain about 'em. When I got certain, I ran three and killed one. They had a bunch when they jumped Floyd Milton and Downes. Then Tait came along and they cut stick. Four to one seems their idea of a fair fight."

None of the three answered. Pony led the way to where Chink had fired his first shot. Step by step over the line of the running battle, he could follow the double trail, past Mig's dead black and on to the tree behind which he had dropped Chink. But—there was no body there, no sign of blood on the dead leaves.

"Well!" Pony said slowly, with frowning stare around.

It was the place. There was no doubt in his mind about that. He had the cowboy's telescopic eye and automatic memory for landmarks. Someone had carried Chink away—and taken trouble to remove the signs of his death there.

"Somebody's picked him up," he told the others evenly.

"No sign of anybody ever being here," Jager drawled.

He looked at Britt, who met the stare with lifting brows and began to whistle softly. Both looked at Pony.

"You—couldn't have made a mistake about hitting him?" Britt asked. "I mean—in the excitement of shooting—"

"Let's go on to the old cabin. That seemed to be a kind of hangout for 'em. There was a pallet there and a frying-pan and coffeepot."

In silence he rode ahead to the flat on which the old log house stood.

"If thieves used that old Watterson cabin, they were braver than most of the men around here," Britt said amusedly. "For Watterson was a rustler, years ago. Lived here when he lived anywhere around this neighborhood. He and some of his rustler-friends celebrated in there one night, years ago. There was a row and as the story goes, four men must have tried to kill Watterson—and succeeded. But while he was dying he killed them—the last two with a knife. Of course it's said to be haunted."

Pony rode into the open, motioning them to spread out. So in a fan-formation they came to the door of the cabin and swung down. Smoothly, Pony had drawn a pistol and held it along his leg. He looked cautiously inside—over the barrel of the Colt. But the place was empty, silent. He went in and the trio followed.

The dirt floor was too hard to show tracks. Stock had passed through, or sheltered there against storms. He found no trace of Connie's feet, or those of her captors. Nor was the pile of old quilts and blankets, the skillet and blackened coffeepot, against the wall.

"Nothing here, either?" Britt inquired softly.

Pony shook his head, spinning his pistol with fore-finger in the trigger guard, whistling tunelessly.

"Not a thing. Some thief has been careful. Yes, sir, some thief was careful."

CHAPTER XX

"We ride for our necks!"

BUT AS HE LOOKED AROUND and considered the situation, Pony found the manner of the three men irritating. Britt looked at Jager, Jager at Britt. The cowboy said nothing, but he held the solemn face of one about to grin.

"Anybody could make a mistake," Jager offered without meeting Pony's eyes. "You know, a man in the brush shoots at you and you shoot back and—and everything happens so fast—"

"It was the sensible thing to do," Pony drawled, as if he had not heard. "If we had identified Chink, it might have led to the other men. Well, Britt! No use killing any more time at this. The body's gone. Makes no difference to me whether you believe there was a dead man, or not. You can't believe that I dropped off to sleep and dreamed it all. For the boy and I did dodge somebody's lead and his horse was killed. And that prize *mañada* of Red Roy's was being pushed this way by the men who shot at us. And Miss Hall was kidnaped."

"If it hadn't been for the dead horse and Miss Hall's account I—well, I admit I might have wondered," Britt told him smilingly. "Because Seventy-Seven and Two Bench stock have drifted through breaks in the fence before this. That sort of thing has happened ever since lines were first put up."

"Right! Absolutely right! But this *mañada* is the one that disappeared when Floyd Milton and my friend

Downes had their fight with thieves. It didn't drift. It was driven. I saw the hoofmarks of ridden horses around it, right up to the place where Chink first tried to part my hair. Well, I'm going to the Two Bench. It's up to Red Roy, what he wants to do now."

"We'll look for the serious sheriff to appear and make his owlish surveys," Britt said, with contempt in his voice. "I don't think Sanford will wear that star after this term. But what we ranchers will probably have to do before his time is out is organize an old-fashioned vigilance committee."

"That's it!" Jager grunted. "That's what I been saying all along! What we got to have is vigilantes and a coil of rope! Sanford ain't worth a hoot. He was Quaid's deputy and a big fighting fool, so he was put in Quaid's place. But he can't see the hand before his face, big as it is—"

"He can see it, all right," Britt disagreed acidly. "But he can't swear it's a hand until somebody tells him. I think I'll take a whirl at clearing up these thefts and run for sheriff myself. Anyway, since Sanford can't do anything, we are going to be forced to forget him and do things on our own. I'll come over and see Red Roy soon, Kirk."

There was little talk among them on the way back to that point where Pony and Mig had first drawn fire and retreated. When they talked, it was of general range conditions. But when they drew rein on the crest of a ridge, to separate, Britt put out his hand cordially, smiling.

"Sorry we met in just this way. But that couldn't be helped. Sorry we didn't find the—dead man. As you said, if we could have carried him to town and identified him, it might have gone far toward putting names to our thieves. Are you staying on the Two Bench?"

"Oh, for a while. It all depends on how long it takes me to put a loop over the dry-gulcher who murdered

Dumpty Downes. Or a slug through him!"

"Luck to you!" Britt said cheerfully. "Tell Red Roy I'll be seeing him. He's not fond of me and I find one or two things wrong with him. But we're in the same boat right now and we've got to pull together or sink."

Pony crossed to 2 Bench range where he had slackened the wires. He tapped the drawn staples into the posts again and went on toward the house, noting ahead of him the trail of the *mañada*. He shook his head at last.

Seems I've been here always, he thought. *I wonder why that is. She's certainly the prettiest girl—and the nicest— I ever met. Seems to be settled here. Of course, if Cousin Roy dies and splits up the property, she'll have a chance to think about that. For the 2 Bench can be sold for a lot of money—if this bunch of thieves is stopped before the place is stripped!*

His thoughts slipped from the girl to Chink and Isbell and the thefts. He was quite confident, now, of his ability to settle the mystery of the thefts; to wipe out the thieves after identifying them. There was nothing of undue conceit about his belief. He had lived some hard and dangerous years which had taught him very well what he could and could not do.

"This can't be as tough a twister as some I've bucked," was the way he described to himself the troubles of Red Roy Kirk and the 2 Bench. "Clubfoot—if there really is a clubfooted boss of this gang snorting fire every time he jumps—can't be a deadlier snake than Alec Sells!"

He planned his campaign as he rode through gathering dusk toward the house. Red Roy, it seemed, did not either trust or wish to lean on him. So he would leave the 2 Bench headquarters strictly alone and, carrying his supplies in the *alforjas*, he would "live out" until he found the thieves' hangout, discovered their place and method of disposing of stolen stock and have all that

information in hand for Red Roy and the sheriff. After
that—

"She's just a kid, in some ways," he told the big chestnut, very softly. "Plenty of fire—and just as much of pretty
ignorance about my kind of man. She thought up to
today that the *buscaderos* riding the high lines, from
Jackson's Hole to Tonto Basin and down to Sonora,
they're just the same as men she's known on city streets."

He shook his head marvelingly.

"Yes, sir! If I'm Pony Kirk, I can't be Chance Fielder,
she says. The kind of life I've led this past year I could
tell her about—if I *could* tell a girl like that about it—
and she'd hear me and she'd know what every word I
said means. But she would no more understand what it's
like to be a human wolf with the hounds and the bulldogs
chasing you— How could she?"

The gray twilight was darkening. From a little ridge
he saw the faraway lights of the house.

"Pretty! The prettiest thing I ever saw. More than
just pretty, too. A lot more! And I— Here I sit, like the
biggest nitwit kid in Texas, even thinking about her!
Making a plain, plumb damn fool of myself. A fugitive
from justice; 'escaped murderer' from the Territory—
ask Bully Witt! A man due to be on the dodge for a long,
long time."

As he rode on and the lights took on their proper
shape of yellow windows, he faced them grimly.

"I ought to be gone from here. If I had two thoughts
more than any old gray goose, I would think of my own
skin instead of remembering Dumpty. I'd pull out and
change names again and cover my trail. But since I
haven't got sense enough to wad a .32 shell, I'll get out on
the range and wolf it with Mig the way I ought to do.
One End Creek— Well, one thing I am and that's a good
stock detective. I'll wade into this creek that bothers

'em all so and I'll come out with its other end and maybe some horses and scalps!"

When he swung down at the corral, Mig came out of darkness to meet him.

"Your cousins have not come back. But the big sheriff is here. He has been here for an hour. We drove the *mañada* into a pasture, then came on. The sheriff had just unsaddled. He stays the night and he is alone and he came, I think, to see you. Is it—something about the back trail, *amo?*"

"That is more than I know. But I will not be trapped. Who is here in the bunkhouse, besides the foreman, Tait?"

"Upshur. He rode toward Needle Rock pasture with Enlow and Cloud as they planned. But his horse grew lame and he came back for another. He will sleep here and go to Needle Rock tomorrow."

"*Bueno!* He and Tait are in the bunkhouse, now? Then we will saddle black Dan and your own horse. You will stay close to the corral, here. If there is trouble at the house—and there *will* be trouble if the sheriff has come about the business behind us!—you will lead out our horses and drive from the corral the others. Then—we ride for our necks!"

Mig grunted and went into the corral quickly and quietly. Pony got Dan easily. Mig had more trouble with his horse, but made even less noise. Pony shifted his saddle and bridle. He held Mig's horse while the boy went noiselessly to bring his saddle. Within ten minutes of his arrival, the two horses stood just inside the corral gate, ready to be mounted.

"I hope this is all useless," Pony whispered. "But I do *not* think of this big sheriff what some seem to think; that he is all teeth and no brain. Life, my son, is very much like the great game of poker. And when I play poker it is my custom to expect that the other player *has* the high hand he *might* have! Listen, now, for a shot, or my call!"

He went on to the house and met nobody until he was inside. Voices carried from the dining-room. He walked softly up to the door and looked in. Sheriff Sanford sat on one side of the long table, Connie Hall on the other. The girl was talking, the sheriff eating his supper.

"Certainly lucky for you that cousin of yours was along," he said as Pony stopped to listen—and look. "That's a right salty young fellow, Miss Connie. Plenty salty! I hope he'll bring in the man he—Chink, I mean. I never heard of anybody nicknamed that, but I think I place him. Reckon you don't know Leon Creek, being new in the country and—Leon Creek not being the kind of place you'd see—"

"I've heard of it. Cousin Roy has said several times that it's a disgrace to the county and—"

"And he couldn't see why I let it spoil the top of the ground," Sanford finished for her. "Uh-huh. Well, I know as well as anybody else what kind of bunch uses around that clutter of stores and saloons and—joints. It kind of gethers in all the riffraff of the county. And *that* is why I just kind of ride herd on it, instead of wiping it out. Because when you know where to find your riffraff, you're better off than if you have to go combing each riff and each raff out of the bushes all over the county!"

"Why—I can understand that! You're not so—"

"Thickheaded as folks believe and say," he helped her again. "I'm right slow; no denying that. But I know I am! And that helps a lot. I ain't a quarter horse, so I don't try to sprint. But I aim to cover the ground and I fit my gait to my size and weight and, so far, I managed to come under the mark a finisher."

Pony watched the grin flicker on Sanford's weathered

face and nodded to himself. His feeling had been cor-
rect; this big, slow man was nobody's fool and he would
win over many of those who laughed at him. But—what,
exactly, did he think of Pony Kirk?

Besides calling me plenty salty? Pony wondered.

"What I started out to say," Sanford drawled, "is that I
know right well, generally, who's in the county and what
about 'em. This man by your tale is one that's hung out
with Ike Isbell and some others I count pretty shady, at
Leon Creek. If your cousin brings him in, we can say for
sure. If he don't—"

Pony had studied the dining-room flashingly. Now he
decided to go in. They looked at him when he appeared
inside the door. Connie smiled a welcome; the sheriff
nodded placidly. Pony went around to take the chair on
Connie's right. There was a window behind and to the
right of him. It was screened, but the sash was raised. He
spoke briefly to them and took off his belts and pistols to
hang them on his chair as the sheriff's hung on his chair.
He sat down and looked across at Sanford.

"Heard what you just said," he told him wearily.
"Reckon you guessed what might happen. Well, it did.
Not a sign of our Chink. Miss Hall tell you what he
looked like? I have been wondering if you could identify
him by the description."

Sanford nodded and resumed his meal. The waiter appeared with Pony's supper and while he ate Sanford told
Pony about what he had said to Connie, of Chink at Leon
Creek. The girl looked from one to the other, but let
them do the talking. When they sat over their coffee,
smoking, Sanford looked steadily at Pony, without any
particular expression.

"I got back to town right after you and that saddle
tramp rode off. Didn't go to Leon Creek, account I met
a man and found out Isbell wasn't there. Nate Azle come

in about the same time and he's painted up for the war trail, young fellow! I went over all the business about Jean Elam and Kane Gravis and I'm plain to tell you, if I'd been there, that inquest of Zink's would have been different. Far's I can see, Zink and that dang nitwit Shack Rolison, they just listened to what you and the dance-hall floozy told 'em and believed every word of it. She was the only witness and you'd been filling her up with drinks and naturally she talked for you!"

"Just between us," Pony said solemnly, "I rode into town to rub out Elam and Gravis. I was getting behind on my tally, you see, so they just had to go. They made the dozen for the month. Sad! But when a man's got a mark he has got to make it!"

"Funny, huh? Well, it won't be so funny when Nate Azle comes after the man that killed his foreman—"

"Whoa! Wait a minute! It was a buckshot out of the bar gun that killed Elam. Kane Gravis is all I'm responsible for. So the Ladder U hasn't got a thing to comb me about. Not but what I had intentions! If Gravis hadn't killed Elam by accident, I would certainly have got him—on purpose! So Azle's clouded up, is he? Well, maybe Red Roy will protect me. Seems that he can handle the Azles by the cowpenful and I don't believe he'll let one of his young kinfolks be rubbed out."

"Nobody knows what kind of slug killed Elam," Sanford admitted reluctantly. "I rode out to hear your tale myself. It seems funny, to me and Azle both, that Elam would have come at you the way Beatrice says he done."

Pony punched out his cigarette in his saucer and finished his coffee. Then, in a flat voice, he told the story he had given to Zink and Rolison, almost word for word, while Connie listened with widened eyes and Sanford stared fixedly.

"It still sounds funny!" the sheriff exploded at the end.

"Beatrice ain't reason enough for all that scheming—Elam having Gravis bushwhack you. Nate Azle says that, too. He—"

"Oh! Has the Ladder U lost any stock?" Pony thrust in lazily. "I thought about that, afterward."

"Yeh. Azle says this gang of thieves has lifted some horses off him, too. Why?"

"Elam was his ramrod—and somehow I just didn't see Elam as the kind of man I'd likely get to love and—trust. If ever I saw a face I thought was owned by a hard proposition, he had it. But ne' mind that, for a minute. Did you find the man that killed Pink Snake Casselberry?"

"Ah, that bunch of Mexicans either never saw a thing or they're afraid to talk! Some day I may git to the bottom of it, but the chances are, then, it'll be plumb accident."

"I think Elam killed him," Pony said calmly. "Killed him for the same reason he tried to kill me. Because I was trying to uncover the blue shirt the Criterion bartender saw going out of the saloon—the blue shirt on the man who murdered Quell. Casselberry promised to tell me something about that shirt. Elam overheard us talking. Casselberry went down to the Luna to wait for me. I went across to Delrio Dolly's to see if Beatrice knew anything. I think Elam drifted to the Luna and tolled Casselberry outside and knifed him, then came on to hunt me. Why? Because—Elam was one of the thieves!"

"Say! Did you tell Shack and Zink any of this?"

"I told Shack some of it. Not about Casselberry."

"And he never told me a word—"

"Likely you wouldn't have listened," Pony drawled caustically. "Even if you could have heard him through all the bellowing about me and Zink's verdict I'll bet you were doing. I—"

From somewhere outside there carried into the dining-room the hollow sound of a shot, then a high yell that Pony recognized as Mig's. Then there was silence.

Automatically, both Pony and Sanford twisted and got hands on pistols. Pony stood, turned to the window and unhooked the screen, and went out like a cat—as he had thought to do if the sheriff attempted his arrest. He ran down the house and rounded it to look toward the corral. Now he heard the sudden distant thudding of hoofs, but only for a few seconds.

CHAPTER XXI

"Saddle's all bloody"

THERE WERE STILL LIGHTS in the bunkhouse, but no sound came from its open door. Pony studied the darkness, and the ground where it was dappled by light. There was nothing to see. So he called Mig and, getting no answer, ran to the corral. The bars were still up and some, at least, of the horses were there. He moved a step away—and checked himself with a startled grunt when his toe touched a body on the ground. It was Mig and he was limp and still when Pony put away his Colts and lifted him with arm under the shoulders. From the shadows by the house Sanford called and Tait or Upshur answered from the bunkhouse to the effect that the speaker knew nothing about the shot, the yell, the retreating rider.

"It's the boy!" Pony said savagely. He was straightening with Mig's light weight over a shoulder. "I—I think he's dead. Somebody shot him and high-tailed and—"

He carried Mig very gently to the bunkhouse and eased him to the floor under the wall lamp. Blood was flowing down Mig's face, turning cheek and neck into a scarlet mask. But he breathed and Pony, finding no body wound, probed through the dark hair and suddenly grinned.

"Just creased!" he announced. "*Dios!* But it had me scared. He's got a gash in his scalp that's going to put an ache into even that coconut. But that's all. Let's have that water, Upshur. Stay back, Connie. I'll wash him— the *diablito!*"

"We was setting here," Vic Tait said frowningly, "when all of a sudden we heard the shot and somebody yelled and a horse pounded off. But it never looked judgmatical to stick my nose outside and I couldn't see from the window."

Pony sponged the boy's head deftly. At the bunkhouse door Connie called to old Hung On, the cook, and he padded imperturbably in to hold out clean cloths for bandages. Mig groaned softly and opened his eyes.

"Take it easy, *hombrecito!*" Pony ordered. "Wait till I get this millinery on you."

"It was a man—I think a thief meaning to steal the horses from the corral," Mig said gaspingly. "I saw him and I spoke quietly to him, standing in the dark by the corral as he sat upon his horse with some light showing him. He jumped his horse at me and I shot at him. But he struck me—with the barrel of his carbine, I think. And that is all I know."

"What did he shape like?" Sanford asked, scowling. "You kind of sky-lined him, huh?"

"He seemed very big. That may have been because of a tall horse. But I think he was big. His shoulders looked very wide. But more than that—"

He shrugged. Pony finished the tucking-in of the bandage and grinned at him paternally.

"Now, young sprout, you turn in! If he was a horse thief—and I reckon he was, by the way he acted—he didn't get a thing but a scare. For the corral bars are all up and the *caballos* are inside. I looked when I came out of the house."

He helped the boy to his bunk, unbuckled his shell belt, and drew off his boots, pushed him flat, and covered him with the blanket. Mig asked for his pistol.

"I reckon you dropped it out there. I'll find it."

"I bet you I know what that fella was after!" Vic Tait said suddenly, looking at Sanford. "Yes, sir! He was after your bay horse, Sanford. He wouldn't have hit the Two Bench feeling safe *just* because you're here!"

He began to laugh, and Sanford regarded him steadily. Without replying, he turned to Pony.

"Feel like riding over to the Seventy-Seven with me, tomorrow?"

"No. No, I reckon I'm too timid," Pony drawled, grinning at him. "I'm pretty sure that Ben Britt's not fond of me and I know well enough he's not fond of you. There might be shooting if we both showed up on the Seventy-Seven. I might get hit. But even if I didn't—you know how you act, Sanford, whenever I'm just in the neighborhood of a gun that goes off. You figure out some way to make every busted cap my fault."

Sanford growled disgustedly. He looked at Lyde Upshur and the stocky cowboy shook his head.

"Sorry. But I'm just a hired hand. I have got my powders to work Needle Rock pasture tomorrow, along with some others."

"I'll go with you!" Vic Tait volunteered, grinning. "Maybe Britt don't like me better'n he likes the rest of the Two Bench. But he ain't bodaciously shot at me, yet. I'll go along and protect you!"

Pony went out, Connie beside him. He was puzzling the attack on Mig when the girl said slowly, "You could almost believe that the thieves, having taken most of the stock out on the range, had come to make the stealing complete by raiding the corral! You said Mig kept him from getting anything?"

"Yeh. What I'm wondering is, why he bothered to knock Mig down with his gun, instead of just taking the short cut of shooting him. He couldn't tell it was just a kid. Well—"

He kicked Mig's gun, stooped and picked it up. He asked Connie if Sanford would sleep in the bunkhouse.

"He said he would. He seemed to want to sleep there. Pony, why won't you go to the Seventy-Seven with the sheriff?"

"Well, to tell you the truth—"

"Part of the truth! As usual!"

"Have it your own way, then. To tell you part of the truth, I just don't like to have to wear my hardware when I'm in swimming or teaching my usual Sunday school class."

"Swimming? Sunday school? Now, what nonsense are you talking? What has that to do with the Seventy-Seven, young man?"

"Watch! I'll show you! Stand there and tell me if anybody shows in the bunkhouse door, heading this way."

While she stared alternately at the bunkhouse and at him, as he slipped inside the corral and began quickly to unsaddle Dan and Mig's horse, Pony grinned without humor, occupied with his private plans for the morrow. He poked the two saddles, the bridles, his Winchester and Mig's, through the bars. When he was outside he looked at her, a slim, most attractive shape in the shaft of light from the kitchen.

"Now, you see?" he asked calmly. "Now I want to hang these up."

He took all but the long guns to the saddle shed and came back to where she waited, a Winchester in each hand. He took the guns from her and they went on to the house, rounded it, and came to the front.

"I don't see! Why your horses being saddled, long after they should have been unsaddled, explains those mysterious remarks—"

"Well, I just don't figure the sheriff. He's amazingly uncertain—and changeable! When Mig met me at the corral to say that Sanford was here and anxious to talk to me, I did *not* run right in to say how glad the meeting was and we ought to call it a holiday. Uh-uh! I wondered what brought him out; if he'd made up his mind that I shot Lincoln and he ought to keep me in jail a few years while he studied out my brands. So I left our horses ready to ride. Mig was hanging around, waiting for me. That's why he happened to see that thief."

"But you came in and sat down so— Well, you looked so tired and so uninterested—"

"Ah, but that was just my deceitful nature coming out again! Sheriffs rouse it out, sometimes. Sheriffs like Sanford, picking me because I'm a stranger to hang all their load of suspicions onto. Didn't you notice how I never turned my back to him and how I sat down out of the place I've been using?"

"Why, I thought it was just to be beside me! I thought my lovely personality had at last captivated you! And it was just the window! Not my beautiful dark eyes and the brand-new satin I wore just for your admiration! I like Floyd much better; he has eyes to see and a tongue to compliment!"

"Of course you like him better! You ought to!" Pony said brutally. "He's your kind. I'm *not*—with the big N! I'm a rough tramp cowboy with a life behind me that— Well, the kind of life that was absolutely natural for my kind of man in the kind of country I worked through, but the kind you'd have cold chills if you knew about. I'll even break down and admit that Mrs. Quaid and

Sanford and Red Roy were right, in reading my brand *Gunfighter*. I do kick about *Gunman* because that has come to mean a cold-eyed killer. I— What was I saying?"

"But I only like Floyd a little better, now that I consider," she told him thoughtfully. "In fact, it's not Floyd that I like better; it's his gift for making pretty speeches. I like to be flattered. Every girl does, no matter how homely she may be. That's what Cousin Roy calls the 'peculiarness of the critter'—the 'she-critter'—a woman."

"No difference! Means nothing to me. My herd's all bulls. What I was going to tell you is, I don't know what Sanford's beliefs and plans may be. But I'm not going to let him arrest me and hold me in that *calabozo* of his while he makes up his mind or has it made up for him. If I ride out with him I'll have to be watching him every minute. I don't want to hurt him and I certainly don't want him to hurt me. So I'll stay clear away from him! Now, I think I'd like to use that shiny bathtub. Way things go around here, no telling when I'll get another chance to clean up!"

"Ramon will fix the hot water for you. I'll expect to see you at breakfast tomorrow, bearing with and upon you the secret—"

"Huh? Secret? What nonsense are *you* talking?"

She faced him in the big living-room and laughed. She was completely recovered from the day's shocks and fears, he thought, and the black satin she wore made her seem more than usual what Mig had called her—that day seemed ages past—a creature from the foreign world of the East, a lovely picture from magazine or newspaper.

"Why, the secret of your fatal charm! That overpowers pretty red-haired, green-eyed dancers and persuades them to rush to your defense and tell officers any story that will serve their—captor."

"Aw, shucks! That wasn't nothing." Pony grinned in

spite of himself, at thought of Beatrice forgetting her own interest. "She just says how I make her think of *her* boy, that'd be about my age, now, if he hadn't weakened and got married."

As he bathed and shaved in the most unusual comfort of a real bathroom, Pony found his mind straying from grim plans for the tracking down of "Clubfoot" to a picture much pleasanter, the shapely figure of a girl in black satin. He had never thought except in the vaguest way of marriage—for himself. Men he had known and liked had abruptly carried their war bags out of the rough free-masonry of bunkhouse or line camp and got jobs in town or begun the building of their own outfits. They had seemed to find some woman good enough reason for the move.

But Pony, looking at them, had never seen anything particularly attractive about the new and restricted and complicated life they began with marriage. He had looked at a good many of their households and wondered what about the yellow-haired or brown-haired or red-haired woman in the case his old *compañero* had found so attractive. He had often wondered, too, what the man got in exchange for his freedom that balanced the account.

"They never could tell me," he recalled, now, as he propped a chair under the knob of his door and put a pistol down beside him in bed. "They always talk about how fine it is to be married and how you don't live a right and a natural life until you get your own house and wife and forty-'leven li'l tow-tops hyenaing around to make you happy. Yeh, they talked. But they couldn't tell! And there was that Boston bughunter I guided on the Box O. What was it he said some smart old Frenchman wrote about marrying? 'Every woman should—and no man!' Dad used to tell the boys marrying is something no man ought to make up his mind to do and go into by a plan; it's something to do when you just can't help yourself! I reckon that's the way I've looked at it all my life—like taking sick—or going crazy—you don't think whether you want to or not!"

He moved the Colt a little so that his hand would fall easily upon the butt, if Sanford's plans should bring the sheriff softly out of the bunkhouse and to this door.

"Well, no use my worrying about marrying!" he comforted himself sardonically. "Bully Witt and that printing-press of his will see that I find a warrant plastered on every fence post between this and that, thick as Lydia Pinkham's pictures! But—if it wasn't for that bunch of lying charges, I would sit down right in this neighborhood and give Floyd Milton a run that would wear his feet off right to the ankles. And likely have my run for my pains! Make a bigger *tonto* of myself than usual. I'm not her kind, no matter what I wish."

He saw the sheriff and Vic Tait ride off before he dressed in old shirt and overalls and those dusty leggings he had worn through so many miles of Territory brush. He went to the table and Connie—very bright, very fresh, completely eye-filling—smiled at him with dark head on one side.

"I thought you'd be that 'cowboy shirted all in silk' the song tells about. But, and yet, I can understand how Beatrice simply couldn't help little things like perjury. If you were to say 'flapjacks!' to me, I know I couldn't resist you!"

"I'm certainly saying it," he assured her, standing to look at her. "You know, that black satin suits you the same way your hair suits you. But, that calico you're wearing—"

"It's not calico, as it happens. It's linen. But go on! I have a strange, weak feeling; a premonition that a compliment is about to happen."

"Not a compliment. I was just going to tell you the truth and say you're prettier in that dress than in the other."

"Two compliments! Now, I am weak! I think I'll double my order of flapjacks. The sheriff has gone. Vic Tait went with him. I heard him promising to take care of Mr. Sanford. I am afraid the promise wasn't appreciated."

"Lyde Upshur go, too?"

"I think not—yet. I sent a special breakfast out to Mig and Ramon said Upshur was there. What are you going to do?"

"Ride. Without any company except Mig—if he's in shape to travel. This is going to be a tough one and I hope—"

"I'd like to go with you, but, after yesterday, I'm very meek and timid. I wish Cousin Roy and Floyd would come in. I don't fancy the idea of staying here with only the Mexicans. I never felt that way, before. But after last night—"

"Keep Upshur. He looks to be a good man. Dependable. I don't think Red Roy will mind his staying."

They talked easily during the meal. Then Pony went out to see Mig and tell Upshur that he was to stay at the house until Red Roy or Floyd Milton came back. Mig was up and making light of the gash in his scalp. When Upshur went out, the boy looked frowningly at Pony.

"I did not say, last night, that the man I shot at is a Mexican. Or one wearing the tall-crowned sombrero of a Mexican. I do not know why I said nothing of this, except that the sheriff was here. Why did he strike me, instead of killing me with his Winchester?"

Pony shrugged. He turned over this added information and decided that it meant nothing. The man might be a

Mexican and one of the thieves' gang. He might be a thief having no connection with Clubfoot and the other rustlers.

"Feel like riding, do you?" he said presently. "Well, we will look over our outfits and get ready for some·plain and fancy wolfing. We'll take what grub we can carry in the *alforjas* and see what trails we can cut. I think we can do something, if we forget houses and beds awhile."

"I am ready! I went out as soon as light came, to look at the trail of that man. It leads toward the road to Vasko."

Upshur came back in. He asked Pony where he was going.

"Around the whole line. I want to look at this famous One End Creek and the Spear Hills. Maybe I'll run into my cousins. Anyway, it'll be moving. I can't sit still." .

A horse was coming at the trot toward the corral. Pony looked out and saw a fat young cowboy of cheerful red face, who rode chanting "Lulu Belle."

"Hi," he greeted Pony, as he swung down and stretched. "I reckon you're the gun bulldogger pore old Dumpty used to talk about, that's fell into so much excitement around here. I'm Rory Eads and I hail from Toyah. I been out with the boss and Floyd Milton, but I couldn't find 'em after we split up last night. So I come on in this morning to eat."

"Where'd you leave Red Roy and Floyd?"

"Up close to the Spear Hills, around One End Creek. The boss went one way, Floyd went another and me the rest of the directions. That's rough country. I never seen a thing and I ended up lost. They come back?"

Pony shook his head. Eads stripped the saddle from his horse and turned it into the corral. When Pony had got his saddle and Mig's and reached the bunkhouse again, Eads was eating and talking to Lyde Upshur. Pony replaced some worn lacings on his saddle and was at the kitchen getting bacon and coffee and biscuit from Hung On when Floyd Milton rode into the yard and dismounted. He left his saddle on the ground with sweaty skirts upturned and came wearily to the kitchen. With stubble of beard and streaks of dust on face and clothing, he made a different figure, this morning, from the dude cowboy Pony had last seen.

"Hello," he said. "Vic Tait here? Rory Eads?"

"Tait and the sheriff are over on the Seventy-Seven. Eads just got here. He's eating. Says he got lost after you all separated."

"So did I. Or near enough to it. I suppose Cousin Roy's not back? I didn't see his gray in the corral."

Connie came into the kitchen and asked about Red Roy.

"He and I and Eads were combing those Spear Hills, on the edges. We didn't find a thing, together. So Cousin Roy told us to scatter. I went up One End Creek to look over the forks. He turned downstream toward the Hills. Eads turned back. I expected Cousin Roy to be first in. He would have been closest of us to the house. Well, maybe he found something. We'll hope so. Now, I'm ready to eat like three men."

"Pony found the *mañada!*" Connie announced triumphantly. "The one that was stolen when Clubfoot attacked you and Dumpty Downes. And he—killed one of the thieves and—"

"Found the *mañada!* Where?" Floyd cried, staring.

As briefly as he could, Pony told of the day on the 77.

"Well! That's something to tell Cousin Roy! You'll be the white-haired child in his eyes, John. And I'm only sorry you didn't get a straight shot at the man Jake. But even one is more than we've managed this far. Maybe it's a beginning."

He went in to eat and Pony packed the *alforjas* on both saddles with food. Presently, Floyd came out and turned to the bunkhouse. Eads he sent toward the Ladder U line. Upshur asked for orders.

"You'd better stay here until Cousin Roy gets back, or I do," Floyd told him. "After that try of last night at the very corral, I won't feel right if somebody's not here to watch over Miss Hall. I'm going to check that *mañada* and see if all the mares are there."

After he had ridden toward the 77 and Eads was gone in the direction of the Ladder U, Pony and Mig saddled their horses. Pony went up to the house to speak to Connie.

He had been there only a few minutes when Upshur called him, with a tone in his voice that somehow tensed Pony. He went out fast, the girl following. Upshur was at the kitchen door and with sight of Connie, he hesitated, then shrugged.

"Red Roy's horse just walked up to the corral," he said. "Saddle's all bloody. Looks some hours old, that blood."

CHAPTER XXII

"You're a funny fool"

Pony went quickly to the corral, where Mig stood beside a big gray gelding. The horse showed no sign of hard travel. The split-reins trailed; the blanket had worked crooked under the saddle. On horn and fork was the stain of blood. Pony studied the marks.

"I'd guess that he was shot; that he put his hand to the place, then caught hold of the horn. But he slid off."

"Shot?" Connie gasped, leaning close to his shoulder.

"Oh, Pony! Isn't there a chance that he—he was just hurt a little bit and got off and—and the horse ran away? I can't believe it! Not Cousin Roy. He was so—so kind under his gruffness. I—won't believe it! Go look! You, too, Upshur! I'm not worried about staying here alone. Not now! Go on, Pony! Fast!"

"Saddle up, Lyde," Pony grunted. He was more moved by the girl's show of concern and quick, warm feeling than by thought of Red Roy. He patted her arm awkwardly. "Chances are, you've hit the answer, Connie. He might've got piled or hit by a limb or—or lots of things might have happened. But we'll see."

"Take my buckskin!" Connie called to Lyde Upshur. "He's the best horse in there. If Floyd comes back— I'll send one of the vaqueros after him. He must know about this. I'll have him found and he'll come to help."

Upshur led out the buckskin at the end of a catch-rope and got his saddle, bridle, and Winchester. Pony sat Dan, hands folded on the horn, looking somberly down at Connie. Again it came to him that she was the prettiest girl he had ever known, the most attractive girl, the most desirable girl. He shook his head viciously.

"Come on! Come on!" he grunted to Lyde Upshur. "Mig, you start. You're better at this than we are. We want to get as far as we can before dark and it's crowding noon, and from what I hear One End Creek's a long way. Be seeing you, Connie. Soon as we can."

He twisted Dan and followed Mig, who was gone proudly at the gallop, leaning from the saddle occasionally to look at the ground. Upshur loped after him and when he came up to Pony's stirrup he jerked his head toward the buckskin.

"She was right. It's a horse!" he grunted. Then, a little later: "Not much chance of finding him alive, huh?"

"Afraid not. He was by himself—what with that fool

notion of his for 'em to separate. If they knocked him out of the kak, they would naturally see that he was dead. Even if they had to give him the old *tiro de grácias*—the shot of thanks. There's a chance, though, that he got to cover and stood 'em off. His carbine scabbard being empty is a good omen—even though the Winchester may have dropped out while the gray was coming home. Well, we'll make the best time we can!"

Mig kept well ahead of them for most of the afternoon. Occasionally he was checked by stony ground or a stretch of arroyo bed where the gray had walked slowly. But, in the first grayness of dusk they came to the swift creek called One End, to look down at the racing stream from a rocky bank twenty feet high. Pony stared downstream toward the hazy lift of the Spear Hills, where One End Creek was said to pour into the underground cavern that never gave it up.

"I see no more of the trail," Mig reported irritably. "This ground is very hard. Too, there have been horses tramping up and down—perhaps the horses of your cousins as they searched for the *mañada*."

"Well, one thing's certain," Pony consoled him, "we're on the right track this far. The gray's trail led up to the creek about here. We'll split. You go upstream, Mig. Lyde, you keep close to the bank. I'll ride out a hundred yards or so and sort of parallel you. Mig, if you find anything, you shoot twice, then wait while you count fifty, then let go one shot. We'll do the same."

Mig nodded and turned his horse. Pony rode away from the water, watching the ground, the clumps of mesquite and low ridges. When he turned again, Upshur was fifty yards in advance, keeping close to the creek. They rode for several hundred yards through the clear, gray light, then Pony pulled in short and stared off to the right. He could have sworn that he had heard the soft fall of a walking horse's hoofs. But there was nothing to be seen, nothing to be heard—

A flash of something moving, seen blurrily out of an eye corner, jerked his head. Automatically, he lifted his Winchester. A high-crowned sombrero had whipped over a ridge thirty or forty yards beyond him. He saw an elbow, a rifle, rising, had a glimpse of dark face over them. Then the man fired, and Pony cocked his own Winchester and returned the shot, snapped down the lever, and fired again.

The Mexican vanished, with thunder of hoofs. Pony looked toward the creek to see if Upshur were coming, before jumping Dan after the fugitive. Upshur was on the ground and looking his way. But as he straightened, seeming to strain to look, he fell backward with a startled yell.

Pony hesitated. He could hear those racing hoofs, going farther and farther away. But Upshur yelled again, and he swung Dan with a furious oath, to send him like a stone flung from a sling, back to the creek. He spun him so close to the crumbled edge which had given way under Upshur that Dan's feet kicked stones into the water.

Upshur's face showed white and strained in the middle of the foaming stream. Then he went under.

Pony ran Dan down the bank, getting down his rope. He had dropped his carbine careless of where it struck. Now he shook out a loop and when Upshur's head bobbed up once more he called desperately to him and threw the loop, wishing that it were not the short lariat of Texas and the Territory. Upshur snatched at the loop, missed, and went down with a gurgling groan and thrashing of arms.

Dan jumped forward as Pony whipped in the lariat. The bank was lower, farther along. He gathered himself for another throw, shook his head, then unbuckled shell belts and let his pistols drop. Dan stopped short and Pony dived into the boiling current that roared just ahead over jagged rocks. He held the loop of his rope and it was paid out, taut, when he struck the water flat with force that drove the breath from him. Upshur was rolling past him.

Pony swung himself, clinging to the little loop, to make scissors of his legs and catch the cowboy. The current dragged at them like a thing alive and Pony's arm felt as if it were being pulled from the socket. But he set his mouth grimly and reached up to get the rope with left hand, too. They went like a pendulum-end toward the bank and banged on rocks. Upshur was not moving, now. Pony shook water from his eyes and looked up.

The bank was sheer, at this point, but a few feet above was a short flat. He began to bend his arms and drag them upstream. It seemed endless, muscle-cracking effort. But at last he sprawled at the edge of the water, out of its force, and could put a stiff hand down to Upshur and haul him up.

After minutes of panting, he got shakily up. It was almost as hard to get the limp man up two yards of bank, and when that was done he could not rest. He kneeled beside Upshur and pumped his arms to start him breathing. It was not a long process. Upshur opened his eyes at last and presently he was drawing long breaths without help.

"You must've—disappointed Saint Pete!" he whispered, trying to grin. "He'd just—dusted off—the doormat!"

Pony collected wood enough for a small fire and they squatted by it when he had recovered his pistols and, riding Dan, gone back to get his Winchester. For he had not forgotten the Mexican who had shot at him.

"Probably the same one Mig cut down on, at the corral," he thought. "Maybe the man who shot Red Roy."

"Certainly lucky you got to me when you did," Lyde

Upshur said slowly, as they dried themselves. "I owe you whatever my fool neck's worth. Lucky you can swim, too! I can't."

"Swim?" Pony repeated. "I can't swim, either."

He worked arms and shoulders and grimaced. He was tough as leather from many months of steady riding and lean diet, but now he ached in every muscle and his palms were chafed.

"You can't swim!" Upshur cried, staring. "You—you just jumped into that water and risked your life to pull me out? You're a funny fool. You are that. But I'm certainly obliged to you, and the—the Upshurs and the elephants have got lifelong memories. You'll find that out."

"*De nada!* It's nothing! You heard me shoot?"

He told of the Mexican and Upshur listened frowningly.

"I wouldn't be a bit surprised if you're right, about that being the man at the corral. But why he'd take a shot at you, Pony— Well, we have still got Red Roy to find. Not much light left, either. I was looking at a track when the damn bank caved with me. But it was pretty old. Not the gray's."

"I'll bring in your horse and see if your Winchester went in when you dived. Mig ought to be along pretty soon."

But he caught the buckskin and recovered the dropped carbine without seeing the boy. When he had come back to the fire, he looked downstream again.

"You stick here and wait for Mig. I won't be long at my looking. But as long as there's some light I want to hunt."

He kept back from the treacherous edge of the bank as he rode. Presently he got down and walked with Dan following, bent over, studying the hoofprints old and fresh that marked the ground. As he moved steadily he thought of Upshur.

"Plenty backbone in that hairpin," he told himself. "Not a squawk out of him when he was in the water—and it takes a man who can't swim and has been about to drown to know how scared you can get! A salty hairpin, yes, sir. He's the kind you'd pick to ride the river with. Off the same bolt with old Dumpty Downes and Pat Curran—poor devils!"

He was more than a mile from the fire, and the darkness was growing too thick to let him see more than a yard or so when he stumbled on a battered black hat no more than a yard from the edge of the bank. It was Red Roy's. He knew the narrow strap with leather-covered buckle that was Red Roy's hatband. He looked from the hat to the edge of the stream.

There was a crumbled place in the bank—as if something heavy had rolled over it. There were jumbled hoof-prints all around. He squatted and whistled softly, looking about.

A big clump of mesquite grew forty yards from the water. It offered ample cover for a horseman, against the eyes of anyone here. He could easily build a picture of what probably had happened.

"Red Roy was sitting the gray, right here, looking around. Or he'd got this far and was riding. Somebody behind that mesquite opened up on him. He was hit and he slapped his hand to the bullet hole. Then he grabbed at the horn. Maybe he was hit again; or he was hit so hard the first time that he went out of the saddle. From the look of the ground—no blood on it—he went right over the edge into the water. Maybe the gray jumped at the shot and jarred him loose."

He shook his head grimly. From his own experience with the grip of that surging current, he felt that a wounded man who had fallen into it was now as dead as if the bullet which had struck him had gone squarely through his head. For he would be drowned like a rat in that underground cavern into which One End Creek plunged.

"If that guess is right," he muttered, peering over the broken bank, "I'll find footprints by the mesquite. Maybe plain enough to be checked with those up the way, of the Mexican who shot at me. If they're the same—"

He saw orange flames blossom upon the mesquite, heard the roar of shots, and in the same split second felt a terrific blow upon his head. It was as if the top of his skull were driven in. Then he felt nothing.

Out of sheer blackness came the hazy idea that he was in the bathtub at Red Roy's. He was soaking himself in the water. But it was cold, now. He would get out— Something struck his head hard and blackness came again.

He floated out of that pitchy sea, hearing a dull and steady roar all about him. It grew louder as the darkness thinned. He moved and found that he was sprawled on a lumpy shelf—and wet. When he turned so that he lay face upward light shone in his eyes. He blinked and groaned. That light was from the moon and it showed him a rugged cliff on his right hand, foaming water on the left.

He was lying at the edge of One End Creek, a spur so firmly caught in rocks that he could not move the foot. The current set in toward the bank, here, and swept against big boulders. Hardly fifty yards downstream reared the jagged heights of the Spear Hills. From there the roaring seemed to come.

He sat up carefully and worked at the spur which had caught and held him. Then he crawled away from the water to a place where he could sit. Blood ran into his eyes and his head ached. There was a furrow from forehead to crown in his scalp, still seeping blood.

"Must've lost plenty blood," he muttered. "I'm weak

as a barber's cat. Let's see— I was looking over the bank when somebody parted my hair. Must've tumbled over the same way Red Roy went. Hadn't been for that spur catching, I'd be halfway to China now!"

He shivered, looking down toward the forbidding cliffs where One End Creek disappeared. Then with sodden neckerchief he bandaged his head.

His pistols he still had, for the straps had been down upon the hammers. He worked up the bank, to sprawl full length upon level ground. The moon went under a mass of clouds, then reappeared. He got up after a while, feeling not so weak. Downstream to the cliffs he went slowly, now in darkness, now in bright moonlight, until he could look at the low, wide cavern that caught the creek water.

Goes in there like a blacksnake into its hole, he thought. *And I was close to going with it!*

He turned quickly away, studying the problem of his immediate future. He had all the cowboy's natural dread of walking and he knew that he had been carried well downstream from the place where he had gone into the water. The moon's height told him that midnight was near. He wondered if Mig and Lyde Upshur were hunting him.

"More important," he grunted suddenly, "I wonder if they bumped into my bushwhackers! Lyde was a plain target, by that fire. But after what I said about the Mexican, I can't see him staying in the light."

He dived abruptly for the shelter of a great boulder. For a horse and another and still a third had flashed out of an arroyo fifty yards away, the clatter of their hoofs drowned by the roar of the creek. They trotted toward the cliffs while he flattened himself along the boulder. More came into view, all riderless, a dozen, twenty or more of them. He did not move when the last one had disappeared.

Were they only drifting of their own accord from one part of this range—and whose range it might be he had no idea—to another? Or were they driven? And who drove them?

Again the moon was blotted out by scudding clouds. He sat up—but with a Colt in his hand, now. Then from close ahead someone cursed the clouds, but broke into a laugh.

"Still, good dark has been fine for us, Fancy. Reckon we oughtn't to kick. But this is creepy country. I'm always scared I'll git lost and tumble into that damn creek and end up down below, the way old Red Roy and that leather-slapping hellwinder cousin done!"

Pony began to move toward the voice, but ready to hug the ground if the moon shone again. The talkative one continued his comments. As they drew away from the creek and closer to the cliffs, the roaring of the water diminished and Pony could hear the clink of steel shoes on rock, where the riders walked their horses.

"He was piling up a tally! Ain't a chance Ike'll pull out. Wonder is he made it to ride this far out of town with them holes in him. He was lucky about Kane Gravis slamming the buckshot into Jean Elam, but I swear I believe he'd have killed Jean anyhow. Jean was plenty tough, but not so much with a cutter. Then Chink on the Seventy-Seven, and busting Jake's arm and scaring Shorty half to death—I tell you, when I seen him tumble over with our lead in him, I felt lots better. I— What's the matter?"

"Loose shoe," another voice growled. "Wait a minute."

Pony worked closer, looking up strainedly at the clouds, putting his feet down with infinite care.

"It was downright funny," the first voice went on. "Us gitting him right where you'd got old Roaring Red Roy.

With them two down in One End Cellar, reckon we won't have to drive to the Hole no more! What One End dabs her loop on, she certainly gits hogtied and never turns loose."

He laughed raspingly as the other grunted.

"But, I tell you, I likely never will git shut of the wrinkles I collected, when Ambrosius and Big Otto seen us. It was nothing but plumb luck that Ike and Jean could make town in time to shut 'em up. You reckon Dumpty Downes really knew anything. Fancy? He was a mighty cute, salty li'l devil and he never let his face know what his mind was doing. Good thing you rubbed him out. But I'll bet you Red Roy was glad when he heard about it that it was Dumpty got killed and not his pilgrim cousin!"

He laughed again as the other man growled.

"No use," the latter snarled. "Fix it later on."

Pony was within ten feet now. If there had been light he would have ignored everything else to try killing them both. Nor had he any doubt of his ability to kill them as if they had been two snakes in the trail.

"But they won't get away! They won't get away!" he promised himself over and over. "The man who killed Dumpty and Red Roy! And he's right there—and not guessing that I'm right here!"

Again the horses went forward and he took up his careful course behind them. His boots had never been intended for walking and the stony ground made the going painful. But he ignored the pain of chafed skin and followed grimly the sound of clinking shoes. One more amused comment he heard from the talkative rider —with the usual grunt from the other.

"Sanford can buy him a gold-topped cane and spend his declining years telling how-come he never caught that slick Clubfoot! He can tell us, Fancy!"

They drew slowly away from Pony and he came finally to what seemed the blankest of cliffs. He worked back and forth without finding a passage and sat down behind a boulder to ease his feet and wait with Apache-like patience for daylight.

But within twenty minutes two more riders came up the trail. They were trotting their horses like men who knew exactly where they went and how to get there. They passed his shelter and he followed, around a great bulge of the cliff and along a passage no more than two yards wide. A quarter hour or so in this fissure of the cliffs and he saw the light of a fire ahead.

CHAPTER XXIII

"They'll give up or—"

THERE WAS A WIDE OPENING ahead of him. He could guess at its size by the distance between him and the fire and the size of the riders silhouetted against it as someone threw on wood and it blazed high.

He walked boldly out upon grass. Unless the moon came out, he was not likely to be noticed. The phrase that talkative man had used recurred to him—"the Hole"— and he guessed this to be the place meant, the holding-ground for stolen stock. Men on foot moved about the blaze as he came down to his belly and worked closer. One talked loudly, waving his arms. The word "Fancy" carried to Pony.

Must be my talker, he thought. *He and Fancy came in together. Then the two I just trailed. Four. And likely there was a man or so here before they came. And this is the holding-ground. Well, you couldn't ask a much better hide-out! Red Roy said there were places in the Spear*

*Hills he'd never seen, and this must be one. It might have
paid a lot if he'd been more inquisitive!*

The talker disappeared into darkness while Pony tried
to make a plan. Every one of those five or six men would
be a hard customer, in the phrase of the country. Not all
would be the killer type Fancy was proved to be. But all
were dangerous. Pony thought that he could do little
more than learn something of their identities, then slip
out before he was discovered.

Rapidly, he computed the number of men who could
be quickly gathered for an attack on the Hole. There
would be enough. But first he needed to know these
thieves' names—their given names or nicknames, if no
more; and he had no clue, yet, to show the honesty or
dishonesty of the 77 and Ladder U. Jean Elam had been
the Ladder U foreman, but many a thief worked for a
clean outfit.

He moved to the side—toward the sound of grazing
horses on his right. Quietly as he went, he got very close
to the horses before a voice challenged him lazily. He continued toward the guard, mumbling an indistinct answer. The man was invisible. Then he stood, coming up
like a jack-in-the-box directly in front of Pony. A match
flicked and the man grunted explosively.

He and Pony fired so nearly together that the sound
was of one loud shot. Pony made no stop to see the effect
of his bullet. He ran back past the dark mass of the
horses, still half-blinded by the flare of the shot, to drop
flat. Men came running from the fire, yelling to "Shorty."
Pony wriggled on his belly across the grass, going toward
the fire again and the bulk of a shedlike building he
could see beyond it. He saw the little flames of matches
by Shorty. Then several men yelled fiercely.

"It was Vic Tait! Cut him off from the gap! He killed
Shorty like he's been a-threatening—"

"That's a lie!" a defiant yell answered from the shed beyond the fire. "I never killed him! Never shot at him!"

In the light Vic Tait appeared. Now, Pony recognized his voice as that of the talkative rider he had trailed. So Tait was one of the thieves! No wonder they had found it so simple to raid the 2 Bench; so safe and profitable!

Tait had a Colt in each hand and whatever vices he owned, cowardice was not his possession. He went toward the men about Shorty, continuing to yell at them that they lied. He had not been close to Shorty.

Pony listened to them wrangling, then watched them come slowly to the fire carrying Shorty. When they put him down on the grass and straightened, a man said grimly, "It's nothing to me, Tait, if you killed Shorty Long or not, or if you want to kill off the whole Long family. But if I was in your boots, every time I fell asleep I do believe I would be dreaming about Ben Britt and Anton Jager and Lonzo Troop! And that'd be plenty to wake me up with a cold sweat!"

"The hell with 'em!" Vic Tait snarled. "I never killed him. Not but what I would've, if he'd kept on tangling ropes with me. But I never killed him, and I'm telling the pack of you I'm tired of hearing it said I done it. The next one of you lying sons that opens his trap to say I killed him is going to be right in the middle of more trouble—"

"Who you calling names?" demanded the man who had prophesied so grimly about Britt and Jager. "Why, you think you're something, don't you? I think you're nothing! I—"

"I'm talking to the bunch of you! Nobody's barred! Not you, Vail Oatman, nor you, Askin Judd. Any time you ruffle with me—"

The shots that followed were so rapid, so nearly together, that in Pony's ears they were like one prolonged, rippling detonation. He went closer, straining to see what had happened—or, rather, to whom it had happened!

Two men were on the ground, one sprawling flat, the other on hands and knees. Vic Tait stood with pistols moving in a slow arc, left to right and back. For an instant Pony believed that he had not been touched. But as he watched from twenty feet away, Tait swayed and coughed.

"You had it coming—a long time!" he said savagely to the men on the ground. "Tangle with me—"

The man on all fours collapsed at that moment. Tait caught himself and stiffened, seeming to watch this one. He coughed again and turned away, muttering. A short step, another, then he went forward stiffly, still holding his Colts, to fall face downward beside the fire.

Pony waited, but Tait did not move. Someoné else did, in the shadowy edge of the darkness beyond the fallen man. Floyd Milton, holding a pistol at waist level in each hand, stood looking from figure to figure. The fire played on his strained face and showed his mouth a little open as if he were panting. Another man came up to Floyd's elbow while Pony gaped incredulously at his cousin.

This man passed Floyd and bent in turn over Tait, Oatman, and Judd. Then he came back, shaking his head.

"Always knowed old Vic was fast. But so was they. Judd, anyhow. And he got 'em both while they was dusting him."

"I've got to go to the Seventy-Seven," Floyd grunted. "The sheriff's there with Britt, I think. I've got to see him. I'll try to send some Seventy-Seven men here to straighten things. You watch here, Evans. I've got to go!"

He whirled and disappeared into the darkness before Pony could collect his jumbled thoughts.

"All right, Fancy!" the man Evans called after him. "If

you see Anker Wing, though, he'll be happy about Oat-man and Shorty. He never liked 'em no more'n Vic did."

"Floyd—Milton!" Pony said softly to himself. " 'Fancy!' The sneaking murderer! The slimy thief!"

He stiffened to get up, abolish this Evans with a flashing shot and run after Floyd. He caught himself only in time.

Ah, but he'll pay! he promised the picture of Red Roy that came to mind. *Half of the 2 Bench wasn't enough. He had to soft-soap Red Roy and pick his pockets and shoot him in the back! And Dumpty—another shot in the back! And he had Elam and Isbell kill Quell and Ozment—*

He pushed those thoughts aside. There was work to do here and cursing the traitorous thief and murderer did none of that work. How many men would be here, besides Evans? He thought that the shooting would have drawn any others. But Tait had said that Ike Isbell was dying and the kidnaper Jake had a broken arm—Pony was grimly pleased that his shooting had accomplished so much. Jake might be here and able to shoot from some hidden corner.

He crawled carefully toward the brush-roofed shed behind Evans and got up to its pole wall. And within a yard he put his hand upon the cold face of a dead man and jerked back. The shed was between him and Evans, so he ventured to get out a match from his waterproof case and scratch it. The tiny flame showed the vicious face of Ike Isbell, who had fought with him on Vasko main street.

He put out the match and stood, to walk around the shed and wait grimly for Evans to turn from the fire.

"Up they go, Evans!" he said quietly. "Or—cut loose!"

Evans jerked his hands high and gaped at him. Pony went out and took his pistol from the holster. Evans had a dark, loose-mouthed face. Just now it worked like—

"You look like a man already choking," Pony grunted contemptuously. "You ought to've thought about that before you got into this and began to live by borrowed notions of harder men. Where's Jake?"

"I—I—Britt's got him on the Seventy-Seven. Hiding him. But Tait said you was rubbed out—down in Hell Cellar!"

"Move back—slow! I'm going to hogtie you—same's the sheriff will do when he stands you on the trap for the hanging. You—"

"Listen, Kirk! I never killed nobody—never even shot at nobody! I wouldn't do it. Give me a chance and I'll tell you everything you want to know. Just give me a chance! Fancy's gone to the Seventy-Seven. He rode out the gap five minutes ago. He's going to jump Britt about trying to grab the girl—your cousin! And—"

Pony squatted and got a blazing stick from the fire. He handed it to Evans.

"Shut up! Walk ahead of me into the shed. I want to see if you're lying about Jake. First funny move and I'll kill you. You wouldn't shoot at anybody—no! But you'd hang out with the slinking bunch that did murder-in-the-back by wholesale. Go on! I'm in good killing humor tonight!"

But the shed was empty. Only piles of dirty quilts and blankets were in corners. Sure of this, Pony marched his shaking, mumbling prisoner outside again. As they came into the firelight, hoofs thundered across the open from the gap. Instinctively, Pony looked that way.

Evans twisted like a frightened snake and jumped for the shed. His voice rose shrilly in what seemed a formula, screamed again and again, "Stranger in the Hole! Kill him!"

Pony saw the riders spreading fanwise to sweep down on the fire in a long line. He ran after Evans and from the

charging men came a furious roar—a bellow which he
could not have mistaken, he thought, if he had heard it
ten thousand miles from its native range—the battle yell
of Roaring Red Roy Kirk!

He yelled at Red Roy; yelled his own name; then went
on after Evans. He heard the man running ahead of him
in the dark. He fired, and Evans screamed.

"Come back here! Come back or I'll kill you!" he commanded, running on. "We've got you bottled up!"

"All right! Don't shoot! I'll come back."

He shuffled back to Pony and was prodded back to
the shed. Red Roy was bellowing for Pony. When the
pair came out into the light, the old man was standing by
his horse. His shoulders sagged; his right arm was in a
sling and his neck was crudely bandaged. And the horse
he stood beside was Mig's!

"Who's that?" he demanded. "Ah, Evans! Well—I
reckon I don't need to be surprised. Not now."

He stared at Pony haggardly. Sheriff Sanford's tall figure moved among the riders still mounted. He came forward to look from Pony to Evans.

"You was honest enough, I figured," Red Roy continued dully. "Anyhow, when you rode for me, Evans, I took
you for honest. But there's so much I never figured—so
damn much!"

"Ike Isbell's dead, by the shed there," Pony told them.
"Some horses—maybe the same *mañada* I found on the
Seventy-Seven; I do'no—are over yonder. I reckon we can
take Evans along and say this cathop's finished. Here, I
mean."

"We could handle Evans nice and quiet and—cheap!"
Tap Enlow drawled. "Couldn't we, Dell—Rory?"

"Easy as—falling off a horse!" Dell Cloud agreed, with
the same quiet, deadly note in his voice. "When Five
Aces Holohan knifed Gabe Garratt on the Tincup last

year, we never bothered Sanford a bit. Old Zink wrote Five Aces down for a death from throat trouble, brought on by a rope burn."

"How'd you come to be here, Pony?" Red Roy asked slowly.

Pony told him as briefly as possible—and as vaguely. He said only that the thieves' leader had shot him.

"Right where I reckon you got shot," he added. "How bad are your holes? And how did you get away?"

"I got a burn on my neck and a hole in my shoulder muscle. Nothing to bother. Happens, I can swim like a fish. So I swum! Swum underwater a long piece. I—had a idee. It come to me while I was going out of the hull and over into the water; a scheme—a good scheme. I wasn't knocked out of the kak; I dove! No chance to fight back, me in the open and that bushwhacker dusting me from the mesquite. Ne' mind that. You—got ary notion about this business? I mean—all of it? All the stealing and the killing and—everything? Outside of Vic Tait being a snake-in-the-grass thief?"

Pony hesitated. He had not expected this situation when Floyd Milton walked into the firelight and became Fancy, the chief rustler and murderer. He shrank from telling Red Roy that one of the Kirk blood had been the most complete traitor.

"It was you or Floyd!" Red Roy burst out fiercely. "Which, I don't know—yet. You kind of drag a foot! You won't talk about your back trail! We don't know how long you really been in the country! I don't even know if you're really John Kirk! Floyd told me when he first seen you we'd better watch you—you *could* have made that draggy print they called clubfooted. So I wouldn't let you trail with me. So I never changed my will to give *you* a third of the outfit. I had to be dead-certain!"

He shook his head. Pony nodded quietly. He had

guessed a good part of it and Red Roy's statement of it did not rouse him.

"I got one glimpse of that bushwhacker! An arm and a blue sleeve. And a li'l jerk of the head that both of you have got—and that I have got and my father had—maybe all the Kirk kit has. I went over the bank wondering which of you had tried to kill me. Finally I crawled out and found your boy, Mig, bending over some tracks. I tapped him light over the head and took his horse and rode toward the house. Run into Sanford and the boys coming out and— Which of you was it?"

"It was Floyd!" Evans cried, shrinking closer to Red Roy. "Fancy, they called him account of his dude outfits. He took to gambling and carousing with Ben Britt and Anton Jager and Jean Elam and they got him in the hole —deep. Tait had been helping 'em steal a li'l bit from you and Nate Azle and some others. But when Fancy come in with 'em they really begun to steal. And Fancy figured that clubfoot business for a stall. One of us made it each time."

"Go on!" Red Roy snarled. "See if you can talk yourself out of a loop!"

"I am! I'll tell you everything I know. Nobody on the Ladder U but Elam was with us. Nate Azle never sus- picioned, and we stole some of his best stuff. Britt and all the Seventy-Seven was in. Vic Tait and Anker Wing was the only thieves on the Two Bench. We used the old Watterson cabin on the Seventy-Seven sometimes, for holding-ground. But this place that Elam found we used most. Quell and Ozment seen us driving some Two Bench horses that day you was in town. They had glasses. We figured they recognized Fancy and maybe all of us. So—"

"So Isbell and Elam hit for town," Pony grunted. "They had to kill Ozment and Quell before they could speak to the boss. Horace Palm—a cheap bum who'd do anything for five dollars—and some of his kind started a fight with Cousin Roy. Isbell killed Ozment; Elam killed Quell."

"And if they had told you," Evans took up the tale matter-of-factly, looking at Red Roy, "you'd been rubbed out on the road home or right after that. Fancy schemed it all."

"I would've trusted him with anything," Red Roy muttered, in the tone of one sitting by a deathbed. "Anything! He was so—so— I'm glad he never wore the name Kirk! It ain't much to be thankful for, but it's something!"

Suddenly, he stiffened, squaring his shoulders.

"That's over! Sanford, we're riding for the Seventy-Seven. *Por dios!* I took on anybody that wanted to tangle with me, when I first got the Two Bench. Maybe I'm a li'l grizzly, now, but I can still hit a barn awing. Come on, Sanford. You being along makes everything plumb legal. We'll clean out the Seventy-Seven. They'll give up or—"

CHAPTER XXIV

"I won't kill you"

THEY RODE DESPERATELY FAST and recklessly behind old Red Roy. Pony wished for black Dan, but the horse which had been Shorty's was fast and strong. In the darkness before dawn they pulled in their panting, sweating mounts two hundred yards from the 77 house and Red Roy wondered aloud how many men might be there.

"Britt and Jager and Lonzo Troop, anyhow," Evans volunteered eagerly. He had seemed fairly sweating to help against his former partners. "Maybe Anker Wing, too. And Jake—but he has got a busted arm and he ain't much on the fight any time. And—Fancy. Floyd Milton."

"If we could just get that door open," Pony said slowly, "it would save a lot of trouble. A log house, like you say it is— Well, they could put up a regular 'Dobe Walls Fight from inside."

"We can try it," the sheriff grunted. "Want me to tell Britt I'm back?"

"Nah. Let's have Evans try it. Pony, you slip up to one end of the house. Tap, you take the other end. Rory, you and Dell slide to the back. Sanford and me'll wait just behind Evans on this front face. Come on. We'll move up slow and git close."

They walked the horses quietly forward until the black bulk of the log house showed ahead, then split as instructed. Red Roy started Evans for the door.

"Better remember," he warned him grimly, "we'll all be watching you hawkeyed. Most of us are right good shots. You just call Britt outside. Talk like you're plenty worked up."

"I'll try! But—you watch him, too!"

As Pony moved cautiously toward the end of the house he heard Evans's shaky yell. A dog began to bark. Evans continued to hail the place. Someone answered from inside.

"Evans? Well—come on up and come in."

"Can't!" Evans answered, with artfulness that surprised Pony. "Got to hold this damn— Stop it, you fool!"

The door opened squeakily. Pony was almost at the house now. The dog continued to bark. Britt's voice was clearer as he demanded of Evans what he held; what he wanted.

Pony began to move along the front wall from the end, working toward that door. From the other end came a crashing noise, of someone falling over an obstacle. Inside a man yelled quick warning.

"Men at the back, Ben! It's a trap!"

Britt's shot roared in the doorway and Evans yelled. Pony jumped forward, afraid only that Britt would slam that door and make a siege necessary. But instead Britt leaned to shoot down the wall in the direction of that stumbling one—Tap Enlow, Pony thought. Pony fired at the flash of Britt's shot; fired twice. He squatted at the doorway and past him Britt fell, half in, half out. For there was shooting all around, now—at the front, the back, the ends, inside.

Red Roy and Sanford thudded up, dropped from their horses, and joined Pony and Tap Enlow at the door. Sanford yelled to those inside to give up. Shots roared in the darkness of the house; bullets sang viciously through the door. But none there was exposed and they poured lead blindly into the room.

Quiet came. Presently, Sanford called once more to any in the house, but got no answer. Pony got out a match and struck it, let the flame creep along the stick, then tossed it inside. There was no shot and he turned to Red Roy.

"Looks like the windup," he said flatly. "But there's no use taking a chance. Day will be soon and we can see."

Yells from the back accounted for all of the party. Tap Enlow had a snagged arm, he reported. Rory Eads had been hit by someone's bullet from a window.

"If he hadn't had his big mouth wide open," Dell Cloud said sardonically, " 'way it always is, he would've lost some teeth! Slug went in his mouth and out his cheek! Never touched his tongue, even—worse luck for us!"

With gray light, they looked into the big room. Sanford stood beside Pony, muttering, "Jager! Anker Wing! That big Jake! Lonzo Troop—he was a salty one! Britt right here. Evans ain't declared hisself since he fell off his horse when Britt first shot; reckon he's rubbed out, too. But—"

"But not Floyd Milton," Pony finished for him.

"I'm glad you seen it yourself," Red Roy told the sheriff. "Saves plenty trouble trying to tell it all to you. We have got to clean all this up. Reckon Dell better hit for town and bring out Zink—he'll likely come down flat on his nose when he sees the place! Pony—"

"After while!" Pony checked him shortly. "After— while."

He went quickly back to where his borrowed horse stood. So Floyd had somehow avoided this trap. That would mean Floyd at the house, with Connie. Pony could not picture Floyd harming the girl, but—

The man's capable of anything, in cold blood, he thought. *I don't know what he might think of, but if he decided it was best to do anything, he'd try to do it!*

He mounted and spurred off. He was in no mood to appreciate the flush of rose and gold in the sky, before the sun came up to work magic on the lightening clouds of the night. It was better light to ride by, that was all. He pushed the horse relentlessly, over the 2 Bench wire and across Red Roy's range. The miles seemed endless, but at last he dropped off at the corral—which had sheltered his approach. The big gelding staggered, but Pony looked into the corral and with sight of a sweat-streaked horse there, he nodded grimly.

When he went toward the kitchen door, he walked wolfishly light, his hands swinging stiffly over the bone handles of his Colts. The kitchen was empty and he passed on. In the living-room he heard the murmur of voices. They came from Red Roy's office. Connie's voice —and Floyd's. He went that way.

"And that's the way it was—unfortunately," Floyd was saying. "But whether he was an impostor or a renegade Kirk doesn't matter to me now. Neither Cousin Roy nor I ever decided just what we thought he was—more than a very deadly sort of young man. But I keep thinking of poor Cousin Roy!"

"I—think of them both!" Connie said, in tone so low that Pony could hardly hear her words. "I—I hardly know what I think."

"Of course not! But if you'll get away from here for a little while you'll feel better. I've got to establish what we know—the fact of Cousin Roy's death. I think there'll be no trouble about that. One End Creek is too well known in this country. He wanted us to have the place. And—somehow I believe that he'd have wanted to go out fighting, as he must have done, instead of dying in bed. He said so—"

From the kitchen carried an unmusical humming. Pony went noiselessly out to confront the wizened little Chinese cook.

"Hung!" he whispered. "You go tell Missy to come here. Say something to see. Bring her here. *Sabe?* Don't tell her I am here. I want to talk to *him* in the office."

Hung On gaped at him, then nodded. Pony, catching sight of his reflection in a glass cabinet door, could understand the cook's nervousness. Beard-stubbled, dirty, with the bloody bandage about his head, he was a savage figure.

Pony went out and around the house to the window of the office. He heard Hung's emotionless voice and Connie's reply. He waited until the footsteps had died away. Inside the office was only the rustling of papers. He lifted himself, pistol in hand, to lean upon the window sill. Floyd stood with back to him. He was whistling, mumbling to himself.

"Red Roy will be here in a minute, Floyd," Pony said softly. "He's riding up now, with the sheriff."

In all his life, Pony had never known a man with such control of himself. Floyd turned to look at him with precisely the shade of amazement—that changed to pleasure

—one would have expected of—

Of the man who had not done exactly all the things he has done! Pony thought, staring almost in fascination.

"You found him?" Floyd cried. "Why—I hardly know what to say! Have you told Connie? This is the finest thing I've ever heard. I found the place where I thought he went over—"

"They're bringing Evans and Britt with 'em," Pony lied drawlingly. "I just rode ahead—in spite of having to miss some of the tale Evans was telling and Britt was making clearer. Oh! I was the one who killed Shorty in the Hole, *Fancy!* It wasn't Tait. I came in with you and Tait, ahead of Oatman and Judd. Red Roy knows the whole tale, now."

Without expression, Floyd stared at him.

"You seem to have done a pretty thorough job of gun bulldogging," he said flatly. "I'm in your hands."

But it was his hand that moved—down and up, bringing a short pistol from the open table drawer. Pony twitched his Colt to the left a little and dropped the hammer. But Floyd's bullet struck him in the neck, driving him half around, staggering him. He straightened, ignoring the wound, concentrating on Floyd. But the short pistol was on the floor and Floyd stood holding his right arm. Blood began to seep through his gripping fingers.

"I won't kill you," Pony said thickly. "Not even—now. Not even after knowing—the kind of snake—you are. Go out. Get your horse. Disappear. It's murder they want you for. I ought to kill you—for Dumpty Downes. But this much—I'll do for—the Kirk name!"

It was increasingly hard to stand there. His knees were threatening to give. But he clung to the sill and with left hand drew up his shirt to wad against the wound in his neck.

"This way—by me!" he ordered huskily.

Floyd picked up his hat and came to the window, slipped over the sill, and walked steadily toward the corral. Pony followed, propping himself up by the wall. He watched Floyd saddle a horse quickly and ride away.

"Pony!" Connie called from behind him. "Pony! Is it true? Is it really true? That Cousin Roy's alive?"

Her voice came to him faintly. He began to walk slowly toward the kitchen door—a tiny black spot far ahead of him. She caught his arm and steadied him and they got into the kitchen. Old Hung took his other arm and at last he sprawled on a couch in the living-room. Then he fainted.

A long time afterward he heard talking about him and opened his eyes. Connie said "head" and "neck" and Red Roy made a growling answer.

"Head! Neck! No worse hurt than I am. He's a Kirk, same as me! Can't kill 'em."

"What I've always heard!" Pony whispered. "They outlive the undertakers."

"Pony!" Connie breathed. "You've been unconscious for hours! How do you feel?"

"All right, of course. But—starved! I would like a big steak—"

He sat up, weak but able to hold himself erect.

"Boy," Red Roy said, from the depths of a great chair, "I have just been thinking that maybe I got as much out of this kinsfolks notion of mine as I could hope for. I'm glad you let—*him* go. Better for us, that way. And Connie's left and—and you certainly won't leave us—"

"Leave?" the girl cried. "Of course he won't leave! Pony—"

He was very conscious of her widened eyes, even though he would not meet them. The loveliest girl he had ever known, the most desirable— He shook his head.

"I can't stay," he told them harshly. "I—am Chance

Fielder. You would know sometime. I have got to go. Soon. Chance Fielder. Human wolf. Notorious murderer from the Territory."

"*Aggh!*" Red Roy snarled. "I guessed that was your go-by. Gun bulldogger, yeh! Murderer—*aggh!* What'd they do over there? Gang up on you?"

"I guessed it, too," Connie almost whispered. "And I wondered—"

"No matter what happened, I'm wanted for murder. I have got to go. I"—he stopped, looked stonily at her, then went on grimly—"I reckon I never was the kind to settle down, anyway. I just stayed here to get the man that killed Dumpty Downes. That's done. So I'm done."

For an instant, bewilderment to the verge of utter un-belief showed in the girl's white face. Then she flushed and got to her feet from where she had kneeled beside the couch. She went quickly out of the room. Red Roy stared from the door to Pony, and his leathery face hard-ened.

"It's your choice," he said angrily.

He got up and went after Connie. For a long while Pony sat on the couch. He wondered where Mig might be, and Dan, and Lyde Upshur. His belts and guns were on the floor by the couch. He looked down at them. Then a step in the outer doorway drew his eyes. Upshur was coming in.

"Hi!" he greeted Pony gravely. "We kind of got split up, now, didn't we? I heard the whole tale from Tap Enlow. Met him on the road to the Hole while I was hunting you. Pony— We met that fancy cousin of yours— Tap and Mig and me. He was on the prod and—I reckon Tap was, too. Anyway—he went into One End Creek. And he—well, *he* won't climb out!"

Pony only nodded. He bent awkwardly and touched the belts and pistols. Upshur moved and picked them up.

He looked at Pony, holding the belts over an arm.

"You look pretty helpless," he said in an odd tone. "I reckon Bully Witt never caught you this way, naked. Take it easy, Pony. Felix! Oh, Felix! Come on in and identify him."

Into the room from the veranda a big Mexican came at short, catlike step. He stopped just inside the door and looked nervously at Pony—who glared at him with hand clenching and unclenching.

"That—is Chance Fielder," Felix Avila announced. "He—I would like now to go, Señor Couch. He—I will feel better when I am on the road to the Territory. I have been long away—"

"Presently! Presently!"

"So you're Merl Couch, Bully Witt's latest deputy," Pony grunted. "You nearly got me when you holed me up that time at Dog Canyon. Well—no matter. I thought Felix was dead, or I never would have left the Territory. For I swore I'd kill him, after he swore to those lies about my murdering Johnson. And, somehow, sometime, I'll kill you, Felix."

"I don't think so," Merl Couch told him. "Bully Witt sent me after you. I brought Felix along to identify you. I had him in Vasko with me when you came in and got into that row at Delrio Dolly's. But he was too drunk to do anything. You saw me knock him on his ear there, but you didn't know it was Felix. Then he tried to get to me here, but Mig took a shot at him. And—we might as well unload it all—he ran into you on One End Creek—when I tumbled into the water—and tried a shot at you. He was scared. So he shot and ran."

He looked down at Pony's grim face and shook his head.

"Trouble with siding you, boy, is that it twists a man's notions. I studied you like a book from the minute we met in the sheriff's office. You see, I had you handed to me for a cold-blood murderer. But you never would act the part! Then you dived into the water like a nitwit and saved my life— Well, when Felix showed up 1—had a conference with him. When he heard that Bully Witt was killed in Ojo, he was willing to talk and talk straight. He told me about Bully making him lie on the Johnson killing. He'll tell it in court—or, better yet, to the governor. Pony, you're white as snow, in the Territory."

"Against Bully Witt—and Shea—and Rosen?"

"Bully Witt's really dead. I'm acting sheriff and I'll be sheriff. The governor is a mighty good friend of the Couch family. So you don't want to hurt Felix. He's your witness!"

Avila shrank back as Pony stood suddenly erect. But Pony turned, not toward him, but to the door through which Connie had gone. He forgot wounds; he felt no weakness. And he almost cannoned into the girl just beyond that door.

"I'm a liar!" he said breathlessly. "I wanted to be the first one to tell you about it. I'm the awfulest liar in the State of Texas—maybe in the whole United States and Canada and—Connie! I was lying when I said I didn't want to stay; that I'd stayed just to heel Dumpty's killer. If you can stand a wild-eyed wolf like me around—"

"Such a changeable man," she said wearily. "Now he will and now he won't—and who's to say when he'll decide to do something different? I think you'll do better elsewhere. In town, say. At—Delrio Dolly's Palace of Terpsichore. The sheriff said that Beatrice is really a very pretty girl. Older than she admits, of course, but quite pretty, considering."

Over her shoulder, as he stared with incredulity that became grimness, Pony saw Red Roy in the kitchen door staring—no, it was glaring—into his eyes.

"All right," he said evenly. "I'll go."

"Go?" Red Roy snarled. "You bet you'll go. Right now! Your stuff's in your saddlebags and they're on your saddle and your saddle's on your crowbait and that boy Mig's waiting for you at the c'ral. Here's a twenty—pay for you and the boy for a half month's work to even us for what you done. You bet you'll go! This minute!"

"What?" Connie cried furiously, wheeling upon him. "He— You— Twenty dollars! When if it hadn't been for him— And you—so proud of the Kirk name— I suppose you think I'll stay! When he goes I go! I—"

Pony shook his head stupidly, looking from one to the other of them. But when her arm went around him and she pressed close against his shoulder, he was not too confused to put a hand awkwardly beneath her small, stiffened chin and lift the angry face.

"You—really mean that, *chiquita?* You'll go with me?"

"Anywhere! I—heard all that Lyde Upshur—Merl Couch—told you. But even if that weren't all cleared, I'd go with you. As for Beatrice, I— Well, the sheriff told me that she wants to leave Vasko; she's afraid to stay; and I gave him the money for a ticket to San Antonio. Just because she helped you, of course! I'll ride behind you the way the Kirk women used to ride behind their—their men—"

From the kitchen a gasping noise that swelled to a roaring interrupted her. They looked up, to see Red Roy clinging to the door frame, shaggy head thrown back, mouth open to let out bellow after bellow while a huge hand pounded the wall.

"He— He—" Red Roy whooped. "She— She— Try to—put one over—on the Kirks! Son— Pony— Ohhh!"

"It's too—noisy here," Pony told her solemnly. "Come away, *chiquita mia*. I want to tell you lots of things—how I bragged I would wade this One End Creek and come out packing the lost end and a lot of other things and—how what I really found—that's valuable—was you—and—"

"Three Kirks," Red Roy said, in an exhausted, satisfied sort of rumble. "Going to be all Kirks on the Two Bench. Real Kirks. Texas Kirks. Three, right now, and—"

"Hold your horses!" Pony called back to him. "Hold your horses—awhile."